D0431664

BAD
GIRL
GONE

ALSO BY TEMPLE MATHEWS

THE NEW KID
THE RISING
THE SWORD OF ARMAGEDDON

THE GOOD FATHER (AS WILLIAM PAYTON)

BAD

GIRL

GONE

TEMPLE MATHEWS

THOMAS DUNNE BOOKS ST. MARTIN'S GRIFFIN ⚏ NEW YORK

THOMAS DUNNE BOOKS.
An imprint of St. Martin's Press.

BAD GIRL GONE. Copyright © 2017 by Temple Mathews. All rights
reserved. Printed in the United States of America. For information,
address St. Martin's Press, 175 Fifth Avenue, New York, N.Y. 10010.

www.thomasdunnebooks.com
www.stmartins.com

Designed by Anna Gorovoy

Library of Congress Cataloging-in-Publication Data

Names: Mathews, Temple, author.
Title: Bad girl gone : a novel / Temple Mathews.
Description: First edition. | New York : Thomas Dunne Books /
    St. Martin's Griffin, 2017.
Identifiers: LCCN 2017010996 | ISBN 978-1-250-05881-2 (hardcover :
    acid-free paper) | ISBN 978-1-4668-6324-8 (ebook)
Subjects: LCSH: Teenage girls—Crimes against—Fiction. | Murder—
    Investigation—Fiction. | Future life—Fiction. | Self-actualization
    (Psychology)—Fiction. | GSAFD: Ghost stories. | Mystery fiction.
Classification: LCC PS3613.A8275 B36 2017 | DDC 813/.6—dc23
LC record available at https://lccn.loc.gov/2017010996

Our books may be purchased in bulk for promotional, educational,
or business use. Please contact your local bookseller or the Macmillan
Corporate and Premium Sales Department at 1-800-221-7945, extension
5442, or by email at MacmillanSpecialMarkets@macmillan.com.

First Edition: August 2017

10 9 8 7 6 5 4 3 2 1

3361408052831 7

Dedicated to my precious jewels,
Manon Lucy Mathews and Piedad Suarez

BAD
GIRL
GONE

AWAKENING

When I tried to remember exactly how I came to be lying in the cold black room, my mind couldn't focus.

I could feel myself slowly climbing upward, clawing my way out of the clutches of a nightmare. This was usually a good feeling, because you knew you were just dreaming, and the nightmare was over. Except this time it wasn't. My hands felt clammy. I gripped the sheets until I knew my knuckles must be white. *Help me,* I thought. *Somebody please help me.*

I had no idea where I was, and for a terrifying second I couldn't even remember *who* I was. But then I remembered my name. Echo. Echo Stone. My real name is Eileen. When I was a toddler, I waddled around repeating everything my parents said and they called me "Echo," and it just stuck.

Remembering my name and how I got it kick-started my brain. I knew who I was. I remembered that I was sixteen years old and lived in Kirkland, Washington, with my mom and dad. It was all coming back to me. Mom was a dentist and Dad taught middle school English. Good, I could remember parts of my life. But I was still in a dark, cold room and had no idea how I got there. I held back a scream, my chest tightening. *Don't lose it, Echo, keep it together*, I told myself. *Calm down, think good thoughts.*

I pictured Andy, my boyfriend. Six feet tall, broad shoulders, blue eyes, and long golden-brown hair. He loved to feed me cookie bites and called me his rabbit. I called him Wolfie. Sometimes he got the hiccups for no reason at all and usually laughed them away. Thinking of Andy momentarily made me feel warm inside, even though the room was freezing.

Where *was* I? I was shivering and yet also bathed in sweat, my skin slick with it. I clutched for my trusty Saint Christopher necklace. But it wasn't there. Mom gave it to me to protect me when I traveled. Would it protect me now? I would never have lost it. The chain must have broken. And then I had an ugly thought. What if someone had ripped it from my neck? I shuddered. *Where are you, Andy? I need you!*

I opened my eyes as wide as I could. It was pitch black. My pounding heart told me, *This isn't some nightmare—it's real.* I hugged myself and breathed deeply, trying to calm my nerves. My shoulders were tight. I rubbed the sheets beneath me. The ones at home in my bed were soft. These were stiff and coarse. I was somewhere completely and painfully foreign. In my head I was talking to myself in a rapid voice, my fear voice: *What is this?—what is this?—what is this?*

Someone nearby was crying. I had a knot in my stomach and my throat hurt, like I'd screamed for hours. My head hurt, too, and I guessed I must have fallen, or maybe something heavy fell on me. I explored my scalp, gently at first, then more bravely, moving my fingers, searching for a lump. I found nothing . . . no lump, no holes. My skull was intact, though my long auburn hair felt tangled and greasy. I inhaled through my nose, searching for familiar scents. Mom's cinnamon rolls, Dad's aftershave. But nothing smelled even vaguely familiar, and the odors that *did* find my nose were horrible. Smoke. Vinegar. Sulfur.

I reached for my bedside lamp—but my fingers touched something damp and stringy. *Oh god.* The knot in my stomach tightened and I yanked my hand back. I willed my eyes to adjust to the dark, but as I blinked, strange pulsing figures leapt out at me. It must have been my mind playing tricks. Right?

I took five good, long breaths, sucking in through my nose and exhaling through my pursed lips, just like my grandma Tilly taught me years ago. But five breaths weren't enough. So I took ten, and finally my heart rate slowed from a galloping panic to a steady, cautious thudding. Soon I was able to distinguish shapes. Was that a *girl* in a bed next to mine? Her hair was impossibly thick and long, spilling down her back. Her sweaty hair. That's what I must have reached out and touched. My heart returned to its punishing rhythm, a fist clenching and unclenching in my chest. The nearby crying stopped. But then it was replaced by something worse, a ripping sound, like bone being cut by a rusty saw. And then a gurgling . . . followed by a low, feral growling noise. Faraway cackling laughter. *What the hell was going on?*

I was terrified and breathing so loud I was afraid I'd wake up the sleeping girl. Something told me I should lie still and keep my mouth shut. Stupidly, I ignored it. My voice was raspy, my throat aching . . .

"Mom? Dad?"

Nothing.

"ANDY?"

The words sounded weak in the stony silence that followed. My ears strained for the comforting sound of my parents' familiar footsteps—but I was met with more cruel noises drifting through the blackness.

I heard a faraway clock ticking and an odd whimpering, and then a cough. But it wasn't Mom's or Dad's cough; it was the cough of a child—a girl, I think. I desperately wanted this to be a nightmare. So I closed my eyes and tried to float back to sleep. But the terrifying sounds continued: the soft, almost melodic crying; the rhythmic, persistent coughing; the howls and metallic noises; the rushing water. I couldn't take it. I opened my eyes again.

"DADDY?"

An echo from the darkness. Distant. Haunting. Mocking.

"Daddy? Daddy? Daddy?"

I sensed something under my bed. The hair on my neck prickled. I imagined dangling my fingers over the side of the mattress, envisioned them being latched onto, bitten by some creature that would drag me down into its fetid pit. I held my breath and listened. There it was. Someone, or some*thing*, was breathing beneath me.

I slid to the edge of the bed and then slowly lowered my head, my irises widening. I peered into the shadows—and saw a pair of feral eyes peering back at me. Acid panic flooded my veins as I jerked back, thinking, *Please don't kill me. If you touch me, my boyfriend will hunt you down and beat the living shit out of you!*

I heard a rustling sound, then footsteps. I saw the creature leap out from under my bed. Its eyes found me, then it scampered out of the room, on two legs I think, a flash of white. It looked human, but it could have been something else. Whatever it was, thank god it was running from me. Or wait! Maybe it was going to gather more of its kind and they'd come back for me in a pack. My skin crawled. *Get out!*

I couldn't stay in this room. I had to get up and move. My bare feet hit the cold, wood plank floor. I took tentative steps into the shadows. A floorboard creaked beneath my feet and I froze. My eyes had adjusted to the darkness and I could make out shapes. Up ahead I saw a shallow pool of light. I moved toward it.

I walked slowly, taking tentative steps, my eyes darting back and forth. The hallway felt like a perfect place for an ambush, so I was alert, my muscles taut.

I passed a closed door on my right, another on my left. I caught a scent of smoke. I heard a splashing sound, as if someone was taking a bath right above my head. I kept my gaze fixed on the pool of light that was spilling out from under a large door at the end of the hallway. As I drew closer, I could see that the door was built from thick oak planks and looked like it weighed a thousand pounds. On it hung a thick brass ring. On my right was a tall, old grandfather clock, ticking away like a metronome but with no hands to tell time with. It made me afraid and angry. What was I doing in a place *with a clock with no hands*?

I stepped closer to the thick door. My stomach tightened in fear. Something was terribly wrong. I was lost, adrift, not only in the wrong place, but I felt as though somehow I was the wrong *me*. I was jolted by a terrible thought. What if I never saw Andy again?

I raised my hand to grasp the knocker but stopped. Because I felt someone behind me.

"I wouldn't do that if I was you," said a voice, barely above a whisper.

I turned and saw a slight boy, thin as a reed with long, snowy hair, eating a red candy apple. The hair on the nape of my neck rose.

"Wow. You're a pretty one," he said.

I might have blushed. I'd never thought of myself as pretty. My nose is crooked, and ever since someone told me my eyes were too far apart, I've been convinced of it.

"Want a bite?" he asked, holding out the apple.

Too bewildered to speak, I shook my head no. My shoulders began to tighten.

"Peeking at me under the bed like that . . . you scared me," he said.

His hair was so white I figured that must have been what I saw as he dashed from the room. "You were under the bed?"

He nodded, took another bite out of the apple. He was utterly strange looking. He looked damaged and sad.

"Where am I?" I asked.

He ignored the question.

"I'm Mick. Sometimes my own room scares me. So I sleep under other people's beds. You freaked me out. That's why I ran. Did you enjoy it?"

Did I enjoy *what*? I was about to ask him when the heavy door opened on hinges that creaked like the gates of hell, bathing the hallway in harsh light. Mick with the white hair took off, leaving a trail of wet footprints. WTF?

I shielded my eyes from the light and peeked up through my fingers at a tall, broad-shouldered woman dressed in what looked like a cross between an old nurse's uniform and a nun's habit. Her hair was black with a shock of silver cutting across one side. She appeared vaguely avian, had sallow skin, and for a moment peered at me curiously, like she thought she knew me or something. Then she stared at me like I was a cockroach. I wanted to ask her what was going on but the words were stuck in my throat, clogging my windpipe. I somehow remembered to breathe. I could feel beads of sweat forming on my upper lip.

"Can you tell me—" I croaked, but she raised one of her talon-like hands. I shut up and locked my shaking hands under my armpits.

"You're new here. You don't know the rules. So I won't discipline you. *This* time. But rule number one is No Wandering the Halls Alone at Night. Now go back to bed!"

The last thing I wanted was to go back to that bed. But her

voice was commanding and stentorian and she looked like she could kill me with a flick of her wrist. I had to do what I was told; I was too afraid to do anything else. I backed up into the darkness and found the room and lay down but was way too afraid to sleep.

Sleep claim me now—help me escape this madness.

My dad always told me if I wanted to sleep I should think of good things, things that made me happy. So I remembered a time with Andy. I was fourteen. It was a warm spring day and his father wasn't home. He was shooting baskets in his driveway. I was leaning against an old oak tree, trying to appear nonchalant. The ball bounced off the back of the rim and he jumped for the rebound but missed it. So the ball rolled right to my feet. I thought, *Did he plan that?* He came trotting over with his sexy lopsided grin and warm, friendly eyes.

"Hey, neighbor."

I hated it when he called me that. It sounded so generic. I picked up the ball.

"Um, I suppose you want this back . . ." Man, I was soooo smooth.

"I'm not in any big hurry," he said.

He was *flirting. With me!* My heart skipped.

I was like a frightened filly and, ball in hand, I bolted past him, dribbling a few times before flinging the ball at the hoop. It was either the best or worst shot of my life, depending on how you looked at it. The ball missed the entire backboard and hit the garage dormer window. A sickening crack ensued.

"Nice shot." He was smirking as he approached.

"God, I am so sorry, I'm such an idiot, I'll pay for it, I'm so stupid, I shouldn't have done that, I flunked gym class, my brain is a big bag of mush and I just . . ."

He took me in his arms. Was he going to?—yep, he just flat-out kissed me. An explosion rocked the earth. Or at least it felt that way. When he stopped kissing me, he was grinning again.

"It worked," he said.

"What worked?"

"Me kissing you."

"Wha . . . what . . . ?"

"It shut you up," he said.

I was shocked and hurt and flabbergasted and my mouth opened wide. He kissed me again, presumably to keep me from babbling like a lunatic. When the second kiss was over, he smiled and touched my cheek.

"I was kidding before, about shutting you up," he said. "I like the sound of your voice."

"Thank you," I croaked.

"You're a good kisser," he said. "Where'd you learn to kiss like that?"

"Um, from you, I think, just now." I was telling the truth. Up until this point, the vast majority of my kisses had been planted on puppies and stuffed animals. This was way new territory.

"Don't sweat the window," he said.

He grabbed the ball and dribbled.

"We'll have to do this again sometime," he said.

"I . . . don't want to break another window."

"I was talking about the kisses."

Remembering that day with Andy had worked. I relaxed, exhaustion took over, and I was pulled down into a sleep that engulfed me like a wave. My last conscious thought was that I was glad I was falling asleep because I couldn't wait for this insane nightmare to be over.

WATER

I had poisonous dreams. I was being chased by shapes through darkness. Then I stopped and experienced an odd sensation. A slow, warm wave started in my hand and quickly spread to my stomach. The dream changed. I was running to the bathroom and of course the stupid door was locked. Then I heard a click, and I opened it, but it wasn't a bathroom—it was an arena with white carpet floors stretching to infinity. I turned and ran. I couldn't hold it any longer and felt heat between my legs. My God, I was pissing on the white carpet in the arena! And then my sheets felt wet.

Opening my eyes, I saw a dozen kids crammed into my tiny room, staring at me like I was a lab rat. No one laughed or talked; they just stared with their cold eyes. It creeped me out.

Mick, the wispy kid with white hair from last night, held a bowl of warm water, within which lay my left hand. Okay, so now I knew for sure that the old "hand in warm water" trick really worked. I jolted up and screamed at the top of my lungs.

"Get the hell out!"

They didn't budge. A bulky girl made a growling sound deep in her throat, and they simply filed out as the water bowl clanked to the floor. Mick must have spilled some on himself, because just like last night, he left damp footprints behind. I sat for a moment in my own pee, humiliated beyond belief. The girl with the long hair wasn't in her bed. I was all alone, having been tricked into pissing my pants by a group of adolescent cretins. Perfect. Just great. I looked around for my phone to call Andy or my parents. No phone. I saw no TV or computer in the room, either.

The tall, birdlike woman appeared in my doorway, scowling.

"Aren't you a little old to be wetting the bed?"

"I didn't—" I protested, but apparently she never allowed anyone to finish a sentence.

"Since you'll have to wash your sheets and clothes, I'm putting you on laundry detail. You'll find a wicker basket in every room. The laundry room is in the basement."

She pointed down the hallway. I was looking at her but her eyes kept dancing away, like I was so ugly that she couldn't stand the sight of me.

"End of the hall, down the stairs. You'll find it."

I looked down at my wet pants and sheets. Ugh. When I looked back at the doorway, she was gone. She moved fast, couldn't wait to get away from me. But I wanted answers and I wanted them pronto. I rushed into the hallway and shouted at her broad back.

"Hey! *Stop!*"

She turned around very slowly, her eyes cautious, maybe even fearful, but she recovered, and her gaze went angry and now her eyes narrowed and cut into me. I was scared, but not too scared to speak. "Where am I and how did I get here? I want to know *now*."

I blinked and suddenly she was right in my face. She was big and strong enough to tear my head off and looked like she wanted to, the veins on her forehead pulsing.

"You are in *no* position to demand *anything*. You are now a resident of Middle House. I recommend that you do as you're told, follow orders, and if you do . . . I will *eventually* answer all of your questions. For now, do *not* question me again."

She turned and walked away. This time I didn't chase after her.

Middle House?

I went back to my room and stood for a moment, taking in the surroundings. There were two beds, two bedside tables with lamps, and one window with the shade down. I slowly raised the shade to look outside and saw trees and a high stone wall. I was a prisoner. I tried to open the window but it was painted shut, so I closed the shade and decided for the time being to do as I'd been told. I would find an opening, and when I did, I was gonna go for it like my butt was on fire.

Angrily, I stripped the sheets and blankets off the lumpy, old mattress. Someone had folded a pair of beige cotton pajamas and set them on the chair next to my bed. I peeled off my wet clothes and got into the pajamas. Then I put everything into the battered wicker basket in the corner and, using the big rope handle on its side, lugged it out into the hallway. The air around me felt cold and thin.

My foot slipped on something and I almost went down but caught my balance. I reached down and felt the moisture on my foot. Blood. Not mine. But definitely blood. They were trying to scare me and doing a damn fine job, because my stomach rose into my throat, my skin felt cold, and my heart thumped.

I picked up the basket and moved down the hallway. In my peripheral vision, I could see a few of them staring at me from inside their dark rooms, the whites of their eyes creepy and glowing. My lower lip quivered, but I was determined not to cry. I clenched my jaw and lugged the basket along.

The first room I came to was like mine, with two single beds. The sheets and blankets had been stripped off the stained mattresses. The laundry basket in the corner was overflowing with soiled bedding, shirts and pants and underwear. I started to pick it up and stopped suddenly. Panic shot up my spine. There was a *finger* poking out of the pile. I took a deep breath. They were messing with me again, just like with the blood.

"Very funny. You can come out now," I said.

Nothing. I flicked it with my fingernail but it didn't move. It looked gray. Oh god. I couldn't help myself and touched it. It wasn't just a finger, it was part of a whole *hand,* and it was cold. Shuddering, I grabbed the hand by the finger and pulled. It came out of the basket, a bloody stump. I screeched and flung it across the room where it bounced. My stomach lurched— until I saw it was just some stupid rubber hand. Another prank. Great. Welcome to the nuthouse. I shook my head. Enough of this bullshit. I decided I wasn't going to let them get to me. I was going to go and do the stupid laundry and, in the process, find some way out. If I couldn't find an exit, I would go and have a heart-to-heart with the tall woman and find out what in the hell Middle House was.

The possibilities of how I got here swam through my mind. I was thinking natural disaster, a flood or an earthquake maybe, and I must have gotten knocked out, lost in the storm, and wound up in this place. Ugh. I saw another hand in the laundry basket. I grabbed it angrily, ready to toss it across the room, but this time the hand grabbed me back!

I shrieked and yanked away and fell back on my ass as a stubby boy crawled up out of the basket. He had a large head and was bald, had a thick neck, and had diagonal scars like zippers on his skull. I felt dizzy. Now kids were staring in at me from the hallway, their eyes wide, their sinister faces expressionless.

"Stupid newbie," one of them said.

I sat in silence for a few seconds and calmed my throbbing pulse. Then I rose and picked up the dirty laundry. What else was I going to do? I was obviously in this place for a reason, and toeing the line for the time being seemed like the best strategy. Let them have their stupid fun.

Down the hall I slogged, lugging baskets by their handles. My back was killing me. I found the end of the hallway and carried my smelly cargo down the stairwell. On the way down, I heard noises, as if the walls were filled with scurrying rats. I heard howls and a moaning, too, but I ignored it all, vowing to get out of this place as soon as humanly possible. I couldn't wait to go do something normal, like a bike ride or a walk in the park with Andy. I hoped he was okay. If I'd ended up here, where was *he*?

The laundry room had a single naked light bulb, so dim that darkness crowded around a huge old boiler, hissing and clanking away like some dying beast. The concrete walls were sweating, and there was one window, barred, against the far wall. I wasn't even going to try it. I found the soap and loaded up the battered old Maytag washers. I remembered all the times I had bitched and moaned to Mom about having to help her do laundry. If I could only be with her right now, I'd gladly do laundry all day long. I turned the first washer on but nothing happened.

I kicked it—always worth a try—but as soon as my bare foot hit the side of the washer, someone yelped. More hazing. Just what I needed. A head popped up from behind the washer. It was a boy, around my age, with dark hair hanging down over his eyes. When he brushed his bangs away, I saw that he was actually trending toward handsome. He had nice eyes—hazel and friendly. He had nice lips, too, but they were curled in a sneer, which he probably thought was sexy but instead reminded me of a neighbor's nasty Siberian husky that once took a chunk out of my leg.

"I suppose you all think you're very clever," I said. "But you're not really scaring me; you're just getting on my nerves."

He reared his head back like I'd just slapped him.

"I wasn't trying to scare you. I'm fixing the plug. That's why the machine you were brutalizing didn't turn on."

He held up a plug that he'd repaired with electrical tape, and then proceeded to plug it into the wall socket.

"Try it now. Maybe without the kick."

I did, and the machine started chugging away dutifully. I suppose I should have thanked him, but I was in no mood to thank anybody.

"Do you always go around kicking things that don't cooperate?" he asked, pushing the bangs out of his eyes again.

"Who cares what I do?" Ms. Petulant. Nice touch.

"I suppose that is the question now, isn't it?"

"No, the question is . . . where am I?"

"You don't know?"

"If I *knew*, would I ask?"

He smiled. It annoyed the crap out of me. I was going to tell him as much but then he answered my question.

"You're in Middle House."

"Middle *what*?"

He looked at me like I was some kind of idiot.

"Middle House. It's an orphanage."

"How the hell did I get here?"

He gazed at me a long time, slowly squinting his eyes as if he were nearsighted and trying to focus on something far away.

"We all come to Middle House in different ways."

"Well, thank you so much for the entirely vague and mysterious answer. Here's the thing. I don't belong here. I'm not an orphan. My parents are very much alive."

He gazed thoughtfully at me and was about to speak when a bell rang.

"Breakfast," he said, and then left the basement, taking the stairs two at a time.

I wanted answers, but I also happened to be hungry. Starving, actually. I had two choices. I could stay in the damp, smelly laundry room watching the clothes churn while I sulked, or I could follow Hazel Eyes upstairs. I climbed the steps and followed the scent of frying bacon to a double doorway.

DINING

The dining hall was full of kids sitting at long, low wooden tables, hunched over their bowls and plates, chowing down like wild animals. I wondered why they even bothered with utensils, because bits of food were flying around and milk was slopping out of their bowls onto the tables and everybody was acting like this was perfectly normal. A black cat darted past me into the room and zipped under a table to lick spilled milk.

Fingers crossed that I'd been properly hazed and that initiation was over, I entered, which caused a slight lull in the gobbling. Dozens of eyes locked on me as I glanced around eagerly for a seat. Hazel Eyes happened to have a place next to him. He saw me and waited a painfully long moment before grudgingly waving me over. Not my first choice—he'd been verging on rude in the basement—but everyone else in the place looked worse, so I approached his table. A lanky boy with freckles, long red hair, and buckteeth was sitting on the other side of the open seat. He coughed loudly into his hand and more gazes fell upon me.

I took the seat between Freckles and Hazel Eyes. I almost jumped back up, because the seat was absolutely freezing. It felt like my butt was on a block of ice. Confused, I slid my hand under my rear end. The wood felt cold enough to freeze water on contact, but there was no ice there or anything else that would explain why the seat was so cold. I shivered. This place was getting weirder by the second.

The voice in my head was looping, telling me, *I don't belong here. I don't belong here. I don't belong here.* I'd always thought I had really good karma. WTF? What did I do to deserve this?

Every single kid was staring at me, including Mick with the long white hair. I stared back—for what seemed an eternity—until they began to look away and went back to feeding. They didn't just eat the food—they demolished it noisily, hoovering away like it was some kind of contest or something. I shook my head, my grumbling stomach protesting as I searched for my usual breakfast fare of fruit and yogurt with a few walnuts and raisins sprinkled on top—the morning meal my mom had been preparing for me for as long as I could remember. But there was no fruit and/or yogurt in sight. I scooped some sickly looking scrambled eggs onto my plate and grabbed a piece of toast.

"Name's Cole," said Hazel Eyes as he pushed a plate of donuts and maple bars toward me. I took one. Mom would kill me. I tended to eat unhealthy when I was stressed, and I was totally stressed on this particularly weird and spooky day.

"You got a name?" he asked.

"My name's Echo."

"What are your parents, hippies?"

"Hardly. When I was two, I apparently repeated everything they said. So they just started calling me Echo."

"What's your real name?"

"I only tell my close friends that."

Cole nodded. So calm.

"Okay, nice to meet you, Echo. You better hurry up and eat while there's still food left. In case you hadn't noticed, we love to eat around here. Go ahead and dig in. Lunch isn't for hours."

I ate the eggs, which were better than they looked. I poured myself a glass of milk and drank some as I munched on the toast. My butt was still freezing, but I ate nonstop, succumbing to temptation and wolfing down a maple bar, and amazingly I wasn't even starting to get full. As I carelessly wiped milk from my chin, I inadvertently let loose with a sizeable burp. All eyes stared at me. Then Mick let loose with a burp, too, and someone chuckled. But the levity didn't last. I was thinking about how odd everyone here was when out of nowhere, I got smacked in the head with a donut. Sprinkles rained down.

"What the hell?!" I yelled.

I had no idea who threw the donut; it was as if the thing decided to attack me and just leapt off the plate on its own. The herd stared at me. My ears burned with embarrassment. I took vengeance upon the donut by biting into it. It was scrumptious and I shoved the rest into my mouth. Chewing like a mongrel, I saw something out of the corner of my eye—it looked like a spark or a streak of fire.

A cereal box in front of me burst into flames. I was scared out of my wits. What was *happening*? I was trying to figure it all out and my head felt lighter. No wonder, because I was having trouble swallowing and it gradually dawned on me that I was choking. Panic spread through my chest. I was turning blue! I opened my mouth to scream for help but nothing came out. I was gagging, waving my arms around like a fool. No one jumped up to help me. Instead they just stared at me with their cold white eyes. I should have been angry at their apathy, but

I was too scared. All I could think was *Please don't die, please, not now, Echo—it's not your time!*

Bees buzzed in my head. I was starting to lose consciousness and I begged God not to let me perish here in the land of creeps. Something slammed into my back, hard, and I thought they were finally doing it—they were ganging up on me and were going to put me down. But it was Cole, thumping the ball of his hand into my back. He was trying to save me but was only making things worse, lodging the deadly lump deeper in my throat. My eyes searched the room for help, but every single kid in there was staring impassively at me. The short boy with the scars, Zipperhead, smiled a tight little nasty vermin smile and made a choking gesture. It drew laughter. Despite my terror, I couldn't believe how cruel they were being.

I turned to Cole, who was eerily calm. His eyes were telling me not to panic, but the truth was I was no longer in control here; fear was rushing through me. My limbs were numb. I was starting to pass out. Cole got up and pulled me to my feet and started applying the Heimlich maneuver, wrapping his arms around my chest and yanking. A jolt of fear shot up my spine as my brain exploded in a kaleidoscope of red and yellow starbursts. I was going to die. I fought back, using my last reserves of strength to scream.

"Let go of me!"

Cole released his grip and I realized that I'd just screamed. He'd managed to dislodge the lump of food that was trying to kill me, and I was breathing again, sucking in air like I'd just broken the surface after a long dive. The kids kept staring like a herd of sheep. No one seemed to give a shit that I almost just died. My face was burning.

"Can't you see that I almost just died! What is *wrong* with you people?" I screamed.

A pause, then more laughter. Sadistic assholes! I scanned the collection of weird young faces, every one of them looking haunted and broken. I was pissed off, but still . . . I almost felt bad for them. They were scary but at the same time looked hopeless. I couldn't help myself and exploded with anger.

"I don't belong here! I'm not an orphan! My parents are *alive*!"

Pin drop. Five long seconds. Then the room absolutely *erupted* with cruel, taunting laughter that sliced my heart to ribbons. Zipperhead oinked like a pig and squealed in a shrill voice, mocking me. "Alive, I tell you—my mommy and daddy are alive!" More laughter. They were enjoying this.

I held my head high and walked out. I wished Andy were here. He would have kicked their sorry asses.

"Echo, wait!" said Cole.

"Echo? That's her *name*?" blurted Zipperhead.

This started an all-too-familiar game.

"Echo . . . Echo . . . Echo . . ."

Ha-ha. I got it, the big unoriginal joke. The one I'd heard my whole life. The life I couldn't wait to get back to.

INTRODUCTIONS

I ran from the dining room, down the hall, and into my room. I wasn't going to let them see me cry. I gave the door an angry slam and threw myself on the bed. Safely behind the closed door, the tears came and I didn't even try to resist. I hoped that releasing them would free me from the pain that was threatening to swallow me whole. It was like I'd not only lost my way but I was getting way too close to losing *myself*. I thought of my mom and dad and Andy. I kept fighting the horrible feeling that something awful had happened. The sobs came from deep within, racking my body until my stomach ached.

There was a knock on the door.

"Go away."

"You don't even know who it is," said Cole.

I was secretly glad it was him and not the tall woman or another gang of sadistic freaks.

"Please just leave," I said.

"Are you sure?"

When I didn't answer right away, he came in. I wiped away tears and curled into a ball. He sat at the foot of the bed. His fingers touched my ankle. I couldn't believe how light his touch was. Wait. Was he busting a move on me *now*?

"I'll help you with the laundry," he said gently. "But we better get it done soon. You don't want to piss off Headmistress Torvous—trust me."

He stood up and then his hand found my wrist. Oddly, I didn't jerk away but let him pull me to my feet. Again I noticed his killer lips. I told myself to knock it off.

"Come on. It'll be cake," he said.

Feeling like a kindergartener who'd just had a time-out, I followed Cole downstairs and we worked on the laundry. I had a million questions and I rattled them off. He thought about each one, and in the end he only answered two. But they were important ones.

Yes, there was a way out, and *yes*, he would help me.

For the first time since waking up in this freak zone, my spirits began to lift. I wanted to know how we were going to escape and why he was helping me, but I didn't press the issues, because I didn't want him to change his mind. We took the stuff out of the dryer and were folding towels when Cole asked me, "Your mom and dad—what were they like?"

The *past tense*—it was like a knife in my gut. I bristled.

"What do you mean '*were*'? I told you, they're *alive*!"

He stayed calm. Even though my eyes were burning with anger. He spoke softly.

"Tell me about them."

I wanted to tell him all about my amazing, beautiful mom, my smart and strong dad, how much they meant to me and how much my heart ached because I wasn't with them now. But I knew that if I started baring my soul, more tears would come. Because this insane fear was creeping up inside me. The fear that, as crazy and unfair as it seemed, my being in this horrible place was somehow justified. That Mom and Dad *were gone*. *No!* Stuff like that didn't happen to girls like me. I chased the thought away and pushed the fear down.

"I've got a better idea. You can meet them. I'll bring them back when you get me out of here, and then you can ask them anything you want."

"I can hear it in your voice that you really loved them."

"Cole, *stop* it! *Love* them. Not *loved*, I love them. No more past tense, okay?"

Right away he was nodding, his eyes full of empathy.

"Sorry. I get it. You love them. You'll always love them. Forever. Believe me, I understand."

But I wasn't so sure he did. I didn't think anybody here did. That's why I had to get out. Every minute I was there I felt like the place was changing me into someone I didn't want to be, and there was no way I was going to let that happen.

We brought the laundry back upstairs, folded and sorted, and delivered it to the rooms. While doing so, Cole acquainted me with some of my tormentors, trying to make nice, which was pointless because I was leaving ASAP. But he'd helped me out and I didn't want to be rude. In room number one, I met his roommate, the other kid who sat next to me at breakfast, the one with the freckles and red hair. His name was Dougie; he was eleven and tall for his age, all elbows and knobby knees. Even though it was super cold in the room, he was shirtless, his skin pebbled with goose bumps. I shivered as he nodded and gave me a limp fist bump when Cole introduced us.

"Sup, Cole?"

"Just showin' the newbie around."

Dougie nodded. "Totally amazing breakfast entertainment. First rate," he said.

Apparently he found himself immeasurably amusing, because he started goose-honk laughing. I plastered on a good-girl prom queen smile.

"Thanks so much. You certainly know how to make a girl feel welcome."

"Relax. Nobody takes stuff too personal around here. It's how we cope. You'll learn," said Dougie. "Man, is it just me or is it, like, sweltering in here?"

Dougie was becoming agitated, slapping his bare shoulders forcefully. "Damn, I shouldn't have hit him—it was just a slap was all, but he cried so hard. He just cried so damn hard," said Dougie.

"Let it go, man," Cole said.

But Dougie was pissed.

"Don't you think I *would* have by now if I could?"

I looked at Cole, who indicated it was time to leave, which was good because Dougie was stripping down to his plaid boxers to endure the "heat." This guy was clearly not right in the head.

Out in the hallway, I stopped Cole and spoke softly.

"What was up with him?"

"His little brother was bugging him, you know how that goes, and he hauled off and smacked him, and the kid cried bloody murder."

"So he can make it up to him, get another chance to be good to him, right?"

"Anything's possible," said Cole. His look told me to drop the subject and I did.

We moved on to room two, where we dumped off laundry for a petite young blonde, Beth, who was reading a book, the edges of which were charred, as though she'd rescued it from a fireplace. A dozen or so candles lit the room, which smelled of lavender. Beth looked up at me.

"Hey, newbie."

"Hi."

"Welcome to Middle House."

"Thanks."

I meant it. It felt good to have another human be civil to me. Beth's roommate was Marsha, closer to my age, maybe fourteen. She had curly hair, and by the looks of her acne and body, she was blasting her way through puberty. She was also a reader and gave me a perfunctory sneer, too cool to speak to me, apparently. "Nice to meet you, too," I said through a sarcastic smile. Marsha clenched her teeth and shot a quick glare at me.

A thick book fell off the shelf and thumped loudly onto the floor. I flinched as half the candles went out. I looked down and saw that the book was entitled *History of the Occult*. And then the candles were suddenly burning again. The falling book and weird flames didn't faze Marsha or Beth in the least. I shuddered for about the hundredth time since I'd woken up.

Cole and I moved on, and he introduced me to Cameron, gangly and dark-skinned, who had sweet, searching eyes. He wore big, black round glasses and snapped his fingers to a silent beat as he stared at a couple of goldfish he had in a big glass tank. The fish seemed to be swimming against some kind of current, but I couldn't see a pump anywhere. Another quirk of Middle House, no doubt. I sent a quiet prayer to the heavens: please don't let me be losing my mind! I didn't want to end up like one of these bizarre residents.

"Nice fish." What a conversationalist I was.

"Thank you," he said, his voice sounding oddly aquatic, as though he were gargling water or something. "One is a comet, the other a fantail. *Carassius auratus*. They're members of the carp family."

Cameron smiled at me. Apparently he really loved those fish. I smiled back, and for a moment we connected as he peered into my eyes.

"Nice meeting you," he said. "Happy hunting."

My heart jerked in my chest a little.

"What do you mean? Hunting what?"

"You'll find out," he said.

Then he closed his eyes, leaned closer to the fish tank, and grooved once again to the beatbox in his brain. More mystery. Great. Just what I needed.

Cole and I moved back out into the hall.

"This place is tremendously weird—you do know that, don't you?" I said.

"Yeah, I know."

I sighed. *Just get through this, Echo, somehow get through this.*

"It's nice of you to introduce me, but it's kind of pointless, because I'm not staying here, you know?"

He gave me another one of his thoughtful looks.

"Whatever you say."

He didn't get it. I was already gone. For the next several minutes we distributed laundry to various rooms, running into one circus sideshow after another. Then we headed to our final destination, my room, way at the end of the hall. I caught a glimpse of the breakfast cat dashing into it. When we entered, there was a girl, about twelve, sitting on the bed next to mine. She was beautiful, with slightly slanted eyes, which made me think maybe one of her parents was Asian. Her face was round as the moon and her hair was super long and full of highlights. She was painting her toenails.

"Lucy, this is Echo," said Cole.

"I saw you in the dining room," she said.

"Really? I don't think I saw you."

"I was there. I just wasn't one of the ones making fun of you."

"Oh. Well, thanks," I said.

I tried out a smile on her. She yawned and stretched, arching her back, and gave me a polite smile back. Words of kindness *and* a smile? I could hardly believe it. There was no sign of the cat, which I figured was under the bed or had scurried out.

"Is the cat yours?" I asked.

Ignoring my question, Lucy got up and started making her bed, moving quickly and efficiently. I started to do the same, and Cole helped me. This felt oddly domestic, and I immediately thought of Andy. I doubted he'd be cool with some guy helping me make my bed.

"I got it, thanks."

"It's no problem."

"I said I *got* it."

Cole backed off, stung. His sudden sadness stunned me. Before I could say anything else, he headed out into the hallway.

"I'll catch you later."

Lucy got up and opened a drawer and pulled out a plastic bag and handed it to me.

"Here. In case you want to get cleaned up."

"What's this?"

Lucy flopped down on her bed and wrapped her arms around her pillow.

"It belonged to Tawny. It's yours now."

"Tawny? Who's that? Where did she go?"

"She was my old roommate. She moved on."

I looked in the bag. Inside were shampoo, conditioner, a brush, a toothbrush, and toothpaste.

"Moved on where? You mean like to some foster home or something?"

But Lucy had already closed her eyes and didn't say another word.

"Lucy?"

She was dead asleep. I felt beat-up and scummy. I looked at the shampoo. Maybe a shower was just what I needed.

SHOWER

I grabbed a towel and wandered the cold hallways until I found the girls' showers. It was a creepy green-tile room with thick rusty pipes running overhead. Thankfully, I was alone. I peeled off my clothes quickly and turned on the water. The old pipes shuddered and rattled in a crush of noise and steam. The water was cold, but I wasn't about to stand around buck naked waiting for it to heat up, so I took the plunge. In seconds my teeth were chattering. I turned up the hot water. The pipes groaned in protest, but finally the spray transformed from freezing to merely chilly to warm to lukewarm and finally, nice and hot.

I soaped up and took care of business as fast as I could. The warm water soaked into my sore bones, but my hair was a disaster. I worked the shampoo Lucy'd given me into my scalp and was feeling almost normal when the water turned scalding hot.

"Ahhhhh!"

My skin was on fire and I had soap in my eyes.

"Dammit!" I yelled.

I reached for my towel but it was gone, along with my clothes. And then I heard it. Laughter. I stood with my eyes closed, stinging, covered in soap. I felt something on my toes. With the heels of my palms I wiped the soap from my eyes and looked down. I wanted to jump out of my body because slimy black *leeches* were wriggling up out of the drain and latching onto my feet. My body convulsed as an ungodly scream burst out of my throat.

I ran from the shower, certain I was going to slip on the slick floor and fall on my ass. But somehow I managed to remain upright, and when I looked down at my feet, the leeches were gone. I'd imagined the whole thing.

I looked over and saw a half-dozen girls laughing as they repeatedly flushed the toilets. Hence the scalding water. I stood there naked, too angry and way too proud to even bother covering myself up.

"Give me back my goddamn clothes!" I roared.

A couple of them flinched. A heavyset girl in pigtails—a truly regrettable choice for her—clomped forward and pointed an accusing finger at me. She was the bulky girl who'd grunted in my room before. I noticed her fingers were short and thick, her nails chewed close. The jumper she was wearing was too tight, and her breath was like a weapon. Ugh!

" 'I don't belong here!' " she said, mocking my breakfast outburst.

"What do you want?" I said

"You think you're better than us? Well, let me clarify something for you, newbie. In Middle House, you're *nothing*. Just like the rest of us. And for your information, you ain't going nowhere."

" 'I don't belong here!' " said another.

"You have no idea what you're talking about," I said. I was trying to sound calm, but my voice was shaky. I spotted my clothes and towel stuffed in a wastebasket and rushed over to get them. My speed surprised me, because I beat two other girls who tried to intercept me. One of them made a grab for my towel and I pushed her hard against the wall.

"Ow!" she yelped.

Pigtails pointed her finger at me again and her eyes narrowed into angry slits and she got right in my face.

"You know what you are? Stupid. You're so stupid you don't even know you're stupid. If you know what's good for you, you better learn to fit in."

"And how do I do that? By torturing people, like you? I don't think so. Besides, I don't have to 'fit in,' because I'm not staying here!"

Pigtails pulled her fist back like she was going to hit me. She made a punching motion but stopped just short of clobbering me. I jerked my head back anyway, so fast I fell backwards. Pigtails cut loose with a horselaugh. I'd had it.

"Please just leave me alone. I won't be here long enough to bother you," I said.

Pigtails shook her head and looked at the other girls.

"What'd I tell you? She's an airhead. She's still in denial."

One of the girls looked like she was going to make a move on me, so I scrabbled up and clenched my fingers into fists. Pigtails sneered at me.

"Oh, look at you, the badass bitch!"

She laughed, her belly jiggling. The other girls laughed along, then when Pigtails waddled out, they left, too, casting spiteful glances over their shoulders. I quickly rinsed off and toweled dry, and in a minute flat I was dressed and hurrying back to my room. Not exactly a spa day.

The remainder of the morning passed without incident. At

lunchtime—an orgy of food not dissimilar to breakfast—I again sat with Cole and Dougie. Dougie politely poured me water from a pitcher. It was so cold it hurt my teeth. Lunch fare was cheeseburgers, curly fries, shakes, six kinds of pizza, root beer floats, hot dogs, fried chicken, Tater Tots, and caramel bars. There wasn't a salad or vegetable in sight.

I felt guilty but I told myself I had no other choice and dug in, piling my plate with two bacon cheeseburgers, an apple fritter, and a handful of fries. I opted for a strawberry shake to drink—god, my mom would ground me if she saw me eating like this. Nonetheless, I proceeded to eat like the world was coming to an end, munching and slurping and burping like every other freak in the dining hall. Across the room, Pigtails was eyeing me. I stared hard at her and she flipped me the double bird.

"I see you've met Darby," Cole said.

"Yeah, we bonded in the showers."

"I hope you'll eventually become friends with her. She can be a powerful ally," he said.

I shook my head in disbelief.

"Believe me, I don't need friends like that. I think she's the pushiest bitch I've ever met. After the shit she pulled, I could have killed her."

Cole touched my hand. Tingles. Again, it was a *wow* thing.

"You shouldn't be so pissed at the world."

"I'm not pissed at the world!" I knew when I said it it sounded exactly like I *was* pissed at the whole world. I felt like an idiot.

"You might be surprised what you need and don't need in Middle House," said Cole.

I calmed down and ate. Just like at breakfast, my appetite was endless. I kept at it until some kids on the lunch detail started clearing the tables. Weirdly, I didn't feel sated. I knew it was because adrenaline had been pumping through my body like gangbusters, but still, all this gorging felt bizarre. I spotted Miss Torvous out in the hallway. I got up and rushed out to her. When she saw me coming, she hastened her pace. She couldn't wait to get away from me. I wondered why she disliked me so much. I raced out in front of her and blocked her path.

"Excuse me, um . . . I really need to talk to you. I know this is some kind of orphanage, and it seems very nice," I lied, "but I really do *not* belong here."

"Are you finished?" she said.

"No. I know for a fact that my parents are alive. I can prove it. Just let me go see them and we can clear this all up."

Cole had come out into the hallway and she signaled to him. He came right over.

"Cole, Miss Stone obviously needs a guide. Will you please handle that? Make certain she's processed, that she fulfills her learning."

"Yes, Miss Torvous."

"Good. I don't want any mistakes. Make certain it goes smoothly."

Miss Torvous turned on her heels and departed quickly.

"*Processed?*" What the hell did she mean by that?

"Echo, listen . . ."

"Oh, for god's sake, leave me alone!"

I'd freakin' *had* it. I ran down the hallway looking for an exit. I was so gone! I had to get out of there before my head exploded. I searched frantically for an exit but all I found were more doors leading to more hallways, like this place was some kind of insane maze. I raced upstairs to the third floor and yanked open a set of heavy drapes. Sunlight blasted me in the face. I could see trees and a lake. Which, in the Pacific Northwest, meant I could be just about anywhere. The window was painted shut. Going farther up didn't seem like a great strategy. So I backtracked, then found a stairwell and tore down it past the first floor into another part of the basement, praying that I could find some kind of subterranean getaway. I heard a voice behind me.

"Echo! Wait! Please stop running away from me."

Screw him. I kept running and reached a door, yanked it open, and slammed it behind me, locking it. I was in a long corridor, with a light flickering on and off at the end. I sprinted down the corridor so fast I nearly ran into the window, which was open. I could smell the fresh air, could almost taste my freedom. There was only one problem. The window had bars on it. Cole was at the door, knocking.

"Echo, open up. Please? You don't have to do this."

To hell with him. I was going to do whatever I had to do to get out of this godforsaken prison. The bars were wrought iron and spaced about four inches apart. For a second, I had this vision that I could somehow squeeze through them, even though I knew my head would never fit. I was seriously about to try this madness when I felt a hand on my shoulder. I spun around. It was Cole. He'd either had a key or was a lock picker.

"How the hell did you get in here?"

He ignored my question and opted instead to slowly shake his head as if I were a little kid asking a stupid question.

"This isn't necessary."

"Cole, I have to get out of here. I *have* to."

"You're going to."

"How?"

"I'll show you. Tonight."

I could tell by the look in his eyes that he meant it. I almost hugged him.

"Thank you."

He grinned, kind of sheepishly. I had no time for this petty flirting.

I thought of Andy. I couldn't wait to see him. And Mom and Dad. They must be worried sick. Tonight. Finally. Tonight was the night.

ESCAPE

I scarfed my way through dinner, another absurdly unhealthy, salty, fried, fat-laced but delicious meal. I was getting more than my share of looks, but no one was giving me the finger and nothing was freezing or catching fire, and the pastries had apparently decided to show mercy and not attack. Zipperhead actually smiled at me. In his own way, he was kind of cute and I wondered what had happened to the poor guy. My guess was he'd gotten hurt in a car accident. By the scars on his head, it looked like he'd gone through the front windshield. He was lucky to be alive.

I got back to eating. Every time I glanced up from my food, I saw someone else looking at me. I could feel the weight of their eyes on me and even though everything was tasty, I forced myself to quit eating and left.

After dinner, I went to brush my teeth—I didn't want to disappoint Mom by showing up with food stuck between my incisors—and then I withdrew to my room where I sat on my bed talking with Lucy. She had an annoying habit of licking her fingers every time she turned a page of the magazine she was reading. I noticed that she licked her lips a lot, too, and once or twice her knuckles as well. Ick. But I warmed up to her when she talked about her parents.

"My mom's an esthetician, and my dad drives a truck. It's not that easy, you know, maneuvering those big rigs around corners and stuff."

What I liked about her was that even though she was an orphan, she talked about her parents in the present tense. I imagined it made her feel somehow closer to them. I wondered how they'd died, but it felt rude to just come out and ask. She'd tell me when she felt like sharing, and I was okay with that.

Later, I changed back into my clean jeans and T-shirt. Lucy loaned me a hoodie and Cole came to get me. We were ready to go.

"Bye, Lucy. It was nice meeting you."

"I'll see you later," she said, stretching out on her bed.

No, you won't, I thought as I left her and followed Cole carefully down the hallway. The floorboards creaked. My heart was racing and I trembled, hoping Miss Torvous didn't come bursting out to confront us. But Cole didn't seem nervous at all. He moved casually; no big deal—we were just escaping, that's all. I had to admit he was pretty damn slick.

Cole led me to a side door. We paused in front of it, and then he pushed the bar—I cringed, waiting for an alarm bell to sound, but everything stayed quiet. I heard nothing but some faraway laughter, and suddenly we were outside, free.

I got my first good look at the building. It was a huge

château, an old, five-story Romanesque stone affair with two soaring cylindrical towers and a steep-pitched slate roof. Perfect, if you like horror movies. I swore the building was glaring at me, so I didn't feel like lingering. I looked up at the high stone walls surrounding the place and wondered how we were going to scale them. Cole took my hand and led me to a bulky wrought iron gate. It was like he was magic or something, because as soon as he barely touched it, it swung open. I smiled and looked into his eyes. They were beautiful. I was so happy I could have kissed him, but I squelched the urge and rushed through the gate—freedom!—and across an expanse of lawn. Looking back, I expected Cole to be right behind me, but instead he just stood by the gate, still as a statue.

"Are you coming?" I asked.

"Some things are best discovered alone," he said.

I'd started to feel safe around him. I was sorry he wasn't coming with me.

"I'll see you later," he said.

"I doubt that very much," I replied. I didn't want to be cruel, but no way in hell was I ever coming back to this awful place. I took one last look at Middle House, then turned and hurried into the night. At the top of the long sloping driveway, I looked back again. He was still there, watching me leave.

I looked to my right and saw what I hoped was Lake Washington glinting in the moonlight. In moments, I was up on a road and started jogging. It didn't take me long to recognize that I was on Holmes Point Drive. My heart leapt and my body flooded with hope. I wasn't that far from home!

For all I'd known, I could have been in a totally different state or even country, but fortune was smiling on me, because I could actually walk home from here. I hiked up Holmes Point Drive to Seventy-Sixth Place and then hung a right on Juanita

Drive. Whenever I saw headlights, I ducked into the bushes. The last thing I wanted was to be snagged by the Kirkland cops for a measly curfew violation.

Moving through the chilly night, I enjoyed this thrilling familiar feeling. I used to sneak out at night with my friend Dani Cooper. We once arranged a classic "freedom sleepover." Her parents thought she was coming to my place and my parents thought I was going to hers. We got dropped off in front of each other's houses, then hid our backpacks and met in front of the junior high school. It was weird to be there at night, the breezeways empty of kids, the old buildings looking dark and foreboding. Our goal was to crash the cheerleaders' slumber party and we had to traverse downtown Kirkland to get there.

I remembered my skin tingling with excitement as we moved from shadow to shadow, avoiding the streetlights, darting around like secret agents. We felt totally vulnerable and yet somehow invincible, too. We ran wild, laughing and shrieking. We were flying high. It was a total rush.

But we never made it. We got caught by the cops, who apparently had nothing better to do than nab a couple of teen girls out after curfew. When my parents came down to bail us out, my mom was beyond pissed off and my dad did his best to act angry, but I think he was secretly proud of me for attempting such a bold maneuver.

And now here I was again, out at night, gliding dreamlike through the streets, determined not to be seen, let alone caught by the cops or anyone else. I jogged along Juanita Drive all the way past the beach where I first learned to swim. Traffic was sparse so I only had to slip into the shadows every few minutes. When I got into Juanita proper, I took a right on Ninety-Eighth. That would take me all the way to Kirkland and home sweet home.

I felt fantastic. Sights and sounds and scents leapt out from the night like I was on some mind-altering drug. I heard crickets and frogs, my senses heightened beyond imagination. I felt so amazingly *alive*. And it was all because of this strange but helpful and kind of cute boy (okay, *really* cute) whom I'd left standing by the gate back at Middle House. I should have talked to him, at least said something nice, and thanked him. But what would have been the point? I was never going to see him again.

I was so amped up I wasn't even tired. I increased my pace from jogging to outright running. I ran until my calves were screaming, but I didn't care—the pain only made me run harder. I was running faster than I'd ever run in my life. The night slashed by on either side of me.

But then my head started to feel strange. The exertion was starting to get to me, I guessed. I was getting dizzy, moving into blackout territory. I didn't care. I had to get home. I had to see my mom and dad. I had to prove to everyone, most of all myself, that they were alive and well.

But deep inside, I was worried, and it was making me have flashes of ugly, violent images and sensations. Misshapen shadows lunged at me. My head felt like it was going to burst from the pain. I had a stabbing ache in my heart. I shook it all out of my skull and held on.

"Stop!" I screamed.

I gasped for breath. Then, with great resolve, I increased my pace, even though I knew at any moment I could have passed out. My parents were alive, and I was going to prove it. I thought about maybe even going back to Middle House and showing off my parents, shoving that fact in the faces of all those freaks.

I pumped my legs. Ninety-Eighth turned into Market Street. I cut over to First Street to get off the main arterial. Then I was on Nineteenth. Then Eighteenth. I lived on Twelfth Street, so I was almost home. Every few seconds, I felt like I was jerking forward, like in a movie where dozens of frames have been cut out. I knew my brain was so lacking in oxygen that it was playing tricks on me. I should have stopped and caught my breath. But something was tugging me forward like a puppet on a string and I rocketed ahead. Fifteenth Street. Fourteenth. I saw headlights sweeping the street ahead of me and looked back. A cop car was right on my ass. I darted into an alley on Thirteenth Street. I'd made a horrible mistake—the alley was a dead end. I ducked into a shadow and flattened myself against a garage door.

I held my breath. The cop car cruised by slowly, pulled into a driveway, then backed around for another pass. It was moving agonizingly slow, tires crunching on gravel, the sound tormenting me. The cops must have been toying with me, I thought, trying to put a scare into a dumb teenager. The cop riding shotgun, a woman, had her window down and gazed vaguely in my direction. My stomach was in my throat. I knew she was looking right at me. I tensed, ready to run my butt off. But her eyes looked distracted by something, like she was deep in thought, and miraculously they kept moving. I could hear the crackle of their radio. The voice of a dispatcher pulled their attention away and they sped off, tires kicking up bits of gravel.

I exhaled. Wow. I had an angel looking out for me tonight. I was alone again in the quiet darkness. I shook my head in disbelief and smiled. *Not busted!* I took off running, racing down to Twelfth, where I cut a right. I was in luck as I passed by the house on the corner, ready for the Siberian husky, Wesley, to bark his damn head off and chase me like he always did. He was in the yard, but tonight he just raised his snout and gazed as I went by, and kept his yappy mouth shut. I kept running.

And then, in the distance . . . there it was. My house. My home. I was elated. I ran closer, then stopped in my tracks, my world knocked off its axis. I was having a hard time letting it into my brain, but my house looked dark and unfamiliar . . . like a death mask, the front door a nose, the two black windows on either side of it eyes that had faded away. Something horrid had happened in our house. Death hung in the air like a fog. Maybe I was wrong—jumping to insane conclusions. Maybe Mom and Dad were just sleeping. But why wasn't the porch light on? They always left it on. Pinpricks crawled across my arms as I walked forward, edging closer to the truth. I blinked, not wanting to believe what I saw. I felt like someone was tightening barbed wire around my stomach. My house was striped with yellow tape screaming CRIME SCENE DO NOT CROSS.

CRIME

I ran to the front door, my brain buzzing, but it was locked. I pulled the hidden key from the fake rock, then unlocked the door and pushed it open.

"Mom! Dad!"

An unforgiving silence greeted me. I reached to switch on the lights but stopped myself. I didn't want a prowling cop car to drive by and see me inside with the place lit up. I got the emergency flashlight from the hall closet, turned it on, and began my search, scanning the entryway at the bottom of the stairs. A lamp was overturned, the burgundy shade torn. A glass-top table was shattered. Family pictures had been knocked from the walls and lay broken on the floor. "Daddy?"

I found his golf trophy picture on the floor and touched it

gently. I swept the beam of the flashlight around and found more broken pictures. It looked bad, really bad. And it got worse. There was blood on the wall. The unthinkable was entering my brain, eating its way in like some hideous insect.

"No . . ." I whispered. "I don't believe it." My voice sounded distorted, like it was coming from someone else. "This isn't happening."

I found a pool of dried blood. My knees buckled. This was it. This was where it had happened. I could feel it and smell it. The crime scene. This was where the murder had occurred.

"Oh god . . ."

Who had the blood belonged to? A voice screamed inside my head. *Mom or Dad!*

I wanted to be brave. To be strong. But tears spilled from my eyes. I sobbed. A piercing ache in my heart overwhelmed me. I wanted to be swallowed by the earth. My crying echoed through the house, but I finally stopped and set my jaw. Why was I jumping to conclusions? I needed more information, so I raced upstairs.

"Mom! Dad!"

In their room the canopy bed was a mess, the sheets, blankets, and pillows strewn everywhere. But no blood! I looked in their bathroom, their closet. But they weren't there. I kept shaking my head in denial. The shitstorm that was congealing into the truth was tearing at my heart. I grasped my mother's bathrobe and clung to it, inhaling her scent. The sense of loss was twisting me inside out.

I kept hoping, kept believing that they were still alive. But everything pointed to the contrary. I'd been placed in Middle House because they were gone. Mom and Dad were gone. Dead. Murdered. All I could think about was how I wanted to join them, wherever they were. I was contemplating ways to accomplish this when I saw a light go on next door on the second floor. It was him! Andy! I ran to the window, opened it, and shouted.

"Andy!"

He didn't hear me. He was wearing headphones. I waved my arms and wiggled the flashlight beam back and forth. But his head was buried in his laptop. I turned to go to his house—I was going to run into his arms and cry. But I saw lights sweep across the bedroom wall. Outside, a car was pulling up across the street. At first I thought it was a cop car, but then I recognized it. It was Mom's blue Camry! Two people were sitting in the front. I sprinted down the stairs before I knew it, moving inhumanly fast. I blasted through the front door I didn't even remember opening.

The falling rain chilled me as I tempered my pace and walked toward the car. I had to make sure it was actually them—I didn't want to sneak up on some strangers and scare them to death. Twenty feet from the car, I heard crying. Coming from the woman in the driver's seat. Fifteen feet, a man's voice. Sounded like my dad. I drew closer, trembling with anticipation. I knew it! I *knew* they were alive. I walked in a cautious arc so I could clearly see through the front windshield.

My father, so handsome, gray around his temples, a receding hairline but good, strong, refined features, was consoling my mom, who was behind the wheel. I noticed suitcases piled in the back seat. My mom was a beautiful woman but right now she looked horrible, her face blotchy, her eyes red from weeping, her hair unkempt. She was crying hard, her chest rising and falling with every sob.

"Mom, it's okay!"

She was crying so loud she didn't hear me. They must have thought I'd run away! My heart was lifting up in my chest. This would all be over now. My family's collective nightmare would come to an end and we would hug each other so tightly we wouldn't be able to breathe.

"Mom . . ."

I stepped toward the car. My father was hugging my mother now, wiping away her tears. I could see that he was crying, too. He looked out the window but I couldn't tell if he saw me since he gave no sign; there was no recognition in his eyes. Maybe I looked like some crazy girl wandering the night.

"Don't cry, you guys! I'm okay," I said.

Mom abruptly started the car. They must have wanted me to get in. They probably couldn't wait to get away from our house and the scene of the horrible tragedy that had occurred here, whatever it was. As I reached for the back door, intending to climb inside—the Camry shot forward, the tires chirping against the asphalt.

"Wait!"

My eyes bugged out. What the hell was going on? Mom didn't stop; instead, she sped up.

"WAIT! I'M RIGHT HERE!" I screamed.

It didn't seem possible but in their grief, they didn't see me. The Camry sped down Twelfth and turned left. They were heading out for the main drag, Market Street. I gritted my teeth. No way was I letting them get away. I started running, racing, trying to catch up. I tore down an alley, moving so fast I surprised myself. Then I bolted into the street, right in the middle, and the headlights of the Camry were in my eyes. I squinted at the brightness and waved my arms.

"Stop! It's me! It's Echo! I'm okay! I'm alive!"

I smiled through tears of joy, knowing they would stop and get out and run into my arms for the best family hug we'd ever have in our whole lives. But something was terribly, terribly wrong. The Camry was. Not. Slowing down. WTF?

"No! Stop! Mom! It's me!"

The lights kept coming. I knew I should jump out of the way but I couldn't.

"I'M ALIVE!" I screamed at the top of my lungs.

I spread my arms out, Christlike, as the world shifted into an altered, blurry state of slow motion. I wasn't going to move. They were going to hit me head on. I didn't want to die, but something was forcing me to stand still, my feet glued to the pavement.

"Look at me!" I screamed.

Then the impossible happened. My mom's Camry, with her and Dad in it, passed right *through* me. It felt like a whoosh from a gale-force wind, and the experience filled my mind with a myriad of sights and sounds and memories and a hundred other sensations from my past. In one second that felt like a lifetime, it was over. I turned slowly and watched my parents speed away into the night. My body felt like it'd been pummeled. Then the horrible truth occurred to me.

You were right all along, Echo. Your parents are alive. But you're *not.*

At that moment, I wished I was dead. But I knew . . . my wish had already come true.

LOVE

I ran as fast as I could through the backyard and into the adjacent park. I had to get away, from here, from the memory, from everything. I thought maybe if I ran fast enough, I could run through this nightmare and come out on the other side awake and alive.

I ran into the deep, old woods. I hastened my pace, wanting to put distance between me and the pain. I couldn't be dead! I ran and ran. At one point, in a clearing, I lifted my arms and I could feel myself rising off the ground. I stopped, and floated back down. It was a hard truth to swallow, that I was deceased, and I refused to embrace it. There had to be some way out of this.

A fleeting hope raced into my brain.

"Andy!"

Andy would help me! I took off running again, flying out of the forest back toward our houses. Now I knew the truth. The reason I'd been able to run so fast wasn't because of the adrenaline, it was because I was lighter, my corporeal being having been left behind. My life was over. Sixteen years, gone in a blink.

No! I screamed to myself. *I'm alive!! I'm not dead! I can't be!*

I needed Andy, needed him so bad then that my heart ached more deeply with every beat. I ran like crazy and reached his house in a blink. I stood in the side yard looking up at the light in his window. The nagging fear voice in my head spoke again.

You're only setting yourself up for more pain.

I wondered how I was going to get up to his room. As though obeying a thought command, I found myself climbing the side of the house like a gecko. *This isn't real. This is a dream.* But I knew it was real, that this was my new normal. I shuddered with revulsion—it felt so weird to be climbing like some freaky creature, but I was spurred on by the belief that I was going to go and hug my one true love, cling to him like he was the last person on earth. I reached his window.

Somehow I was able to hold on to the side of the house, as though my hands and feet had a sticky substance on them. I stared in at Andy. His eyes were bloodshot. He'd been crying. My heart sank. I saw the open bathroom window to my left. I slid over and climbed in, taking care not to knock over the stuff on the sill.

My feet felt light on the carpet as I moved down the hallway. Andy's door was partly open and I slowly pushed my way in. I didn't want to frighten him. Fear spoke. *He won't see you.*

"Andy?"

My voice was barely a murmur. I waited, my heart thudding. He didn't look up. He still had the headphones on. I could hear the music. It was "Love Me Anyway," by Manon Denat. It was our song! My heart was melting. I took another step forward and in my peripheral vision I could see his bulletin board, crowded with newspaper clippings and Internet printouts. But there was no time to stop and gaze anywhere else but at his amazing eyes. I waved my hand to get his attention and spoke louder this time.

"Andy?"

He didn't look up. He was writing on his laptop. He paused to wipe away a tear and then resumed. I knew I was invading his privacy, but I had to know what he was writing, so I moved closer, shifting behind him, and peered over his shoulder. I read, my eyes savoring every word.

My sweet Echo. I love you more than life itself. I want to hold you in my arms. I want to kiss you. I want to tell you everything that I'd always wanted to tell you but was afraid to because I didn't want to scare you away. Now I know I should have spoken those words; I should have stood on a mountain and shouted them to the sky, should have told you a thousand times, I love you, I love you, I will always love you. Now, it's too late, and every waking moment is a nightmare for me.

A tear ran down my cheek.

"It's not too late," I said.

He didn't hear me.

"ANDY!"

I was screaming now, repeating his name over and over.

He can't hear you, said the troublesome fear voice in my head.

He can, too! He will!

I took a big breath and screamed his name again.

"ANDY!"

"Andy?"

It was like my voice had a reverb—I was hearing it twice. It was haunting. The echo—my namesake—contained a deeper, foreboding tone. Andy looked up. Right into my eyes. I gasped. My insides flooded with relief and my whole body tingled.

"Oh baby, I've missed you so much!"

He blinked.

"Andy?"

The reverb voice again. His bedroom door opened all the way and his father Hank entered. I felt like I'd been kicked in the stomach. Andy wasn't looking at me at all; he was looking right *through* me—at his father.

"What are you working on?" said Hank.

Andy deftly closed his laptop before his father could read the screen. Hank looked over at the bulletin board and fingered the clippings on it. My eyes followed him and I felt a creeping nausea as I read the headlines:

Local Girl Found Murdered
Lake Washington Teen Dead
Girl Killed, Burglary Suspected

There were a dozen more articles fighting for space on the board but I couldn't look at them. Except for one. The one featuring my yearbook picture—the one I loathed—staring out with a surprised gaze, a forced smile plastered on my face. I'd hated that picture since the day the yearbook came out. I thought I looked particularly clueless in the photograph, like a girl who didn't have the faintest notion of what she was going to become. Like she feared life. Now that photograph seemed eerily prescient, as though I had known something terrible was going to happen to me all along.

"It's not going to do you any good to dwell, Andy," said Hank.

He reached up and pulled out a pushpin from one of the clippings. It fell from the corkboard and fluttered to the floor. Andy jumped up from the bed and grabbed it.

"I'm not going to just forget her!"

"Nobody's asking you to."

"That's funny, because it sounds like that's exactly what you're asking me to do! She's not even in the ground yet and you come in here like this! Jesus, Dad!"

"Don't talk to me like that." Hank's eyes hardened.

"I'll talk to you any way I want. You don't get it, do you? I loved her!"

There it was, like a sledgehammer to my gut. The *past tense*. I was past tense, gone. Truly and wholly gone. The concept, in all its ugly finality, was beginning to sink in.

If I wasn't even in the ground yet, that meant they hadn't had my funeral. Seeing as I'd apparently been murdered, they were probably doing an autopsy. I pictured my body on a marble slab being cut up, and an involuntary shudder slithered through me.

Andy was so close I could smell him. I reached out with my hand and tried to touch his face, but I couldn't make contact. I was an ethereal being, transparent, without form or substance. He couldn't feel me. I spoke to him, praying that somehow he would hear my voice.

"Oh baby, I'm so sorry. I miss you . . ."

I closed my eyes and begged the universe that I might dream myself away from there, away from that room, from the awful truth. I wanted to dream us both away to a place, *our place*, down by the river, the soft grass on a spring day, holding hands, staring up at the clouds, listening to the wind rush through the tall, leafy reed grass, giggling at everything and nothing, lost in the moment, content in the simple pleasure of each other's company.

I heard soft crying. It was me. I heard my fear voice again. It felt like a cold hand on the nape of my neck and sent shivers sweeping down my spine. The voice said, *You have to let him go.*

I can't.

You don't have a choice.

What if the voice was right? What if I didn't have any choice but to leave Andy and forget about him? It was unthinkable. Andy and his father argued. My head swam. Their voices sounded muffled and distorted, as though *they* were the ghosts and I were human. I felt faint, deprived of oxygen. My knees grew weak and my heart rose in my chest. Andy's eyes narrowed and a wisp of what could have been fear flashed in his eyes. *No, no, no!* He was staring right at me when he screamed.

"Get out!"

It was like a cold slap in the face. Stars exploded in my head. I was jolted backward by my own revulsion and whooshed out through the wall and landed on the lawn below. I heard Andy scream again.

Get out!

The words reverberated in my head. *He was talking to his father.*

Wasn't he?

I held myself against the cold. I had to face facts. I was dead. Dead as the nail in a coffin.

RULES

I tried to think back, tried to remember what had happened in my house, but every time I tried to go there, a blinding flash of pain jolted my brain. And the harder I tried to remember, the more intense the pain became. To say this *sucked* would have been the understatement of my lifetime. Or whatever. I was getting really pissed off. What did I ever do to deserve this? I'd followed all the rules—I was supposed to be having a wonderful life! And so I ran with rage, without direction, but not without intention. I wanted to meet my murderer head on and choke them until they confessed why they did this to me.

Who would want to kill me? And why? What the hell did I ever do? My anger and confusion made me run faster. I ran through a fence, a car, a man walking his dog. I was like a power-ful wind blowing furiously through the night.

I stopped, expecting to be tired, but I hadn't even broken a sweat. I wondered if I even sweated anymore, now that I was a ghost. Did my pits stink? I ran again, this time just racing away, my feet a blur. I blasted through a thicket of saplings and onto a street. I saw headlights. A car roared by me, dan-gerously close, but the driver didn't even notice me. Why should she?

I had driven my mom's car only a few times, practiced in the school parking lot on Sundays with Dad as my copilot. He was scared out of his wits but pretended I was doing a great job as I lurched and braked, lurched and braked in a clumsy, fear-ful rhythm. We did it over and over until I finally got the hang of it. Now, I thought, what had been the point? Thanks, Dad, for teaching me how to drive. I'm sure it's going to come in really handy now that I'm dead.

I sat down smack in the middle of the road. I was trying to kill myself all over again. Cars roared through me with no more effect than a puff of wind.

I began to cry. With each tear came another thought, another image. Losing Mom and Dad. Losing Andy. Never going to prom. Never graduating. Cars whooshed over me and I didn't even bother to look up. Instead I just stared at the pavement. I had no idea what I should do. In my mind I was wandering aimlessly, like an animal lost in the forest. And then it hit me and I stood up. I knew exactly what I had to do. I was going to find out who killed me and make them pay. I vowed I would find my killer if it was the last thing I did on earth.

But the question was, how? Where to start? I walked around Kirkland, up and down the streets where I'd grown up. Every memory brought up buckets of tears and I cried inside for what seemed like hours. I wondered if time passed the same for me now that I was . . . dead. Did ghosts tell time? What was I capable of? What could I do and not do? I had so many questions and gradually came to understand that the only way I could even begin to comprehend myself, to get answers, was to return to the place I'd found so horrible, Middle House.

With grim determination I backtracked down Market Street, not bothering to run, but still moving incredibly fast, reaching Juanita Drive in minutes. I turned left and headed up to Holmes Point Drive. I jogged and closed my eyes, taking great leaps through the air.

Cole was waiting for me in the same spot where I'd left him, as if no time had passed at all. He was tranquil and his eyes were full of compassion. He moved to an old carved-stone bench and sat down, motioning for me to join him. I did.

"Welcome back."

I was too numb to speak.

"What did you find?" he said.

I couldn't stay mute. I had to let the truth out.

"Um . . . my parents are alive."

"Good."

"And I'm . . . dead."

He let that hang there for a few seconds.

"Yeah, I know. Echo, I'm so sorry."

I stared at a nearby towering Douglas fir tree. Its bark glistened and pulsed with life. My vision was incredible. It was as if I could see each individual fiber of the bark. My senses were enormously acute. I could feel life vibrating from everything around me. It was ironic. All this life, and there I was, deceased.

Cole gently placed his hand on mine. I wondered how I could feel a ghost hand on my own ghost hand. I wondered about a lot of things. Even though it felt good—his touch was so tender—I pulled my hand away. Andy. I wouldn't betray him, not even in death.

I looked at Cole. His eyes were crystal clear and steady. Swallowing the lump in my throat, I spoke, my voice halting and tentative.

"You knew, didn't you? You knew what was going to happen when I went home."

"Yes."

"Why didn't you warn me?"

"It's *the learning*. You needed to find out yourself. In your own way. We all had to do it."

I nodded. It made sense. The other kids could have talked to me until they were blue in the face and I wouldn't have believed them. I had to go and find out on my own. But I still yearned for answers.

"There are some things . . . I want to try and understand."

"I know. You must have a million questions."

"Why don't I remember anything? I mean dying, or being killed, murdered, I guess. When I think about it, try to search in my mind, all I get is a massive migraine."

Cole opened his mouth like he was going to answer my question, but he closed it as he glanced to our right.

One by one, they emerged from the shadows. A clutch of the Middle House kids. Now I saw them for what they were. Ghosts.

Zipperhead was the first to speak.

"When people die a normal kind of death, like from sickness, and they're surrounded by their loved ones, they pass from their mortal life on to the next one smooth-like, no problemo."

Cameron, the dark-skinned boy with the goldfish, piped in.

"But when you're murdered, killed in cold blood, it's radically different."

The black cat from the dining hall darted out and stopped two feet in front of me. It stood on its hind legs. I watched as the cat morphed into Lucy, my Middle House roommate with the long hair. I felt faint.

"Being murdered, it's appalling. It happened to all of us at Middle House. The experience is so traumatic that your soul's consciousness is shattered like a pane of glass into a thousand fragments."

Pigtails Darby appeared and shook her head as she pushed Lucy aside.

"Well, that's all very poetic, Lucy, but how about someone just tells it like it is?"

Darby moved closer to me, again in my face.

"This business takes time, and a hell of a lot of effort, to bring back the memory of your death. You can't just demand it or force it! It sucks, but it's a process, got it?"

She had her hands on her hips and looked like she wanted to slap me around just to make sure I got her message.

"Yeah," I mumbled.

I remembered Miss Torvous using that word. *Processed*. If this was being "processed," I didn't like it one bit. I stared at the Middle House kids who now surrounded me. I looked them in the eyes one by one. Zipperhead, Lucy the cat girl, Fish Guy Cameron wearing his glasses, Pigtails Darby, Snow Hair Mick, and freckled Dougie. I didn't know what the hell had happened— but whereas they were menacing before, now they all, even Darby, kinda, looked so damned *friendly*. My lower lip was puffing up and I could hear the tremor in my voice as soon as I spoke.

"Why were you all so *m-m-mean* to me?"

Darby clamped a beefy hand on my shoulder.

"All newbies get hazed. It toughens you up. It's not like it's a picnic being a ghost. You gotta have balls!"

Great. Now not only did I have to adjust to being dead, but I was supposed to grow a set of balls, too. It was all too bizarre. I'd gone and died. Maybe, I thought, I'd already *gone* to hell.

CONFESSIONS

Now that I knew the other kids were ghosts, I noticed things about them that I'd been ignoring before. Their skin was different: pale to be sure, but it was more than that. They almost glowed, as if lit from within by a pastel moon. Mick, the wet-feet kid, pulled a candy bar from his pocket and bit off a hunk. I realized something and was thinking out loud.

"My god, I ate like a pig and didn't even feel full. Because I'm a . . ."

"Say it!" snapped Darby.

"No . . ."

"Go on; don't be a pussy—just say it!"

"I'm a . . . ghost . . ."

The word hung in the air and echoed through my brain.

Zipperhead grinned, then spoke. "Being a *ghost* has some perks. We can eat all we want. Cheeseburgers, fries, cupcakes, candy, ice cream—you name it."

Darby patted her thighs.

"Yeah. Just like regular teenagers but ten times as much. We get to eat like horses and we don't gain an ounce! I used to worry about my stupid weight all the time. But not anymore. I'm a BBB. A big, beautiful babe. And anybody who says different I'll kick their butt to the curb!"

No one stepped forward to contradict her. I looked at my body and shook my head in disbelief.

"So . . . I'm going to be like this . . . the same hair . . . same weight . . . as when I was . . ."

"It's cool. Go ahead and say it," blurted Dougie. "You were killed. Murdered. Snuffed out."

I kept looking down at my body. A memory rushed into my head. I remembered being in a Krispy Kreme donut shop, wolfing down two maple-glazed crullers. My eyes were red from crying. I'd been in a fight with Andy. That was my therapy, the donuts my meds.

Before my untimely demise, I had been stressed out—about almost everything in my life, not only Andy—and I'd taken to pigging out on Krispy Kreme donuts and had gained two pounds, up to 114 from 112. Great.

"This is totally harsh. What did I ever do to deserve this?" I said.

What I got back from the group was a bunch of dirty looks.

"You didn't DO anything!" said Cameron. He was suddenly angry as hell, as was Darby.

"You think any of us *did something* to deserve being murdered?" she said. "Jesus!"

"Sometimes bad things happen to good people," said Zipperhead. "There's no accounting for it. Shit happens, and then you die."

I'd heard that depressing statement so many times before but in this moment it was oddly comforting. I felt a little relieved, as I'd been telling myself that I could have *only* wound up like this if I'd done something terribly wrong. Of course they were right. I was innocent. I was starting to feel better, but the reality that my old life was gone was overwhelming.

I wanted to take off running again but I knew it was too late for that. There was no outrunning this afterlife. I'd been flung into purgatory. I looked at my Middle House roomies. They read the question in my eyes. I wanted to know how they had died, if any of them knew. They didn't say anything, so I gave them a prompt.

"How did all of you . . . ?"

Mick said, "Missing from my stepfather's yacht, presumed drowned. Body never found. So far."

I had an "aha" moment. Drowned. That would explain the wet footprints he left behind wherever he walked.

Zipperhead said, "Pushed from a sixth-story balcony." He pointed to the zipper scars on his head. "These babies . . . were the result of my head saying 'howdy' to a couple of wrought iron fence spikes."

"With a head like that, how could they miss?" said Dougie.

"Tell the rest of it," said Cameron.

"Oh, and the wrought iron fence was struck by lightning. While I was impaled."

Zipperhead rubbed the scars on his head and the action caused sparks to fly. It was the strangest thing I'd ever seen. I had a feeling there was more to come.

Dougie and Cameron lost it, shoving each other as they hooted and hollered with laughter.

"It was an electrifying experience!" said Dougie.

"Oh, I'm so going to die from laughter," Zipperhead said sarcastically. Then he continued explaining to me. "The docs tried to save me, but my brain was mush. I died on the respirator."

"Okay, okay, check this out," said Darby.

She pointed to herself. Her visage changed as bullet holes appeared—four in her chest and one in her forehead.

"Shot five times. Mistaken identity, had to be. I mean, who would ever want to shoot me, huh?"

Dougie and Zipperhead started to laugh but Darby stifled them with a hard look, then got back to schooling me.

"It took a lot of pain, but now I can remember it happening. I can see the moron with the gun, his face like a pit bull. I still haven't found the shooter. He was a stupid gangbanger, and when I find him, I'm going to haunt him so bad he'll want to shoot *himself* five times. In the face. Although, when I think about it, that would be kind of hard to do."

"I'm . . . so sorry," I said.

Darby looked like she was about to spit out some harsh words but instead just nodded at the ground.

Hearing them all vent about their own murders was freaking me out. I had so many questions spinning around in my head that I felt like if I opened my mouth to speak, the words would fly out like bats from a cave. I tried to stay silent but I couldn't.

"This isn't fair! I can't be dead! Who killed me?!"

"Things will come back to you— memories, in bits and pieces," Cole said.

I shook my head.

"What does being a ghost even mean? I mean, what *am I*, exactly?"

"You're just like us," said Lucy. "You're an in-betweener."

"And in-betweener?"

She continued.

"You're not alive, obviously, but you haven't moved on yet, either, to the final place, the eternal place, where you wait for rebirth. You asked about Tawny, how she moved on? Well, she did it by finding her killer and paying him back. That's what Middle House is all about. It's where we go, where we wait until we resolve our issues."

"And once we do that, we get to move on, with the Afters, to await being reborn," Mick said. He looked hopeful.

I thought about being reborn. The concept calmed me, but only for a moment. The image of Andy entered my brain. I couldn't shake it and knew I never could. I wanted no part of any kind of existence without him.

"It took me three months to find out who killed me, but I remembered," said Dougie. "I was just cruisin' along, not trying to remember, you know, when all of a sudden I heard a random door slam, really loud, and bam—it just came to me. The door slamming triggered a memory. I remembered being locked in a freezer. By my freakin' uncle. Slowly freezing to death while screaming for help and pounding and clawing on a six-inch-thick steel door 'til my fingers bled? That is a messed up way to go, I can tell you that right now."

I felt so sorry for him.

"What a horrible way to die."

"There ain't exactly no good way, missy," said Darby.

"Your uncle. Did you haunt him, or kill him, or what?" I asked.

"Not yet—he's out of the country. He, like, imports processed meats and bails out of town for weeks at a time. We'll get the SOB one of these days. My dream is that we get him so good that he confesses, to my whole family."

The others nodded. Cameron patted Dougie on the back.

"We'll nail him—you can take that to the bank, bro."

Cameron drew in a long breath, then shared his story.

"I was hit at the base of my cerebellum," he said, lifting his hair to reveal a hideous hole. "It was a powerful blow, right there to the nape of my neck, probably by a hammer. I was working on my aunt's roof. It might have been her—everyone said she's crazy; she has eleven cats."

Lucy sneered. "And the problem with that is?"

Cameron ignored her and continued.

"It might have been my cousin Cindy, my aunt's freaky goth daughter, who had a thing for me, which I didn't particularly reciprocate."

"Particularly?" I said.

"Well, not after the first time. She had dog breath. I just wasn't into her. It might have been her crazy-jealous boyfriend. Who knows? I never saw it coming."

Now Lucy told her tale.

"Mine was poison. People said it was my mom, but I think it was her best 'friend,' Centa. Mom and Dad were taking a break and I was staying with Centa. Mom was there, but I just kept getting sicker and sicker and Centa's a Christian Scientist, so we just prayed. And . . . here I am."

I looked at them, this group of kids who'd all met untimely deaths. I felt so incredibly sorry for them for a moment that I forgot about my own troubles. I hugged myself and as I felt the touch of my fingers on my arms, something occurred to me.

"Hey, if I'm a ghost, how come I can feel myself?" Then I reached over and touched Cole. "How come I can touch you and feel *you*?" I bent down and picked up a rock. "And how come I can touch this and feel this?"

"Ghosts can touch and feel each other, but not the living. The living can't see or hear or feel us," said Cole.

"And we can touch stuff and move it around," added Zipperhead. "And sometimes when stuff touches us, we barely feel it, it passes right through us. Weird, I know."

Even though I didn't really comprehend, I nodded. This was all going to take some getting used to.

"We better get a move on, guys," said Cole, looking at me. He meant I should go with them.

"Um, do we have something important to do?" I asked.

"As a matter of fact, yes. We have an appointment."

"With who?"

"My stepfather," said Mick. "Mister Joshua Everett Mowrer. Are you in?"

"Don't bring her," said Darby. "She'll just get in the way."

"It's up to Mick," said Zipperhead.

"If you want to come, it's okay with me," said Mick.

"Call me crazy, but I'm not going anywhere unless I know where we're going and what we're doing," I said.

"We're going haunting," said Dougie.

Cole patted me on the shoulder affectionately.

"That's all you need to know. Let's go. Stay close to me."

They took off into the night. I hung back, wondering what I should do. Then it hit me. I had to follow them. To find my killer, I was going to have to watch, listen, and learn.

REVENGE

The group moved incredibly fast; we weren't flying, actually, but running so swiftly it felt like I was riding a mini hurricane. We whooshed through the streets, phantoms unseen by humans. Only an occasional dog or cat or squirrel took any notice. I tried again to remember what had happened to me.

I saw a hallway at school, then an image of me driving my car, fast. Someone was chasing me. I was on the verge of remembering when my brain throbbed with pain. I reeled and clenched my jaw. *Come on, Echo, remember!* Darby was watching me. I was expecting another tongue-lashing but her eyes softened a little.

"You're trying to force it, aren't you?"

"Yeah, I guess so."

My head felt like someone had hit me with a rock.

"And it hurts like a sumbitch, right?"

"Yeah."

"So don't go there; back off. Think of something else."

I did. I thought of Andy. The two of us in his bedroom one afternoon when his dad was gone. We kissed. And touched. It was heaven. My headache subsided. Darby was watching me.

"Better?"

"Yeah."

"Hey. You'll find out who did you in. And then maybe if you don't piss me off too much, I'll help you kick their stupid ass," she said.

She was the meanest of the mean at Middle House, and now I was starting to like her a little. Cole was right. She was going to be a powerful ally. She lifted up into the sky and flew. The others followed. I was running fast, but fear kept me earthbound. Until Cole turned around and waved me up. Even though I'd felt myself lift off the ground a while ago, I had no freakin' idea how to fly. What was the first step? I ran faster, my legs a blur, and began to imagine myself airborne, and then it happened—I lifted up into the sky and flew. I soared over Kirkland, looking down at the lights below. It was like a dream. I almost felt joyful. But the reality of my situation intervened. I suddenly hoped this *whole thing* was a dream. But it wasn't. I was D.E.A.D.

We arrived at the Kirkland Marina, circling overhead. Cole took my hand and helped me land.

"Um . . . thanks. That was . . ."

"Amazing?"

"I was thinking awesome, but yeah."

He smiled at me. I was feeling a little bipolar. Hey, I'm dead, *but by the way I can fly and he is really cute.* I told myself to knock it off. I had to get a grip and somehow find a way back to my old life with Andy.

The parking lot was mostly empty, except for a few boat trailers and some pickup trucks. Mick climbed the marina clock tower.

"Nine fifteen. He should be here any second."

After a few moments, a Mercedes-Benz pulled into the lot and parked. A tall man stepped out. He was slender and had that "I know I'm handsome" smugness about him. I immediately disliked him.

"There's the asshole now," said Mick. "My beloved step-father."

"He's the one who . . . ?" I said.

"Murdered me? Yeah. I'm about ninety-eight percent sure it was him."

"So what the hell have we been waiting for?" said Darby. "That's good enough for me. Why are you being such a wuss, Mick?"

"Because he wants to be one hundred percent certain, that's why, and he's right," said Cole.

I watched as the man, Joshua Mowrer, popped the trunk of his wine-colored Mercedes and lifted out two blue gym bags. They made a clanking sound as he dropped them on the pavement. He locked the car with a chirp and picked up the bags, his shoulders sagging under their weight. The mooring docks were gated and he let himself in with a key. The mesh fence tickled my stomach as we slid right through it.

Mowrer walked to a forty-foot cabin cruiser, the *Well Earned*. He climbed onto the yacht with the gym bags, which he set down on the rear deck. We floated onto the yacht, joining him. He looked at me and I flinched. But of course he couldn't see me. It was a miserable feeling, knowing that the living couldn't see us. Mowrer tossed a guilty glance back at the parking lot, making sure no one was watching him. He thought he was safe. No one *alive* was watching him. But *we* were.

He fired up the yacht's powerful engines and chugged out of the marina.

"Come on," said Cole. "Let's enjoy the ride up front."

He took my hand—again I noticed his gentle, not entirely unpleasant touch—and led me to the bow of the cruiser, which was steadily thrusting into a stiff headwind. The wind felt different as a ghost. It didn't buffet me like when I was alive. Instead it passed right through me, which I had to admit was unique. I closed my eyes for a moment to get a better feel for the sensation. It was like I was flying into the stars. After a few seconds, I felt a tug on my jeans, down near the heel of my shoe. I blinked my eyes open and looked down. I had risen upward like a balloon and Cole was holding the hem of my jeans, making sure I didn't float away into the blue-black sky.

"Whoa!" I said.

"You're okay," he said.

"How do I get back down?"

"Just kind of push, with the core of your body."

I did, and landed back on the bow.

"Thanks."

Cole was giving me that look that boys do when they're about to bust a move on you. But that wasn't going to happen. I inched away from him and his lips.

"What are we doing out here?" I asked.

Cole turned and indicated Mick's stepfather back in the raised bridge, piloting the wheel.

"He comes out here two or three times a week to the same spot and just drifts. It's like he's keeping an eye out for something, and we have a pretty good idea what it is."

"And what would that be?"

"Mick's body."

That was a creepy thought. And it reminded me of my own

body, lying somewhere. It occurred to me that I had to somehow make sure that they didn't cremate my body. I'd never discussed it with Mom and Dad, but I wasn't so keen on having my body burned to ashes and kept in a vase.

Mowrer pulled back on the throttle, briefly put the cruiser in reverse, then neutral, effectively stopping. He cut the engine and we drifted. An ivory moon was out and bathed the lake's surface with a dull glow. Mowrer dropped a heavy anchor over the side.

"Let's just do him now and get it over with," said Darby.

"No," said Mick. "We wait. Like always."

Darby sighed and spit over the side of the boat. It passed through the water without a ripple.

Mowrer moved right next to me, and I couldn't stand the feeling of being so close to him so I rushed to the right. The boat caught a swell. To steady himself, Mowrer suddenly lurched left and—whoosh! I collided with him. But instead of passing entirely through him like I would any other solid object, I *entered* him.

I was bombarded with fast, ugly images from his brain. He was a sick and twisted man, his crowded thoughts a whirlwind of repulsive memories. I saw Mick's face. Mowrer was remembering how he killed Mick by hitting him in the head with a pipe wrench—it was so horrible, playing in slow motion in the sicko's brain—and then tied Mick to something and dumped the body over the side of this boat. I was nauseated. I had to get out of the freak's brain. I lunged sideways with all my might. With a weird sucking sound, I was out. I turned and looked at him standing there, puzzled and abhorrent in the night. I wanted to punch him in the face.

Mowrer recovered from our *experience*, then shook his head and went below. Mick was staring hard at me.

"Did you . . . go *inside* him?"

"Um, yeah." I nodded numbly. He saw that I was shaking.

"You all right?"

"It was bizarre. I thought his thoughts, right along with him. He definitely killed you, Mick. I saw it all."

"I knew it," said Mick.

"All right, time to parrrrtay!" said Darby. She punched me lightly on the shoulder. "Maybe you're more than deadweight after all."

I was still stunned over the experience of rattling around inside Mowrer's brain.

"Does that happen a lot? Going right *into* people? I mean, do *you* guys do that?" I asked.

"No. I once heard about a kid who could do it. But nobody I've ever met at Middle House can enter the living," said Cole.

"What does it mean?"

"I don't know for sure. But I'll help you find out. Trust me. It'll take some time."

There was that word again: time. Ticktock. Even though I was dead, I felt like I was running out of time.

Cole went over to Mick, who had followed Mowrer and was watching him through the porthole. Down in the cabin, his stepfather peeled off his clothes and struggled into a wet suit. Mick spoke evenly. "He was rich, some stock market loan thing, but he got greedy and lost it all. I guess he must have known he was going down, because he bought an insurance policy on me."

"He killed his own son? For *money*?" I was incredulous.

"He's not my real dad. My real dad died. This creep just swooped in and took over my mom and all her money."

Mowrer emerged from below and outfitted himself in full scuba gear. He tied off a long yellow rope on a deck rail and tied the other end to the blue gym bags. He had a mesh bag full of zip ties on his diving belt.

He tossed the gym bags over the side. They sank quickly, emitting a burp of bubbles. Then he masked up and grabbed a waterproof light and plunged into the water.

"Here we go," said Mick.

Mick, Darby, Cameron, and Dougie all jumped in the water without making a splash. Lucy climbed on top of the pilothouse. Her long hair flowed in the breeze.

"I'm gonna pass."

Right. Of course her feline side hated water. I didn't blame her. The lake was cold and black and the prospect of leaping into it was daunting. But Cole had me by the hand and pulled me with him as he jumped over the side.

WATER

I held my breath. Panic jolted me as we slipped right through the surface without so much as a ripple, then dropped down and down. It was only slightly slower than moving through thin air. Cole saw me holding my breath.

"You don't have to do that, Echo. We can breathe down here. Ghosts can breathe anywhere, even buried underground."

Great. What a lovely thought. I was so conditioned to holding my breath underwater that my pulse was racing, but I went ahead and sucked in a breath through my nose. It worked! I could breathe just fine. Echo Stone. Fish girl. Again, weird.

"Why are we down here?" I asked.

My voice sounded weak and far away but Cole could hear me loud and clear.

"Mick wants to see his body."

Mick's stepfather dove down until he was almost at the bottom, around 120 feet. He swept the powerful diving light back and forth slowly through the murky depths. Silt and seaweed swirled around. Chinook salmon, cutthroat trout, and yellow perch darted about, avoiding the light. Mowrer kept up his sweep. He looked frustrated. I heard Zipperhead's voice.

"Oh god, I found what he's looking for."

Zipperhead was moaning and rubbing the scars on his head, creating dim sparks that lit up briefly then quickly dissipated. But it was enough to draw Mowrer's attention. He trained his light toward Zipperhead. And there it was. A body, tethered by a chain to a cinder block, floating ten feet from the bottom of the lake.

The creatures of the lake had nibbled and chewed and ripped bits of flesh from poor Mick's face and arms, which were floating skyward, as though reaching for help. I felt sick as I looked at his empty eye sockets.

Mowrer swam quickly to the body and used the zip ties from his net bag to secure more weights from the blue gym bag to Mick's decaying corpse. Eventually he attached so many weights that Mick's body sank all the way to the lake bed. To finish the job, Mowrer found heavy rocks and stacked them on top. Now Mick's body would never be found.

But Mowrer was going to have a rude awakening. Because Mick's body *had* been found. By us. We lifted ourselves effortlessly to the surface and hopped back onto the yacht.

"Man, I never thought I'd ever look that disgusting." Mick shuddered.

"Forget about it," said Zipperhead. "Just concentrate on what's about to go down."

Mick nodded. The Middle House kids now stood in a line and held hands. Cole took mine. They spoke in unison.

"We, the jury of Middle House, find you, Joshua Everett Mowrer, guilty of murder. Let the punishment fit the crime."

Mick's stepfather broke the surface and climbed onto the yacht. He went below and Dougie followed him. As soon as Mowrer removed his wet suit, Dougie waved his hands.

"Time to freeze your nuts off, asshole."

In a few seconds Dougie dropped the temperature in the cabin twenty degrees.

"Jesus!" shrieked Mowrer.

Shivering, he pulled on pants and boots and a thick wool sweater and angrily yanked a down parka out of the closet. He was blinking, confused at seeing his breath, trying to wrap his brain around the fact that there were ice crystals forming on the windows. His teeth were chattering as he cursed.

"This is *insane!*"

"You ain't seen shit yet," said Darby.

Lucy, in her black cat form, sauntered into the cabin.

"Wha-what the hell?" Mowrer stammered.

He tried to kick Lucy, but she was way too quick and side-stepped him, then floated up right in his face, hissed loudly, and with a powerful swipe, scratched his cheek, leaving four bloody streaks.

"Ahhhhh!"

Mowrer ran out of the cabin, up onto the deck, and looked around frantically, then began to haul in the anchor.

We all floated up above the boat and watched as Cameron waved his hand slowly.

The water swirled around, creating a vortex that spun Mowrer's *Well Earned* cruiser in a circle. In seconds, the lake became turbulent and deadly. Cameron waved at the sky.

"Chance of precipitation is one hundred percent."

Clouds formed quickly. The sky rumbled. Rain and hailstones pounded down.

"This can't be happening!" screamed Mowrer.

"But it is," said Mick. "Just for you."

Knowing as I did now how he had brutally murdered Mick, this all felt kind of spectacular. I wondered if I should feel guilty enjoying watching another human being suffer. I'd always believed in karma. Now I was seeing it in action.

Looking almost gleeful, Darby got into the act, opening her eyes as wide as a circus clown. A vision of Mick's corpse appeared on the yacht.

"Wow. That's some kind of power you got there," I said.

"It's just a hallucination, but it feels totally real to him," she said. "He's going to crap his Dockers."

Mick's stepfather clutched at his chest.

"I'm sorry, I'm so sorry—God forgive me!" he wailed.

"A little late for that," said Mick.

I watched as Mick floated down and opened the engine hatch and Zipperhead grabbed a diving knife from the gearbox and sliced a fuel hose, sending gasoline spewing. Mick hovered over his pathetic, murderous stepfather.

"This was fun, 'Daddy.' I hope Mom finds someone decent, you scumbag."

Mick was done. He couldn't help but crack a smile as he looked at us. But the smile didn't last. He began to look a little sad. I believed a part of him would be sad forever.

"Let's get out of here."

We soared back and stood on the water. Literally *on* it. Incredibly—I couldn't believe my eyes—we just walked on the surface. Mick led the way back toward the docks and we followed, everyone walking on the water except Lucy, who hitched a ride on Darby's shoulder. I turned to Cole.

"So . . . Mick just wanted to scare him? He's going to let him live?"

Zipperhead let out a little snorting laugh.

"Just wait for it," he said.

Mick now spoke to Zipperhead.

"Would you mind doing the honors?"

Zipperhead grinned and rubbed his zipper scars vigorously with his hands, which began to crackle with electricity.

"Adios, amigo," he said.

He pointed his fingers at the *Well Earned*. A long arc of electricity fired across the water and struck the yacht. An earsplitting boom echoed through the night. I flinched as Mowrer's yacht erupted, exploding in a roiling ball of flame. My heart was pounding.

"Holy shit."

I'd just witnessed my first kickass haunting and retribution.

We flew to Briarcrest, a gated community outside of Kirkland, to Mick's old house. Mick stood in his driveway, gazing in the window. His mother was playing a baby grand piano. Beethoven's "Moonlight Sonata." The notes hung strong and mournful in the night air. I'd never heard anything so beautiful. When she finished, she stroked the piano like an old friend, and then closed the keyboard cover. Mick was weeping silently.

"Good-bye, Mom. I hope to see you someday."

I could feel my heart squeeze in my chest. Mick hugged each of us, then raised his arms and floated upward, glowing more and more brightly as he rose like a balloon. I was stunned and couldn't help but murmur a dumb question.

"Where's he going?"

"He's moving on," Cole said. "To join the Afters."

We craned our necks, watching him drift up and up until he was just a tiny point of light and became one of the twinkling stars. I hoped he would find peace beyond the cruel clattering of this world and carry nothing but loving memories with him.

"Is this how it happens?" I asked. "You pass through to the next afterlife once you've brought your killer to justice?"

"Yeah," said Zipperhead. "The sooner you move on, the sooner you can be reborn."

"What do you mean 'reborn'?" I asked. "You mean like a newborn baby?

"Yeah. We play our cards right and we get another shot," Darby said.

I was learning. It wasn't like I was getting used to being a ghost, but in its own weird way, things were beginning to make sense to me. An eager yearning took hold of me. I *had* to find out who'd killed me.

OBITUARY

Back at Middle House, we entered quietly. Everyone headed for their rooms. The light in Miss Torvous's room was on, and passing by her door, I heard the sad love song, "Ain't No Sunshine." It sounded like Miss Torvous—though hard to imagine—was or had been in love. I stopped and listened more closely and heard a faint crying. I thought about trying to pass partially through the door to get a better look, but just then the crying—whimpering, really—stopped, and then so did the music. She must have sensed me outside her door. Her light flicked out and I heard footsteps.

I pushed away as quickly as I could and flew down the hall, ducking into a doorway just as Miss Torvous yanked open her door. I could hear her uneven breathing. She looked in my direction but I was flat against the door and she didn't spot me. I waited a beat, then poked my head out far enough so that I could see her. Her eyes were red, and she wiped away tears and then shut her door, hard. I wondered what was going on in her life.

Cole appeared and walked with me to my room.

"She was crying," I whispered. "She seems so strong. What could possibly make her cry?"

"Torvous, crying? She's got a heart of stone. You must have imagined it."

"No, I definitely heard her crying."

"She's always been alone. I know she's not happy. But I have no idea what could be tormenting her. I mean, besides being dead," he said.

"I was kind of wondering if she was really dead, because she looks so real, so healthy. You know, healthy in a creepy kind of way."

"That's her power. She can appear to be human to the living. That's how she's able to maintain this place. You know, dealing with the groundskeeper and the occasional curious soul who happens by. They probably think she's some kind of crazy old cat lady."

"And *we're* the cats."

We reached my room and I opened the door.

"Kind of a big night for you, I know," said Cole.

"Gee, ya think?"

When I remembered all that had happened in the last few hours, my heart raced and I got so dizzy it felt like my head was going to fall off. Cole reached for me. As soon as he touched my cheek, my head cleared. I looked at his eyes, which were beautiful even in the dim light cast from the candle that Lucy had lit in my room. Cole didn't seem eager to speak, or to leave, for that matter. His eyes were shining, and he had a wry, Mona Lisa smile going on. I was definitely attracted to him. But what could I have possibly been thinking? Even though I was dead, I was still crazy in love with Andy. My soul mate forever.

"I know this is all going to take some getting used to," Cole finally said.

I felt the heat from his fingertips. I was out of my head in that moment, under the spell of a handsome boy. A ghost. And I was letting myself drift toward bliss.

"I don't think I can ever get used to . . . this . . ." I mumbled.

"You will. Trust me. Good night."

I stared at his lips. Was he going to kiss me? No. He turned to go. I felt a sudden jerking, a twinge of loss. As though he could sense my feelings, he stopped and came back.

"Echo?"

"Yeah?"

"Can I hug you?"

Whoa. Talk about being pushed and pulled. I nodded, trembling, and he wrapped his arms around me. Our bodies fit together perfectly. Now I knew for sure that even ghosts get turned on. The hug was achingly brief but potent. I felt like I was in the arms of . . . family. As he pulled away, I could see that he was blushing.

"Even though it sucks being dead, I'm glad you're here."

"I wish I could say the same thing," I said.

He frowned.

"I didn't mean . . ."

"I know what you meant. Good night," he said.

He averted his eyes and departed, this time for good, disappearing down the hall into his own room. The feeling of the hug lingered on my body.

In our room, Lucy was already asleep, purring. *Yeah, this is going to take some getting used to,* I thought. I plopped down on my bed to rest my weary bones. Wait, I wondered, did I have bones? It felt like it. I felt the same, like my body did . . . before. I touched my arms, my legs. They felt solid to me. But I knew the truth. I was imprisoned in this in-between existence, terrified, cheated out of the life I was supposed to have. I closed my eyes and prayed for sleep. I wanted to dream about Andy. I tossed and turned, but couldn't fall asleep.

"Lucy? Are you awake?"

She rolled onto her side and opened a cat eye.

"Sure, I'm a light sleeper."

I knew I'd woken her.

"Sorry."

"It's okay. I nap on and off all day long."

"Why does every kid at Middle House have some amazingly cool power?"

"No one knows. Except, it's kind of like whoever created the universe gave us something special to help us through this in-between time. What was done to us was rotten. So it's like he or she or it knows we need some kind of advantage to right the wrongs done to us."

She yawned and curled up—her tail appearing briefly and twitching—and in seconds she was purring again.

I lay there for what seemed like forever, pondering my future, which appeared bleak, at best. I closed my eyes and tossed and turned, unable to sleep.

How could this have happened? Who had done this to me? I wanted so badly to learn the identity of my executioner and pay him back. Or her. The pain and anger were draining. I was exhausted and eventually sleep claimed me.

I found myself in a disjointed dream. My father was holding my hand and we were on Patterson Bluff overlooking Puget Sound, one of my most treasured places.

"Echo?"

"Yeah, Dad?"

"No matter what happens, just remember that I love you with all my heart."

I nodded. My stomach tightened up. Whenever someone said "no matter what happens," you *knew* something was going to happen—and it was NEVER good. I stared up at him as the sky changed from gray to black and stars skidded by in the heavens. I wanted to speak, wanted to ask him, *What do you mean?* But I was too scared. Then the cliff fell away and I was plummeting down.

The dream shifted. I was with Andy, looking into his eyes, which were sparkling hazel, and that was weird, because I knew darn well they were brown. I was momentarily confused but it passed. The dream continued. I was younger, totally crushed out on him, and I was crouching down, staring at him through a crack in the old fence that separated our yards. He was cutting his backyard grass with a push mower. He took his shirt off. His arms were taut and muscular—he had guns for sure—his stomach hard and flat, but not ropey-rippled like those fake-looking Abercrombie guys. I was wondering what it would be like to feel his warm stomach against mine. I prickled with little points of light that danced from my scalp to my toes. Fear and desire were waging a battle.

The dream shifted. Another day, a scorcher in the throes of summer. On a long walk. I trembled as I took his hand. Every time I was around him, I thought of dark, exciting things. We walked in silence, the only sound the rush of a nearby creek. When we reached the soft, green grass of the riverbank, he embraced me.

"I love you."

"I love you more."

Our lips were about to meet when Andy's image dissolved, the scene shifting now to my parents' house. The creek turned bloodred. In a brutal torrent, it flooded into my parents' house, bringing the walls down. Red rain seeped up from the ground and lifted into the ashen sky.

In the morning, when I woke up, I thought I was back in my old bedroom, alive. But no, I was here, in Middle House. Dead, thank you very much, universe. I closed my eyes again. Maybe if I just stayed there for a really long time and kept my eyes closed, I could shut out the freak show. I could clear my mind of everything and become one with the cosmos.

That lasted for about thirty seconds. *Oh, the hell with it.* I got up, my stomach grumbling, and headed for the dining room. I intended to eat until the food begged for mercy.

Cole and the others from last night's haunting weren't there, so I found a seat and helped myself to the offerings—French toast and pancakes—piling my plate high and digging in. I loved the fact that I could eat until my stomach should explode.

Cole appeared in the dining hall doorway and made a motion like "follow me." I could have eaten another two or three slices but something in his manner made me super curious what he was up to. I got up and followed him.

"What's going on?" I asked.

"I have something to show you."

He led me down a stairwell until we came to a big green door, which he opened, ushering me in like a real gentleman. It was a storeroom, with boxes stacked floor to ceiling, office furniture piled up in dangerous-looking heaps, and old textbooks by the hundreds, spines broken, shelved for eternity. Cole found an antique rolltop desk in the corner, upon which sat a vintage CRT computer monitor. It was attached to an ancient IBM computer slumped ingloriously on its side on the floor.

"It's a dial-up modem, if you can believe it. It's horrendously slow, but it works. Anyway, I got curious, so I looked online and found something I thought you'd want to check out. *Eileen.*"

It was agonizing waiting for the bogus, old contraption to

make the connection, the modem whirring and beeping. But the screen eventually popped on and loaded, slowly, page 8 of the community section of the *Seattle Times,* and on the obituary page, in print so tiny I had to squint, I read a sentence that stopped my heart.

> A memorial service for Eileen Stone, beloved daughter of James and Carolyn Stone, will be held Tuesday, September 17, at 11:00 a.m. at Green's Funeral Home in Kirkland.

Cole and I exchanged a look. The concept hit me in about two seconds. I was about to do something gonzo weird.

"Cole, am I going to do what I think I'm going to do?"

"Yeah. You're gonna go to your own funeral."

FUNERAL

Green's Funeral Home was situated on a lush hillside on the outskirts of Kirkland and sat adjacent to the sprawling, tree-lined Kirkland Cemetery, no doubt the final resting place for my mortal flesh and bones. Which was totally ironic, because as a little kid I used to play there, dancing amongst the tomb-stones, flaunting disrespect for the departed. Now it looked like some kid was going to be dancing on my grave. How wonderful.

Cole and I approached, and he was grinning, even though his eyes seemed sad.

"Can I call you Eileen?"

"If you do, I'll kill you."

"Sorry, someone beat you to it."

I wondered how Cole had died. I knew he'd tell me when the time was right.

I stared at the funeral home. I was out of my mind with fear. I felt like someone was holding me back with a choke collar; Cole had practically dragged me here, explaining that it might be the best place to jog my memory.

We entered the main building and followed the strains of "Time to Say Goodbye" down a hallway flocked with floral wallpaper. I was feeling extremely sad.

"This is so creepy," I said.

"Yeah. Hang in there," he said.

"I don't know . . . if I can do this . . ."

"I'll be right here with you."

We came to a chapel, where my friends and family were gathered to say sayonara. Mom and Dad were there, of course, along with my uncle Daniel and aunt Liz; my cousins, Vincent and Brandon; my basketball coach, Miss Reiger; and my favorite faculty member, Mr. Hemming, the psychology teacher who also taught photographic arts. His precious camera was hanging around his neck as usual. Tons of kids from school were there, some of them friends, some not so much.

And there was Andy, his strong shoulders slumped, his eyes portals to untold pain. Sitting a few seats away from him was Dani Cooper, the only other girl I knew whom he ever took to the movies, my old friend until it became clear Andy and I were so much more than just neighbors. Sitting behind Dani were creepy Denise Wiggins and her clique of rich acolytes.

I looked at my casket. It was a baroque, très élégant affair, the wood the color of gingerbread, the handles sparkling brass, the lining pink silk. I slowly moved closer. And then I was *staring* at my dead body. I was sure I'd be frightened, but all I could think was, who in the *hell* did my makeup? I'd never worn aqua eye shadow before in my life and my lashes looked crusty and way too thick, like someone had plastered little black caterpillars on my eyes. And why was my hair coiffed up and all puffy? I was starting to get mad, thinking I could *not* go off into eternal rest looking like a country-western singer! But then I softened a little when I saw that Mom had chosen my favorite cotton print dress, the vanilla one with the tiny red roses weaved into it. I loved that dress. Because it was Andy's fave.

People were making speeches about me. Denise—of all people—stepped to the podium. She was blonde, and today was a big-hair day for her and she toyed with it, shaking it from side to side and touching it with her fingers. Apparently she wanted everyone to worship her hair as much as she did.

"She was an *amazing* girl, one of the most *amazing* I ever knew, and one of my dearest friends. I'm . . . not sure how I'll be able to cope."

I thought I might throw up, and I wanted to do it *on* her. She was snuffling away like a beagle now, dramatically wiping away tears and yammering on and on, every other word *amazing*. What a hypocrite! *Me? One of her best friends?* That bitch and her clique banished me to the hinterlands of the severely unpopular during the first week of school.

"You're almost pretty," I remember her saying, having cornered me in the hallway, "but your accessory choices are rather unfortunate."

That had brought on a slew of giggles from her snotty entourage, and I had been dumbstruck, too shocked and frightened to defend myself. Denise loved an audience, and now here she was, at my funeral, using my tragedy to spew her drama-queen bullshit.

I returned my attention to my dead self. *Was* I pretty? The girl in the casket looked like some oversized porcelain doll, not like the self that I'd always imagined I was. My father once told me that as humans we all had illusions about ourselves. The key, he said, was to be ready and willing to reject those illusions and see ourselves for who we truly were. I was all for taking an honest inventory of myself, my character, but how could I possibly see and accept who I was now? *Dead? Really?*

My head was beginning to cloud with a growing sadness. I was on the verge of crying and couldn't help but think how pathetic that would be. Me, staring at myself, grieving over myself, blubbering like a baby at my own funeral. It was ridiculous.

"Are you all right?" Cole asked.

"Um, I think I'm doing okay. For someone staring at their own dead body. Yep. I'm good. I'm fabulous." But of course I was a wreck.

People were standing now and marching up to view my corpse. I was losing it. I had to get out of there. A scream was working its way up my throat and I stifled it, muting it into a beastlike, sorrowful moan. Overwhelmed, all I could see were stars rushing at me, bursts of white illumination. I fled as fast as I could, blindly, into the mass of blazing lights. I shut my eyes as tightly as I could and ran.

I was moving fast toward the door and with a jolt I found that I had *entered* someone, just like I'd entered Mick's stepfather on the yacht! The ache in my heart—the one that plagued me ever since I woke up in Middle House—now took firm hold of my soul, sharpening, intensifying, growing monstrously painful. My vision was blurred, and I screamed like I was on fire.

It was so weird, being inside another human being. Looking down through a blizzard of swirling lights, I saw a hand holding a hunting knife—which had been shoved into my chest! It was all very blurry and disjointed—but I could see that the knife had pierced my skin, sliced between my ribs, and found its way into my heart. My chest flooded with blood. Game over. I was seeing my own murder! But who was it? My eyes wouldn't open! *Come on, Echo, look, look! Is it a man? A woman? An adult? A teenager? Please, please let me see!*

Flashes from the murderer's ugly mind assaulted me. I saw

hallways at school. Girls casting fearful glances my way. Now darkness, the dull glow of a yellow light. A candle? I couldn't tell. The murder weapon, that heinous hunting knife, being buried. This person was so familiar! But I couldn't tell who it was; it was only a shape. *Who was burying the knife? Man hands? Boy hands? A woman's? I couldn't tell; the images were too unfocused and rushed. Come on, Echo! Concentrate! See! See who it is!*

I tried with all my might. But the transmigration only lasted a few seconds. The trauma was severe. Every cell of my being was on fire—I felt like I'd been dropped into molten lava. I screamed until my throat went raw.

Then it was over. I was outside the funeral home now, lying in the grass with Cole hovering over me. The blinding lights dispersed and gave way to normal vision. I was blinking, grateful now to be able to see a red-breasted robin in the oak tree above.

"It happened again, didn't it?" Cole said. "What happened on the boat . . ."

"Yeah. I went *in* someone."

"I think you've found your power."

"I found more than that."

"What do you mean?"

"Cole, it was the person who murdered me! I saw the knife; I remember now, being stabbed. Right in my heart."

I looked down. For a moment, my image transformed. I could see blood gushing out of a gaping wound in my chest. Oh. Shit.

"Who was it?"

"I . . . I don't know. I couldn't see."

I gulped in breaths as fast as I could, my ghost heart pounding in panic.

"Cole, what is *wrong* with me? Why couldn't I see them?"

"Take it easy. Try to be calm. Breathe."

I did. Five long, deep breaths. The images of gushing blood

stopped. Cole pulled me to my feet as my spectral body returned to normal. There. I was good.

"It was someone from school. I saw things . . . at the school."

"Good. That's a great start."

Progress, though incredibly painful, had been achieved. I now knew that the same person who killed me, who brutally stabbed me in the heart, was right there at my memorial service. But who was it?

BURIED

My casket was being carried out and loaded into a hearse by Andy, my dad, my uncle, and Ethan Johns, one of my only other friends from school, a science geek. He was a loner, tall and strong as an ox. I never liked the glee he displayed while dissecting animals and we'd once had a nasty argument about animal rights. He had a violent streak, but I doubted he would have ever taken the time away from his video games to kill anyone.

The boys bearing my casket looked uncomfortable in their stiff shirts, cinched ties, and tight-fitting suits. My body was driven two hundred yards up the hillside and unloaded. Cole and I moved to my grave and I stared at the living people as the minister spoke familiar words.

"Ashes to ashes, dust to dust. May the soul of Eileen 'Echo' Stone be welcomed into heaven, where the Lord's compassionate hands will comfort her with eternal love and forgiveness."

Well, *that* didn't happen. Not yet anyway. I scanned the assemblage, carefully studying the faces. Mom, Dad, Andy, my aunt and uncle, my cousins, Dani, Denise and her tribe, other kids from school, a few neighbors and teachers. Try as I might, I couldn't convince myself that one of these people had killed me in cold blood. But one of them had.

The minister finished his spiel and last respects were paid. Weeping, Mom and Dad placed daffodils on my coffin. Dad had to tug at Mom in an effort to pull her away. She didn't want to leave me. I wanted so badly to comfort her.

"It's okay, Mom, I'm okay, I'm right here. I'll never leave you."

I rushed and hugged her, wrapping my ghost arms around both her and Dad. She couldn't feel me, but I think she sensed me, because she stopped crying and when my dad started to speak . . .

"Carolyn—"

. . . she shushed him.

"Shhh!"

She listened intently as I spoke to her again.

"I will always, always love you. I'll never leave you. You'll always be in my heart."

Mom looked confused, then pained. Had she heard me? I turned to Cole, who was by my side.

"Can she sense me? Hear me?"

"She can never hear you, Echo. Anything you do like this will probably just freak her out. She'll think she's crazy."

I wasn't totally convinced he was right, but I backed off.

Mom allowed Dad to pull her away and they walked slowly, sadly toward their waiting limo, each step now part of a long march of grief. I did feel as though I had touched her. And I wasn't going to give up trying. But I knew that the time had to be just right.

Now my eyes found Andy, who held a lone silver rose, a beautiful thing, my absolute favorite flower, and placed it gently on my coffin. He was so handsome; I yearned for him so much I was wild with despair. Tears flowed from his reddened eyes and streamed down his cheeks. As he wiped them away, he moved his lips, his voice a whisper.

"Good-bye, Echo. I'll love you forever."

After these six words, the love of my life—my soul mate—turned and walked away from my grave, his eyes cast downward. I felt as though I had stones in my chest.

A cry lifted up from my throat, growing louder and louder—at least in my world it was deafening. It turned into a high-pitched keening so loud that a flock of sparrows shot like bullets from a nearby maple tree.

Cole looked like he wanted to offer some encouraging words but knew well enough to keep still. Better for him to wait this one out.

"Andy, wait! Don't go!"

I ran in front of him and struggled against his progress, but my spectral self had no earthly substance, so he continued walking, staring intensely at the ground. He passed right through me.

"Why can't I enter him?" I screamed at Cole. "Help me!"

"I don't know how your power works. I told you I only heard of one other kid at Middle House a long time ago who had it. I think maybe you can only enter people who are scared."

But I didn't want to scare Andy. I wanted to take him in my arms and hold him forever. I wanted me and him to become *us*, forever. A gust of wind swept in off the lake and Andy paused, feeling it caressing his face. I prayed he was feeling me, but it was probably just my hope. But what else was love *but* hope?

"I swear, I *will* find a way back to you," I said.

He started walking again. I couldn't just let him walk out of my life. I rushed ahead of him and, trembling, I screamed as loud as I could.

"ANDY, LISTEN TO ME!"

He stopped and slowly lifted his gaze from the grass to a point somewhere behind me.

"Echo . . ." he said very quietly.

"Yes! Yes, Andy, I'm right here!" I shouted.

My ghost heart thumped. I wanted so hard to believe he could hear me.

"I loved you so much . . ."

Wait, what was he talking about? *Loved?*

"Andy, don't leave; stay here with me a minute—please, baby? Show me you can hear me. Lift your hand, like you used to do when you would touch my neck."

I waited, begging the universe to let this one small thing happen. But his hand stayed by his side. He shook his head, steeled himself against the world, and walked away from the cemetery. I collapsed to the ground like a rag doll. I looked at the world upside down. Cole's feet came into view. He kneeled down.

"Echo, you have to get up. This is important. Someone here is your killer. You said so yourself. Please. Get up."

Reluctantly, I allowed him to help me to my feet.

"He didn't . . . I wanted . . ."

"I know. You loved him."

"I still love him!"

"Right. You love him. And he loves you. But to him, you're gone now, and if you want to find out who did this to you, then you better start taking a good look at everyone here."

There was an edge to Cole's voice. Was he jealous? No, I wasn't going to go there. I had a mission.

As the cemetery worker began covering my grave with the mound of dirt, people were departing, fanning out to their parked cars.

Dani, Denise, my aunt and uncle and my cousins, people

from my school, Coach Reiger, Mr. Hemming. I concentrated to see if I could glean some hint of guilt or malice from their eyes. Nothing. I lowered my head in defeat.

"It's hopeless."

I couldn't bear to see the final scoops of dirt heaped upon my grave, so I turned to leave. Cole was beside me when I spotted something out of the corner of my eye. A man, standing behind a tree. I moved to get a closer look. Was he a random stranger? Or a coward watching my burial in hiding? I walked closer until I recognized him. It was someone from school. Old Mike Walker, the creepy guy with frizzy red hair who ran the lunchroom. His face was stoic, his thin, beady eyes bloodshot. But his eyes were *always* bloodshot because he was a boozer. He sucked on peppermints but you could always smell the liquor on him anyway.

As usual, his craggy face was dotted with bristly stubble. Why was he here? He was no friend of mine. He was a pathological liar, who was always boasting about how he'd been a big Hollywood producer back in the day. The truth was he hadn't done much of anything except lie. Today he didn't just look hungover, he looked guilty. I remembered helping him once on lunch detail and he came and stood behind me, like he was smelling me—yuck!—and touched my shoulder and told me I was pretty and offered to put me in the movies. Yeah, right. I flinched at his touch and couldn't help but blurt out "Eeew-www!" Later that day I'd gone into the supply closet and someone wedged the door shut with a doorstop. I kicked at it so hard I thought my foot was going to break. Walker came to my "rescue" and acted apologetic, like oh, how could anyone have done such a thing. I knew it was him and took off immediately. Creep city.

As though he sensed my anger, Walker tossed a fearful glance over his shoulder and retreated to his beat-up old pickup truck covered with right-wing nutjob political bumper stickers. He started it up and left, the back wheels spitting up clippings and leaves. There was only one reason he would be here. Guilt. At having stabbed me to death with a hunting knife. Had Walker been inside the chapel? Was he the one I entered? Were those *his* visions?

"Cole?"

"Yeah?"

"I think I know what I have to do."

"What's that?"

"Go to school."

SCHOOL

Cole and I flew back to Middle House—I was getting the hang of this amazing flying thing—and once the others heard about my encounter with the killer, they were all champing at the bit to help me call him out and haunt him to his grave. I slept fitfully that night, dreaming of a faceless boy reaching out to me. Was Andy fading from my dreams already? Or was it Cole, struggling to enter them?

In the morning, Cole saved a seat for me in the dining hall. I didn't tell him about my dream, but when I told him I had weird, confusing ones, he touched me again tenderly on the shoulder. His hand lingered.

"You're going to be fine. I promise you."

I tried to deny that he was starting to grow on me in a big

way. But I couldn't. He was pretty much irresistible, an annoyingly wonderful combination of strength mixed with tenderness. And his damn piercing, beautiful eyes didn't hurt.

After breakfast, it was time to get down to business. Cole called the same group—those who'd helped haunt Mick's stepfather—together. I stood before them, my proverbial hat in hand. I kept trying to speak but the words were stuck in my throat like rocks.

"Echo has something she wants to ask you," said Cole.

"So spit it out. I ain't got all day," said Darby.

"Would you guys help me? Find my killer?"

They all looked overly skeptical, averting their eyes and shaking their heads. It looked like I'd alienated all of them and wasn't going to get a stitch of help. Then all of a sudden they began laughing and whooping it up and high-fiving and Darby clapped her hands together like a thunderbolt.

"Hell yes! That's what we do, girl!"

I couldn't help but smile. They'd nailed me.

"I gotta say, it takes balls to go to your own funeral!" said Darby. The way that they looked at me I could tell they were all impressed.

We sailed across the sylvan landscape, passing a flock of geese—oh, hello there—and landed near my school. I was with Cole and my new Middle House friends, Lucy, Darby, Cameron, Zipperhead, and Dougie. Every time I looked at Cole, the nagging voice in my head kept saying, *Boyfriend material?* And I would answer, *That's crazy talk!* Sure. Sure thing. We stood on the crest of the wooded hill overlooking Washington High. It was an old building with several mismatched additions that made it look like an argument between a couple of cranky architects. Though it felt like a lifetime, only four days had passed since my last day in these hallowed halls.

"This Walker guy, what's he like?" asked Cole.

"Everybody calls him 'Grody Toad, the lunch dude.' He's been at the school forever. He runs the lunchroom and works the slop line, spooning out delicious servings of starch. Creamed corn, mashed potatoes, Spanish rice, barf beans. That kind of thing. Let's go."

We moved down the hill. I thought about Mike Walker. He scowled at the boys and leered at the girls. We always held our trays up over our boobs so he couldn't scope us out, and that pissed him off. He had more hair on his arms than the average orangutan and it never failed to make it into the mashed potatoes. He kind of skulked around, most of the time looking like he'd done something wrong.

We floated toward the front entrance, and as I took a sidelong glance at my comrades, I realized that they were a troop of dead freaks. Most of them were too young for high school but didn't seem the least bit intimidated. I guess once you've been murdered, not much else can daunt you. My new clique. Too ghoul for school.

We passed through the front doors. The hallways were crowded with kids slogging back and forth between classes. Zipperhead kept looking at the short girls and I could tell he was longing for them in the worst way. Poor guy. I made a mental note to talk to him about girls. We came upon a flabby Hereford of a boy with a weak moustache who was twisting the ear of a much smaller underclassman, Denny McCarthy. I recognized the fat bully as Gary Magar, a senior and a first-class jerk with a nascent supervillain complex who walked around talking like he owned the school and had once pinched my left nipple. He was laughing as tears formed in the eyes of little Denny. I shook my head.

"God, I really don't like this guy. That kind of crap always made me sick. Nobody ever does anything about it. Might makes right."

"Not this time. We got it covered," said Cameron.

He smiled at Cole, who nodded to Darby, who unfurled a fire hose. Zipperhead spun the valve wheel. Water exploded out of the nozzle and Magar was blasted off his feet.

"Hey! Aaaack! Shit!" he wailed.

He got back up, fiery mad, and they hit him again. The water pressure was so strong it slammed him backward into a locker. Denny's eyes went wide.

"Cool."

Denny took off running. I smiled at Cole.

"Thanks," I said.

"No sweat," he answered.

We watched as Gary Magar crawled away on his knees all the way to the bathroom. Looking eager to get into it, Darby rubbed her hands together.

"That was sweet!"

"I can think of a bunch of other people who need to be taught a lesson . . ." I said.

"Let's get on it!"

"No," I said. "It's probably better if we stay on task."

The group looked disappointed but they followed as I led them down the hall toward Mike Walker's office. As we passed the art room, I spied Denise Wiggins moving around furtively inside. She was the only one in the room and entered a closet, then emerged holding one of my art projects, a garish papier-mâché head with more than a passing resemblance to reality TV star and omnipresent "celebrity" Kody Cosmenkian. My artistic expression had included a meat cleaver sunk in her skull. A nice touch, I'd always thought.

"What is *she* doing?" I asked no one in particular.

Denise covered my artwork with a pillowcase—indicating this act of thievery was premeditated—and slithered past us into the hallway and out a side door. We followed her to a Dumpster.

Now I understood. Denise worshiped Kody, and she'd taken it upon herself to rid the world of my art. That *so* wasn't going to happen.

Feeling in full control of her life, Denise approached the long line of metal Dumpsters and ceremoniously lifted the head out of the pillowcase and stood holding it like she was Perseus having just beheaded Medusa. I tried to imagine Denise ripping the Saint Christopher medallion from my neck and murdering me with a knife, but the image wouldn't stick. Then she opened her stupid mouth.

"You want the *real* eulogy, Echo? Okay. You sucked. I never liked you. In fact, you made me want to puke my guts out every time I saw you. You were 'amazing,' all right—amazingly skanky, you little whore. You got what you deserved for disrespecting Kody. That's why I spoke at your stupid funeral. It was irony, get it? I was pissing on your grave. And oh, by the way, David never really liked you. He only hooked up with you because you put out, you sleazy bitch." She was talking about her boyfriend, David Petterson. The memory hit me like a wave you turned your back on at the beach. Time froze as I remembered:

It was night. I was in the back seat of David Petterson's Mustang. The images were hazy and fragmented, but I knew we weren't studying anything except anatomy. We weren't going all the way or anything, but I wasn't on my best behavior, either. I was shocked. At myself. Obviously my self-image was being called into question. I dug deeper, concentrating, and I remembered why I was doing this. It wasn't to piss Denise off; I was trying to make Andy jealous. We'd had a fight and this was my response. It had worked. Andy had become angry and possessive and had come to me, telling me he wanted me all to himself or not at all. I pretended to think about it, then fell into his arms. I'd been Machiavellian. Echo, the manipulator, doing anything to get what she wanted. My sense of self-worth dipped.

I rationalized what I'd done by telling myself that fear made people do strange things.

I let that memory go, gladly, and I was left wondering if it was possible that Denise's rage had compelled her to jam a knife in my ticker. Not to mention that she was obviously incensed that I'd defiled the great Kody Cosmenkian's iconic image.

Could anyone be so sick with jealousy and celebrity worship that they would do such a thing? I had to consider the possibility. Denise had always held a deep dislike of me, and last fall when someone keyed her car, she accused me. I was innocent, but that didn't stop her and her acolytes from pouring bleach into my locker.

Well, what goes around comes around. She wasn't going to get away with trashing my artwork, and if she was the one who killed me, she wasn't going to get away with that, either. My crew would make sure of that.

Denise opened the Dumpster. Her eyes went all gooey when she saw a black cat inside.

"Aw. What a cute kitty . . . Come here, baby . . ."

Lucy started coughing.

"Oh, you poor thing," said Denise, leaning closer.

Lucy hacked up a slimy hair ball that splattered against Denise's face.

"Ewwww! Ohmigod! Ohmigod! You little piece of shit!"

Lucy leapt out of the Dumpster, howling. Zipperhead ignited a can of solvent that burst into flames. Darby, ever so creative, conjured up a ghostly image of me, then morphed it into a rotting corpse, mouth open in a terrifying scream. The eyeballs fell out of the sockets and hung on the cheeks, dangling by gory veins. The blood drained from Denise's face and she screamed. Boy, I had to give Darby credit. Denise was about to toss Kody's head into the trash when Zipperhead used his sparks to sizzle a message on the front of the Dumpster. The words appeared slowly, ominously.

Do this and you die...

"Oh . . . my . . . god." Denise went ashen. She put Kody's head back in the pillowcase and stepped quickly back from the Dumpster.

"I'm sorry, Echo! I didn't mean it! I swear!"

For a girl who was dead, I was feeling pretty damn good. Log it in the books. Kick-ass haunting number two.

Ten minutes later, Denise was crouched in the main hallway near the front entrance to the school. She had my Kody head placed on the ground, had pilfered flowers from the teacher's lounge, and had made a sign that she taped to the wall above it that read,

WE WILL NEVER FORGET YOU, ECHO.

Nearby, Mr. Hemming was crouched with his ever-present camera, capturing Denise's reverent display.

Our little fright fest seemed to have done the trick. Denise had pulled a one-eighty and created an *altar* to me. But still, although she appeared outwardly shaken, in my book she was still wearing her guilt like a butt-ugly prom dress. I concluded that she was definitely a prime suspect and would remain so until vindicated. I decided I would delve into her world later. For the time being, I wanted to check out suspect number one. Mike Walker. It was time to go Grody Toad hunting.

KNIFE

In the hallway, Zipperhead again gazed longingly at a couple of girls. He looked so sad that I took him aside.

"Listen, don't worry about it. It's going to happen for you."

"I'm short, my head's the size of a basketball, I have two massive scars on my head, and to top it all off, I'm dead. I'm kind of having a hard time being optimistic."

"Number one, you don't know what the future brings. You might come back. And let me tell you something about girls. Sure, they say they like hot guys, but what they really like are guys who are sweet and funny and make them laugh. So no matter what you look like, there's always, always hope."

Zipperhead closed his eyes like he was thinking about what I'd said. When he opened them again, he looked a little less sad.

"Thanks, Echo. Let's go scare the crap out of this creep," he said.

"You got it."

As we passed Mr. Hemming, he stopped taking pictures and glanced around as though he'd felt something. He had. Us. I paused. I'd always had a soft spot for him. He was divorced and rumor had it that his heart had been broken. He was handsome and polite and always talked to us like we were peers, not just a bunch of dumb kids. Memories of Hemming momentarily flooded my brain. He'd always made me laugh and—just like I'd told Zipperhead—that's the thing I liked most about him. I wanted to stay and be with the memories—something was definitely pulling me toward him, like maybe he could somehow help me. But I decided I shouldn't linger; I had to move on. We had another haunting to get to.

Walker's office was way at the back of the lunchroom and we passed through the kitchen, watching as the despondent staff prepared sad-looking trays of chicken nuggets and mozzarella breadsticks alongside bins of broccoli and carrots steamed into mush and iceberg lettuce salads dumped out of twenty-pound plastic bags. The food at Middle House was looking better every day.

Walker's door was painted a bright red. It was slightly ajar, and I smelled something burning. He had a tightly tied bundle of some dried plant by his window, propped in a vase. It was a pale-blue color and the tips were glowing as it burned slowly, emitting thin tendrils of smoke. It was horrid. Within seconds, I was sick to my stomach.

"What *is* that? What's he burning?"

"Sage," said Darby. "The stupid scumbag."

She spat and I looked at the Middle House kids. They were all sick to their stomachs, too. I had to swallow to keep from gagging. I was starting to feel weak.

"I take it we don't like burning sage?"

"It's not dangerous, just unpleasant," said Cole.

I started forward, intending to step inside Walker's office and have a look around. I felt a jolt of pain in my feet and Dougie stopped me and pointed to the floor at some kind of powder.

"Now what?"

"Sea salt, cinnamon, and garlic," answered Lucy, hissing.

"It's been used to ward off ghosts for centuries," said Cole.

I looked closer and saw that Walker had a thick line of powder across his threshold and lining the perimeter walls. The only place there was no powder was the window where the sage was burning. His office walls were nearly covered in mirrors, small, large, round, square, rectangular, and he even had shards taped up.

"Same thing with the mirrors?" I asked.

"They don't bother me, but some ghosts don't like mirrors," said Zipperhead.

"Hmmmm. Why do you suppose he's afraid of ghosts?" I asked.

"Murderers always are," said Dougie.

We stood and stared at Walker.

"He sure looks like a guilty jerk to me," said Zipperhead.

"This sucks!" said Darby. "I can't concentrate with all that crap all over the place. I can't conjure!"

Walker looked up from his desk, his eyes fearful. He sniffed the air, as though trying to draw out our scent.

"Can he smell us?"

"No, he's an idiot," said Zipperhead.

Walker's hairy hands began to tremble and he knocked over his coffee.

"Shit!"

"He senses us. And he's getting nervous. That's fantastic," said Cole.

I was feeling less nauseous and growing stronger.

"What's happening? Why is my stomachache going away?"

Cameron smiled knowingly.

"He's afraid, and we feed off his fear. The more terrified he gets, the stronger we become."

Walker stood now and though his voice was shaky, he tried to remain calm as he issued an edict.

"Depart, spirits! You are not welcome here!"

"And you, dipshit, are totally rude," said Dougie. "How'd you like to freeze your junk off?"

With a wave of his hand, Dougie created an arctic zone and Walker shivered.

"Go into the light!" Walker said.

"So stupid. They all say that," Lucy said.

"It's pathetic. Duh, we *would* if we could, dumb-ass," Darby said.

"There is nothing for you here!" There was a nervous warble in Walker's voice.

"He's wrong," I said, growing bolder as Walker's fear kicked up a notch.

"I think there is something here for me. I think he's hiding something."

"We'll be able to go in pretty soon," said Cole. "He can't hold out much longer."

Cole proved to be right as Walker, buckling under the frigid air and pressure of our presence, doused the burning sage and hastily exited his office, closing and locking his door.

"Follow me," said Cole.

He led us outside and we entered Walker's office through the window, bypassing the powder lines.

Splayed on a side table next to a small couch were copies of magazines: *Outdoor Life*, *Field & Stream*, *Bowhunting*. On the wall between the mirrors hung kitschy paintings of twelve-point bucks and moose.

We searched the office from floor to ceiling. There was no trace of my Saint Christopher medallion. In the closet, we found an aluminum carrying case. But it was locked.

"Stand back," said Zipperhead. He zapped the locks, which popped open easily. I lifted the lid of the case, revealing a set of hunting knives varying in lengths—they were neatly labeled—from four inches to thirteen. They sat nestled in tidy little foam inserts. The eleven-inch knife, the one that most probably found its way into the depths of my heart, was *missing*.

"God, it looks like it's him. What do we do now?" I asked.

"We don't jump the gun. He's innocent until proven guilty. We have to find the missing knife," said Cole.

"How?"

"There are ways. There are always ways," Darby said.

We were feeling pretty smug and emboldened but then Walker came blasting back into his office wielding a fire extinguisher and sprayed me with a torrent of foam. He dropped the extinguisher and stared in disbelief. The foam had of course passed right through me but in the faint mist it left behind a vision, an outline. He could see me!

"Who are you?!"

Well, you should damn well know, I thought.

Cole grabbed my hand and we backed out of Walker's office as he collapsed onto his couch, curling up and covering his ears as he moaned. "No . . . no . . ."

I watched Mike Walker rocking and moaning on his couch. He looked pathetic.

"Now what?" I said.

"Let him be with his fear for a while maybe?" Cole said.

"You're right," I said. "He knows my spirit is here and I'm after him."

"When we come back, he'll crumble like a cookie," said Darby.

We were back in the hallway about to leave the school when I stopped. Andy was standing before the memorial Denise had erected on my behalf. I looked at him and for a moment I saw him so clearly it was as if I could see his lungs, his heart, his ventricles, his arteries, the veins that spread out through him like branches on a tree, as though I could see blood coursing through his body. Far from being gross or macabre, it was exciting. He was an amazing creature, a thing of beauty; he was *alive*.

But he was not, in this moment—while staring at my altar—in any way, shape, or form, happy. The aura of grief that surrounded him was so powerful that I wanted to cry. I'd caused my one true love so much pain.

I floated to him, whispering his name.

"Andy . . . I'm sorry; I'm so sorry."

I tried to embrace him but he was upset and his body shuddered violently. I was thrown backward by his rejection. I wanted to go to him again but somebody beat me to it. It was Dani.

"Andy . . ."

Her voice trailed off.

"It's pretty bad, I bet," she said softly.

"Yeah, really bad," said Andy. "Every time I close my eyes, I see her face."

He closed his eyes. I imagined him seeing me and hoped that he was remembering me dancing with him or kissing or doing something other than lying in a coffin wearing dreadful makeup.

"Nobody expects you to forget her," Dani said. "That would be weird if you did. But maybe you can work on keeping your eyes open."

Andy opened his eyes and looked at her. She smiled warmly—not in a creepy way, just a nice, welcoming smile. It seemed to calm him down a little.

"Yeah, thanks, that's a good idea," said Andy.

"I want you to know that I'll always be here for you," she said.

He nodded. He heard her loud and clear. Because she was alive; she had a human voice. This was so pissing me off. Death was currently not suiting me. And it got worse. Dani gave him a comforting hug that I judged to be not only too tight, but way too long. His arms hung limp at his sides. And then he did something that felt like a second knife being plunged into my heart. He hugged her back. He sobbed silently and she pressed her cheek against his. She couldn't help herself and actually had a tiny smile on her face.

I was shaking. I wanted to jump between them, pry her from his arms, and shove her into the next state. But Cole and the other Middle House kids stepped between us.

"It's time to go," said Cole.

My brain was going into tantrum mode. I responded the only way I knew how. By screaming like a mental patient and running. Outside, I stopped and looked back at the school— my school—where my boyfriend was with another girl, and burst into tears. I covered my face with my hands. I thought to myself, *Somebody please kill me again.* I couldn't allow this! I felt arms wrapping around me and I thought, *Andy!*

But it was Cole. At first, I resisted. But the heartache was so intense that I capitulated and allowed his embrace. He held me until I cried a few more tears, and then wiped them from my cheeks.

"Better?"

"No," I lied.

His next movement was very deft. I thought he was brushing a tear from my chin but he lifted it. And then he kissed me. I was shocked and thinking two things. (1) What in *the hell* was he doing? and (2) boy oh boy was this guy a fantastic kisser. I let him kiss me for longer than I should have and then pushed him away.

"What do you think you're *doing*?" Me all indignant.

"I'm . . . I'm sorry. I just thought . . ."

He was blushing. The Middle House kids, standing behind him, were peering at us like we were some kind of afterlife social experiment.

I marched off, my body language clear. That was *not* cool. But as I was retreating, there was something I didn't dare admit to myself, or I was going to be in big trouble. When Cole held me and kissed me, I liked it—*a lot*. I may have been dead, but I was still a girl.

I didn't know what to do. I had to get the hell out of there. I'd heard people described as being uncomfortable in their own skin. That was what I felt like now. I just wasn't comfortable in my new form, my new body, my new being. It felt like I was wearing a wet dress. And at times it felt like . . . nothing, like I wasn't even there. So I ran, jogging at first and then picking up speed, going faster and faster, flying. I whooshed up one hill and down another. I zoomed by a man lying on a bench and, as I passed him, he shuddered and held himself tightly as though I were a gust of wind. Of course to him, that was all I was. He couldn't see me but he felt me. I wondered if I felt cold to him, or if I frightened him. I kept going, zooming around, trying to release all the tension I'd built up inside. I needed to let loose, needed to escape, needed to get my old life back. *Yeah, good luck with* that, *Echo.*

DIARY

I landed in downtown Kirkland and looked around. People were walking on the sidewalks and cars came and went and nobody once looked at me. The others from Middle House were nowhere to be seen. I wondered if they'd followed me. If they had, it looked like I'd outrun them. But when I turned around, there they were. Perched on a building, a car, an awning, and a telephone pole, like birds. Just waiting. Cole stepped out from behind a parked truck.

"We're not going to let you suffer this alone," he said. "We're all in this together. We help each other."

It occurred to me that I had lost my flesh-and-blood family and that these kids were trying to become my surrogate one. I didn't want that. But I *did* want their help. Because come hell or high water, I was going to find out who murdered me and make them pay. I figured the best thing to do was to head back to the scene of the crime, so I pointed up the street and started flying. One of the perks of being a ghost is that you can get around really fast. I was outside my house in less than a minute.

I remembered the day we'd painted the porch. A family project. I had bitched about it the whole time and now wished I hadn't been such a brat. Why is it that when we're living life, we don't appreciate the moments we're in—we always have to be thinking of something else? I vowed that if I ever got a second chance, I would do it right.

The others from Middle House showed up a few seconds later. I kept trying not to notice how handsome Cole was, what strong shoulders he had, and how his eyes sparkled whenever he stared at me, which seemed to be more or less always.

"I'm here for you, Echo. We all are."

"Thanks."

My house was eerily quiet. The yellow crime-scene tape still dangled from the door. I wanted to go in. Alone. It felt so personal. My house. My life. My death.

"I need to go in by myself," I said.

It was as though I was ashamed of my murder, ashamed of being dead, ashamed of what had happened to me. What could I have possibly done to deserve such a fate?

"If you're looking for clues, maybe a fresh set of eyes would help," Cole said.

I shook my head.

"No. For now, please just let me go alone."

He nodded and looked over at the other Middle House kids. They just stared stoically as they were prone to do.

I stood at the front door and reached for the doorknob. Then I thought to myself, why bother opening the door when you can just go through it? I did and then moved very slowly up the staircase. On the wall beside the stairs was a picture gallery of me. Some frames had been knocked off the wall but most were intact.

There were younger pictures of me at the bottom—in my crib, now on a tricycle—and me growing older the higher I climbed. Halfway up the stairs I was smiling, a goofy eighth grader. At the top of the stairs I was a full-blown, pouty, belligerent teenager.

I went into my room. I knew right away that Mom had been in there. The bed was made. My clothes were all folded neatly. The things on my desk were arranged in perfect order. That was very unlike me. I was more of a lazy slob than a Tidy Tina type and made my bed possibly once a week and only when Mom yelled at me.

I poked around in my closet and found a shoe box. Inside were some expensive shoes and a handful of costume jewelry. I felt a tinge of guilt as I flashed back to the time when I'd shoplifted those things. I wasn't some kind of master thief, but I was kind of shocked at the memory just the same. Why would I steal stuff when we had enough money? I guess I just had to let the naughty out. Hell, nobody's perfect. I put the shoe box back where I found it. Then I sat down on my bed and flopped backward and gazed up at the ceiling. When I was about seven, my dad had used a stepladder to stick up little stars on the ceiling that glowed in the dark. It was daytime, so they weren't glowing now, but in my memory they shined brightly.

I thought back to when I used to write about my dreams amongst the stars. Then I remembered something. My journal! I got down on my knees and dug under the bed and opened a plastic alligator treasure chest—*Welcome to Florida!*—and took it out.

Lying on the carpet, I read. It was more or less a chronology of my life, just like the pictures on the stairs. At first, the entries were mostly about new toys, Christmas, and birthday parties, being mad at Mom or Dad and about other kids in school, and a couple of silly boy-band crushes.

But once I hit puberty, everything changed. I had discovered love. And lust. And I began to write about the boy next door. Andy. I flipped to the end to find the latest entry. As I read, I felt a rising panic.

Dear diary,

I am so in love with Andy that it hurts. Sometimes I think I'm going to die because of it.

I love him so much every beat of my heart becomes more and more painful. Why? Because I know I'm going to lose him. there's just no way we're going to live out our lives in some storybook way with me being the doting wife and him the faithful husband. It's all going to go to shit just like everything always seems to. And I don't want to be around when that happens. I know my heart's gonna break. It's just going to swell up and swell up and swell up until it bursts in my chest.

I'm so afraid he's going to break up with me. I've seen the way he's been looking at Dani. that bitch. I think about taking a brick or knife or a hammer and killing her. But then he'd probably love her all the more. I don't know if they've even kissed. But I bet they have. I don't know what to do. Every morning I wake up I'm torn. I think I just want to die. Just get it over with . . . just get it over with now. If I kill myself, he'll always love me no matter what. Eternal love! I could do it. I could. I think.

I must have been interrupted while writing. I flipped the pages. Blank. No more entries. I closed the diary and put it back in the box and under the bed. My thoughts were finding new pathways, dark places I was uncomfortable poking around in. I closed my eyes and tried to remember the vision I'd had at my funeral. I tensed up, trying to will it to come to me, then relaxed. I knew I couldn't force the visions; I had to let them come. I felt a sharp pain in my chest and then a sound like thunder banged in my head.

Once more, my murder came to me, and again it was dis-jointed and unfocused, the shapes and colors and sights and sounds bleeding into one another. The knife plunged again, sinking into my heart. I felt a cut on my hand. A defensive wound. But then I saw my own left hand on the knife—for just a split second—and my world tilted. Was there *another* hand on the knife, too? I couldn't tell—it was playing out too fast, the looping vision wobbling, smearing. And the blood. There was so much blood.

Then it was over. I opened my eyes. The room was quiet. I was alone with my thoughts and a very big question. Was it pos-sible that I was so distraught over the thought of losing Andy that I had *killed myself*? I shook my head. Oh god, no—I hated knives, always had. But maybe I'd used that as punishment. Maybe I'd used the very thing I'd feared most to end my own life. How creepy would that be? I felt like something slimy was snaking its way up my spine. But what about my Saint Chris-topher medallion? Had I taken it off myself?

A faint breeze lifted the curtains in my window. A moment later, as I was rising to leave, I sensed someone behind me.

"Cole?"

"I didn't mean to invade your space, but I called out your name and you didn't respond. I was afraid maybe something had happened to you."

"No, I'm . . ." I wanted to say "fine," but that was clearly not the case. My universe had been seriously compromised and I was sick with doubt.

"Cole, how did you die? I mean, you were murdered, right?"

His eyes slid off me and found a spot on the carpet.

"Yes."

"How did it happen?"

He took a deep breath. This was clearly difficult for him.

"Her name was Meryn. She was older. She hung around with a bad crowd, was into drugs and other stuff."

"What kind of other stuff?"

He didn't want to say. But when I locked eyes with him, he spit it out.

"She sometimes sold herself."

"Oh. Crap."

"Yeah. Drugs cost money, and her parents were poor. So she threw it down on the streets. I had a . . . I guess you'd say a schoolboy crush on her. She would lean out her window and kiss me and it was like . . . heaven."

I waited, eager to know what had happened, but I didn't want to push him. I kept quiet and just looked at him. His eyes had tears in them.

"I thought we were, like, boyfriend and girlfriend. I was an idiot. But I loved her. She broke up with me one night and I couldn't take it, so I followed her. Downtown. She met some guys, owed them money, I guess, because they started to rough her up. She fought back, hard. And then one of them had this pipe in his hand, was going to bash her skull in. I rushed to her and . . ."

Cole now lifted the hair from his brow and for a moment his death mask appeared, his forehead split open, brains and blood spilling out. The vision vanished in an instant.

"So you . . . died for her."

"Yeah, I guess so. She got the hell out of there and left me lying in the street. She was really scared, but still—so much for true love."

My heart melted. He'd loved that girl so much that he'd sacrificed his life for her.

I raised my arms to hug him.

"Can I?"

He didn't answer. I took that as a sign it was okay to hug him, and I did. It felt really good, like for just these few seconds, we were human again, with actual human feelings.

"Echo . . ."

He wanted to say something. But we both heard the same

noise outside and turned toward it. We moved to the window, then looked down and saw Walker's truck parked on the street. We went downstairs and outside. Walker carried a silver florist's box and was muttering to himself on the porch, pacing back and forth as he read the crime-scene tape.

"DO NOT CROSS. DO NOT CROSS. DO NOT CROSS."

There was something wrong with this man's brain. I had been holding on to a strong hatred of him, convinced because of the missing knife that he was the one who'd killed me. But I wasn't 100 percent sure. I watched as he knelt down and took the top off the box. Inside there were flowers, a dozen white roses. *Pure Love.*

"My fault . . . so sad . . . my fault . . . my doing," he whispered. "Eileen . . ."

He knew my real name. He must have looked at the school records, or maybe he read it in the paper like everybody else. I would have killed to stay alive just so my real name wasn't tossed around.

"Eileen . . . never should have happened . . . my fault . . . I did this . . . I did this to you."

It sounded like he was confessing, coming to the scene of the crime to make peace with God or something. Tears spilled from his eyes. With his left hand he slapped himself—really hard—right in the face. Then again and again.

"My fault! Mine!"

He sobbed loudly. The other kids from Middle House were gathered around.

"Give us the word and we will spook this creep until he'll want to shove a knife in his own belly," said Darby.

They were good and ready to scare the living crap out of Walker, but something wasn't quite right. He was already terrified and it gave me an idea. I would *enter* him.

"No," I said. "I got this."

DAMAGE

As Walker continued his self-punishing diatribe, I closed my eyes and rushed at him. I felt a violent shudder—and then I was in. As I passed through his flesh, I was more cognizant of the feeling this time. It was like walking into a thick velvet curtain that slides over you.

Once inside, it was a different story. Walker's mind wasn't a happy place. He was having all kinds of thoughts, his brain firing away, juggling images and sounds, a kaleidoscope of dread. When you're in someone else's brain, it's incredibly disorienting, sights and sounds flashing at you like shooting stars from a thousand different directions. I told myself to breathe deeply, and I did, and the images began to slow down enough that I could make some sense out of them.

Walker saw himself on his knees, crying. He wasn't in school; he was in a dark, smoky place, an apartment of some kind. I held on to that image and rode it. It was a memory and I stayed with it. The room he was in—*we* were in—was rocked with explosions and plaster rained down from the ceiling.

The room was spinning but I held on. Now I could see why Walker was crying. He was kneeling over two bodies, a woman and her daughter, both dead from bullets that had ripped through them. They were Iraqis, and Walker was a marine. He had an M16 automatic rifle in his hands. He must have broken down the door and shot them before he even knew what he was doing. Casualties of war.

Images of knives appeared before me now and I saw Walker cursing in his office back at school as he stared at the contents of his knife box. The lock on it had been cut away and he was angry. He replaced the broken lock with another one and locked his knives—all but the missing one—back up tight. He kept hitting himself on the side of his head—doling out his punishment repetitively, forcefully.

He remembered the time I was locked in the supply closet. My being inside him must have triggered it. I'd been wrong about him. He didn't lock me in; I'd somehow trapped myself in there and he'd come to help me, not harm or punish me. He remembered seeing my backpack overflowing with supplies. So I was a school-supply thief, too. My self-esteem, my good-girl image of who I thought I'd been, took yet another hit. I had another thought. Maybe the universe knew what it was doing when it called my number. All along I'd thought I hadn't deserved to die, but what if . . . what if I had?

Walker went back to thinking about his war trauma and his inner pain was threatening to overtake me, so I wrenched myself free from his body. My little venture into the mind of Walker had taught me some important things. He was miserable with guilt over what he'd done as a soldier. It was the ghosts of the woman and her daughter who he thought were haunting him. And the knife from his collection had been stolen from him. He must have read about me being killed with a hunting knife and did the math and blamed himself. That's why he was here now, to try and make amends.

"Leave him alone," I said to the group. "He's not the one."

"Are you freakin' kidding me?" said Darby.

"This is messed up," said Cameron.

My new friends were disappointed. They'd been circling like a pack of wolves, ready to pounce and kill, but I'd called them off. They looked off into the distance, searching no doubt for some other prey, but appeared itchy because they didn't know where or when or how they'd find it.

Walker looked so sad. I took an extended deep breath and started walking, then flying. The others took flight and followed. In minutes, we were back at Middle House. At dinner we ate like ravenous fools. Then Cole walked me to my room.

"Sorry it wasn't him. I thought for a minute you were going to be . . ."

"Free?"

"Yeah, something like that."

"Thanks. I'm so . . . tired."

Cole nodded.

"Sweet dreams."

He touched my shoulder. My stomach tingled. My body tensed as he moved closer. He smelled wonderful. Then his lips, his amazingly soft lips, kissed my forehead. The back of my neck flushed. I wanted to complain, to tell him no, he couldn't just *do that*, but it was too late. The kiss lingered and he was already halfway down the hall, and about three-quarters of the way into my heart.

I turned and crept into bed and pulled the covers up over my head and slept fitfully, my dreams a collection of scattered images. Love and hate. Fear and longing. Life and death.

I woke up during the night bathed in sweat. I swore I wouldn't get used to this, I wouldn't let being in constant pain be my new normal. In the morning I avoided Cole—I couldn't let my eyes meet his or he'd *know immediately* that I adored the feel of his lips—and slipped out a side door. A feeling was pulling me toward school. Maybe I had a sixth sense that I'd find my killer there. Or maybe I just wanted to see Andy again. Either way, I slipped out of Middle House without telling a soul and was roaming the halls of school before second period began.

I passed Ellie Wagner, a girl who I'd always thought kind of liked me. I turned and followed her and the scent of her cheap candy perfume. She was always a little bent. Maybe that's why I had a soft spot for her. She went to her locker, which was a few down from mine. She opened it and pulled out a bag of licorice and bit into a red piece. Brian Gottberg, a freshman but tall and broad shouldered, got all stud-like and sauntered up to her, tossing a look at my locker, which had graffiti scrawled on it. *Angel Bitch*. Weird. You'd think they'd make up their minds.

"Hell of a thing," he muttered, referring to me, no doubt.

"I'm not shedding any tears," said Ellie.

You could have knocked me over with a puff of smoke. What the hell was she talking about? My self-esteem was taking a beating.

"Yeah, I guess she was kind of a bitch," said Brian. He looked uncertain, like he was just agreeing with her so she'd go out with him. "Right?" he said.

"You didn't know?"

"Know what?"

"Well, obviously not. She was a slut. Andy's about the nicest guy in the whole school, and she was cheating on him."

"That sucks," said Brian.

"You might say that."

My body felt heavy, my stomach lurching. I watched them walk away. Brian was making his play, and by his body language, Ellie was shutting him down cold. Me? A slut? Cheating on Andy? What the hell was she talking about? The name David Petterson came to mind.

I wanted to know for sure (was there someone else, too?) but it wasn't like I could go and ask her or anything. I followed her anyway, until I rounded a corner and saw my mom heading right for me. She looked haggard, like she hadn't slept for days. Mr. Hemming, my photography teacher, emerged from his classroom. I smiled immediately, then was struck with a weird feeling, too. I tried to remember what was up with him but nothing was coming into focus. He saw my mom and did a one-eighty, averting his gaze and rubbing his nose as he ducked into the boys' bathroom. Weird. I had no time to ponder him, because I wanted to get closer to my mom, who was heading down the hallway. Where was she going?

It only took her a minute to reach my locker, and she had a slip of paper in her hand. I moved closer and looked over her shoulder. She glanced at the paper, reading my combination as she spun the dial and opened my locker. I moved around her and watched as she slowly emptied it out, fetching my hoodie and a pair of tennis shoes, a jewelry box, and a ball of scrunchies. Then she found my stash. Some cigarettes and pot. Score another one for the bad girl. You think you know yourself and then you go and die and find out maybe you had a side of yourself that you weren't owning up to. Mom tugged at her hair nervously and the skin around her eyes was bunched up. She froze. I saw goose bumps on her arm. Could she sense my presence? She let out a sharp, frightened breath.

I instinctively rushed forward to comfort her. She was frightened and I entered her body. I hadn't meant to, I'd only wanted to hug her. But there I was. I could feel what she was feeling, see what she saw in her mind's eye. Her world was colored by a scarlet grief as images of me swam around in her brain. I saw her giving birth to me—*Push! Push!* Then hugging me, teaching me to read and swim and cook. Then I was a teenager and we had a screaming match over some cranky trifle.

Flashing forward to after my death, I saw her open the medicine cabinet, take out a bottle of sleeping pills, look inside to see how many there were (it was full), and then put it back. I could hear her silently weeping. The sound had an eerie reverb. I couldn't take it anymore and withdrew from her quickly. I ended up sitting on the floor, looking up at her. Her eyes were closed, and she looked for just this moment like she'd found a little peace. Then she bagged my stuff, shut the locker, and left the school.

I had to find my killer. Maybe bringing him or her to justice would help ease her grief. It was time to fly back to Middle House. I had to seek out the one person there who I was sure had some answers. The enigmatic Miss Torvous.

DARLING

I turned the knob on her door. It was locked. I knocked.

"Miss Torvous?"

I put my ear to it. Nothing. The simple thing would be to pass through it but we tried to respect each other's privacy here. So I knocked again. I thought I heard something. The hell with this. I passed through her door. She was lying on her bed, staring up at the ceiling, humming a tune, her voice childlike.

"Baa, baa, black sheep, have you any wool? Yes sir, yes sir, three bags full. One for my master, and one for my dame, and one for the little boy who lives down the lane."

I wasn't eager to crash this little nutcase party she was having for herself, but I couldn't wait around forever for the answers I needed.

"Miss Torvous? I'm sorry to bother you, but . . ."

She sat up abruptly, and her head swiveled like a robot as she spoke to me. She was very different in this moment, her eyes actually appearing warm and friendly.

"Darling . . ."

Darling?

"You could never bother me."

I blinked and felt a tingling in my chest. What was going on?

"Come. Come sit with me," she cooed.

There was hardly any way to put it other than she looked really stoned. I wondered what her dope of choice was. I didn't see any weed or pills or booze in evidence. I wondered if ghosts could even get high. I walked over to her. She patted the bed next to her and I sat down.

"I can't begin to tell you how much I've missed you."

She touched my hair softly and gave my shoulder a little squeeze. Then she pulled out the whopper. She hugged me. Miss Torvous. For real. Hugged *me*. The one person in Middle House who I was convinced wanted to bite my head off now showed me *affection*. Things were getting weirder by the second. I inhaled deeply through my nose and let my breath out slowly through my mouth. Then I made strong eye contact with her.

"Um, I know you know more than you tell us; I'm thinking maybe you know why I'm here."

She blinked, then glanced around the room as though looking for answers. Her shoulders slackened. I had to keep prodding or I was never going to get anywhere.

"Do you have any idea who killed me?"

Wham. She looked like I'd just slapped her across the face. Someone in the room shrieked. My skin crawled. There was no one there with us. Miss Torvous hadn't moved her lips. I slowly realized that the shriek had come from her mind. She'd manifested it audibly. She trembled and stammered.

"What? How . . . h-how could you ask me such a thing?"

She rose from the bed so fast she almost knocked me over. I stood up.

"You must know. In fact, I think you *do* know . . ."

I was scared but I had to get bold here. Maybe I'd get an honest answer out of her. She began to tremble.

"I have feelings, you know," she said, her voice cracking.

"I appreciate that," I said.

"Don't you think I have a heart? Or maybe you just think my heart is made of stone!"

She picked up a vase and smashed it with such force on the floor that shards exploded everywhere. Then she gathered her composure, hugging herself tightly as she turned away from me and snarled in a guttural voice.

"*Get. Out.*"

It was like trying to have a conversation with a wild animal. It was time to leave, so I headed for the door. She whirled around—and had transformed again into Little Miss Wonderful.

"Where are you going?"

She sounded hurt.

"Please . . . don't leave me . . ."

I moved closer to the door. Now her eyes blazed.

"Do not leave. *That* is a direct order!"

I opened the door, looked back at her, and shook my head.

"Whatever happened to you, I'm very sorry."

"WHERE DO YOU THINK YOU'RE GOING?"

Away from this freak show, that's where I was going. I slammed the door on my way out. I waited for her to follow but she didn't. I walked away and heard the same crying coming from her room I'd heard before. Frickin' spooky.

As far as my murder was concerned, I was getting nowhere fast and I had no one to turn to for answers. It was going to be very lonely being a ghost. I walked toward my room but didn't go in, because even though Lucy was perfectly nice, I didn't feel like talking to anyone or listening to her purr. I swung by the dining hall but didn't go in, even though as usual I was hungry. Instead I pilfered a bag of chips from the kitchen.

Sitting on the roof, I could see for miles. I heard a commotion down below but after a minute or so it died down. The sun was setting amber, lighting the world in a soft wash of color, and the surface of the lake was glass. A sailboat knifed by, rolling up a shallow wake. I opened the bag of chips and wolfed down a handful. Then I folded my hands behind my head and lay on my back. The pitch of the roof was steep and the tiles were cold and slippery, but I didn't care. What was I gonna do—slip off, fall down, and kill myself? I looked up at the sky. I wished I could just float up into the clouds and leave this world and join the Afters. But I couldn't. I'd seen how the game was rigged. I'd have to catch my killer and bring him or her to justice before I could ascend. I pondered what I had so far. Walker seemed the most likely suspect but he'd proven to be innocent. It was possible that I'd done myself in, but didn't the kids all say Middle House was for those who'd been murdered? Suicide isn't murder. I thought maybe I should cross my own name off the list. Then there was Denise. She was a first-class bitch but didn't truly strike me as the kind of person capable of killing me in cold blood. I'd have to keep poking around.

I heard Cole coming.

"I was kinda hoping you'd come up and join me."

I lied. I hadn't been thinking about him at all. But now that he was here, I was glad to see him.

"Chip?"

I offered him the bag. He dug a handful out. Tossed one in the air and caught it neatly on his tongue. Crunch.

"It appears that Miss Torvous has lost her marbles," I said.

"Yeah, I don't know what's up with that," he said.

"Every day it gets weirder and weirder," I said.

"I know. I'm glad we have each other." I could see him working some words around in his head.

"I mean, we've only known each other for a little while," he said. Oh boy, I thought, here it comes. Was I ready for this?

"But I feel like . . ." he said, "like I've known you for, like, a really long time, you know?"

I didn't want to admit it, but I had to speak the truth.

"I do."

We watched the sunset together, in no big hurry right then to do anything but just . . . be. Together. I wondered what it would be like spending the rest of my "life" in this state. Cole put his hand on mine. I got a little adrenaline rush and thought that if I could be with Cole, then maybe being a ghost wouldn't completely suck. I'd been feeling so adrift, so disconnected; I ached for a human connection. I was touch starved and the feeling was gnawing at me. So I did the only logical thing in this situation. I grabbed Cole by the back of his neck and pulled him into a kiss. It was a long one, and it made me feel like I had bubbles flowing down my back.

"Wow," he said, when we finally disengaged.

"Yeah. Double wow." I was becoming quite the conversationalist.

We were both self-conscious and blushing. Blushing ghosts. Weird.

"That was totally impulsive and also irrational and I'm sorry if I—"

I couldn't finish the sentence because this time Cole did the grabbing and kissed me. The sun was just going down when he started the kiss. By the time we broke it off, it had completely set.

"Now that was just . . . I don't know. Majorly significant, I think," I said.

"Echo, I have—"

He stopped because I stood up, walked to the edge, and jumped off the roof, my heart pounding. He ran and jumped after me and we flew over the trees, my fingers reaching down and touching the tippy tops. Cole found a suitable branch and landed on it and I landed next to him.

"This moment," I said. "It's kinda perfect."

"Yeah."

"It's not going to last, is it?"

"It could if we want it to."

I pulled away and floated down to the ground. On a soft spot in the grass, I lay flat on my back and looked up at the night sky. Cole joined me. He tried to hold hands but I wouldn't let him touch me right then.

"Up there . . . while we were flying above the trees?"

"Yeah?"

"It was really cool. Until . . ."

"Until what?"

"Until I thought about how it was so much fun I couldn't wait to tell Andy."

The joy of the last half hour dissolved. Cole looked glum. I couldn't blame him.

"I have to find out who did this to me. I can't leave it like this. For me, and for Andy."

"I know. I'll help you. I'd do anything for you."

"I think you would."

"Miss Torvous asked us to make sure you didn't leave the premises."

"But you're not going to hold me against my will, are you?"

He thought about it. Not a good sign. Something awful was up with Miss Torvous and it involved me. I didn't know what it was but I didn't want to stick around and find out. I had business to take care of, and pronto. I left Cole at Middle House. He looked sad as I flew away.

DANCE

I flew through the night to Andy's place, landing softly on his roof this time. No gecko-climbing for me—I had evolved. I passed through the roof and floated down into his room.

"Andy?"

He wouldn't answer. He couldn't hear me. But I liked the sound of saying his name. He wasn't in his room. I lay down on his bed and smelled his scent. It drove me crazy. I rolled over and hugged his pillow. I looked at his corkboard and something stood out. He'd written "Fourth period?" on two separate sticky notes. Andy had a thing for sticky notes. They were goal setters for him. He'd leave them up until hell froze over or until he accomplished his written goal, whichever came first. What did he have for fourth period? I tried to remember—I was pretty sure it was Spanish but I wouldn't bet my life on it. School seemed so far away right now.

I poked around in his room a little longer, touching the shirt on the back of his chair and his black baseball cap. He had a picture of the two of us tacked on his corkboard and I gazed at it, feeling my heartbeat. Everything about me had changed. But I still had a heart.

I heard music playing. At first I thought it was just in my head, but then I moved to the open window. It was coming from below. I went out the window and floated down into his backyard. Andy was lying faceup on the picnic table, staring up at the night sky. He was listening to a streaming station. The same one we listened to together. I moved over and wondered how I could ever get close to him again. I had an idea, but would it work?

My fingers found the surface of the iPad. I chose a different song. Our song. As soon as it started playing, Andy began to tremble. The moon cast a bright blanket of pale white over the yard.

"I miss you so much," he whispered.

"Oh baby . . ." I said.

I could feel the heat from his body. I crawled onto the table and curled up next to him, laying my head on his chest. He couldn't feel me—there was nothing to feel; I was nothing, not even vapor. How could I ever give him what he needed, the comfort of a girl? I cried softly to myself. Then he said, "It's okay, Echo."

My body tingled. I jerked my head up, expecting him to be looking down at me. But he was looking at my picture on the iPad. He was talking to it. But why? Why, when I had just started crying, had he chosen to comfort me?

He knew I was there; he could sense me. As our song continued to play, I was lifted up by hope. Maybe our love wasn't doomed! Maybe it was so strong that not even death could destroy it. Andy propped the iPad on the table and got up and stood still with his eyes closed.

"Wherever you are, I know you miss me like I miss you," he said. "It's going to be okay. It's always going to be okay."

Then he started moving to the rhythm of the song. It was a slow song, so he just sort of swayed. I floated to him and wrapped my arms around his waist, and though I wasn't really touching him, not like we used to touch, I moved in sync with him. We were . . . dancing. In the moonlight. It was almost perfect. The only thing that would have made it any better was if I was actually . . . you know . . . alive. But now I didn't care. I just wanted to savor the moment, bottle it up and make it last forever in my heart.

"Don't worry, baby," he said. "I'll never love anyone but you as long as I live."

I felt a thickening in my throat. It was like a dream. I held him close as he moved in his slow dancing circle. Could he feel me? I closed my eyes and begged the universe to let him feel my body against his. I was trembling.

"Andy . . . can you feel me, my love? Can you please feel me? Just for a moment?"

He stopped moving and his head jerked sideways. I could see goose bumps on his skin. I'd broken through the barrier. I'd gotten through to him!

"ANDY! I'M HERE! I'M RIGHT HERE!"

He shook his head.

"I'm losing my mind," he muttered.

"No, you're not! Kiss me, baby! Kiss me!"

I put my lips to his. He was perfectly still. Was it my imagination or did he part his lips slightly?

"Echo?"

I kissed him deeply and passionately. He did not move.

"Come back to me," he whispered.

It was romance in the moonlight and my heart was thudding

with excitement. In a few sparkling moments, everything was going to be amazing; we were going to reconnect. Then boom—it all came crashing down. The backyard floodlights blazed on. A voice, gruff and unforgiving, intruded into our euphoria.

"*Who the hell are you talking to?*"

Andy's dad, Hank, stepped out from the house. Andy's body stiffened and he flinched, in effect tossing me off. I felt foolish—ragged and betrayed. Hank walked over and turned off the iPad, killing our song.

"For god's sake, son, you've got to stop this bullshit!" he said.

Andy sat down on the table.

"Dad, exactly what part of 'leave me the hell alone' don't you understand?"

"What I understand is that you're getting worse and worse. She's dead! You buried her! It's time to move on."

I wanted to slap Hank so hard it'd make his head spin. But he kept up his tirade.

"She wasn't good for you when she was alive and she's even worse for you now that she's gone. Get it through your thick skull—she's gone!"

Andy's shoulders were tightening up into a knot, his whole body pulling into itself, coiling like a snake.

"Just let her go!" yelled Hank.

And then Andy struck, jumping up and lashing out at his father.

"Shut up! You have no right to bring this shit down on me!"

He swung wildly. Hank had been in the Marines (he never stopped talking about it) and he grabbed Andy's arm, not only stopping the blow but twisting Andy's arm so badly that he cried out in pain.

"Mess with the bull and get the horns."

Hank used the leverage he had on Andy's arm to throw him to the ground. But Andy wouldn't stay down. He jumped back up.

"I'm not going to let you talk about her that way!" he screamed.

Stay down, Andy, I thought, *just stay down.* It was too late—he'd taken another swing at his dad and this time Hank swung back with a cupped palm and slapped Andy so hard I thought he'd knocked him out. Andy went down on his knees.

I summoned up the loudest, most bloodcurdling scream I could muster. It rose up from the depths of my soul and pierced the night—at least in my mind. I wasn't going to stand by and watch Andy get beaten up by anyone. Hank's eyes went wild—like he'd seen or sensed something. I rushed at him, forgetting that I couldn't even touch him, intending to knock him backward, but instead—I entered him.

Like the other times, it was like leaping into a hurricane, with thoughts whirling around madly, sights and sounds and fragments clashing. There was a hideous sound track going on in Hank's brain, a death metal thing with screams and the sound of steel being sawed and bricks smashing. He was angry and frustrated. I was assaulted by dozens of images—some of me even, and I latched on to one of those and rode it into a dark chamber of his brain. Hank was chasing me, reaching for me. But I kept eluding his grasp, which only fed his frustration. Inside him I was spinning wildly, out of control. I knew this wasn't going to last long. If I held on, if I could just hold on, I might find the memory where he killed me in cold blood. My head felt like it was going to explode, and though I tried to stay inside him, I couldn't bear the pain. I pushed with my shoulder and leapt free.

I sat on the grass and stared up at Hank, who looked like he'd just thrown up. He took a step back and felt his heart with his hand.

"This . . . this *thing* you're doing—it's messing with all of us, Andy."

He held out a hand for his son and helped him to his feet. He tried for a hug but Andy would have none of it.

"We're all sorry for her. And sorry for you. But it's time to put it behind us. Come on inside. I'll make us sandwiches."

Hank turned and went back into the house. Andy stared at his feet. After what I'd experienced in Hank's whack job of a brain, I had a hard time believing he was even remotely sorry for me. Maybe he was sorry for what he'd done to me. Maybe he'd ripped the Saint Christopher medallion from my neck and then stabbed me. I'd always known he disliked me—didn't think I was good enough for Andy—but did he actually hate me enough to kill me? That would be one way to break up a relationship.

A wind kicked up leaves. The weather was changing. Andy ran to his Jeep, got in, and took off. I flew after him. He drove like a maniac, running stoplights and careening around corners. I kept up with him and pleaded.

"Andy, don't! Slow down! Do you want to get yourself killed?"

As if in defiance, he sped forward faster, roaring up a hill, fishtailing around a sharp switchback in the road, his back tires sliding, his rear end clipping a guardrail. He looked like he was on a mission to die. I flew in front of the car—right in front of his face—to no avail. Finally he skidded to a halt. He sat for a moment, then pulled off the road onto the shoulder. He got out of the car and walked to the bluff of Chalmers Cliff. Down below, waves crashed on boulders piled next to the train tracks.

Andy had a distant, empty stare going, as though searching for something way beyond what he could see.

"I want to be with you," he whispered.

The implication was not lost on me.

"Oh god, not like this . . ." I said.

His scream echoed into the night.

"I WANT TO BE WITH YOU!"

I'd been so stupid. My adoration, my *truly* undying love, had caused this. If only I'd just left him alone and not reached out! I'd only caused him to become so distraught that he was contemplating the unthinkable. He stepped over the railing and past the sign that read, "DANGER—STEEP CLIFF!"

Tears fell from his bloodshot eyes. He didn't bother wiping them away. He must have been crying in the car all the way up here. He took two more steps, right to the edge, his toes poking over. A strong wind blew at his back. If he wasn't careful, he was going to get blown right over.

"Baby, don't do it . . . I'm begging you," I pleaded.

His ears were deaf to me, his senses shut down. He was jacked up on his own body's fight-or-flight chemicals and had tuned the world out. A car sped past behind him, the stupid driver laying on his horn. Who does that?

I hovered in front of him, pleading, begging, trying to hug him, trying to kiss him, but he was immune to my existence. He teetered forward and back, rocking on the balls of his feet. A jackrabbit hopped out of the scrub and along the shoulder. I was desperate. I flew across the street and screeched a high-pitched wail. The rabbit froze, alarmed—and I rushed into it. A car was coming, fast. I took aim with my new skewed rabbit vision and darted into the road. A screech of tires and wham! I was knocked into the air. The car kept on going.

I could see stars, and some vague images of grass and what looked like a warren of rabbits. Then I saw Andy. He'd rushed over from the cliff and picked me up. I jerked myself out of the little creature and miraculously it jumped out of his hands and hopped off into the night. I'd only succeeded in getting clipped by the car, not run over. But it was enough to bring Andy out of his death-wish trance. Shoulders slumped in despair, he walked to his Jeep, got in, and drove off. I didn't follow him. I'd done enough damage to the boy I loved.

PRISONER

As I flew toward my new home, I contemplated how badly my play for Andy had gone. The last thing I wanted was for him to leave the world of the living. I had to do something to stop him from such madness, but I didn't know what. How could I save him?

Fog was rolling in off Puget Sound. I soared through the mist. A mile from Middle House I saw an orange glow. I flew faster and landed. My mouth fell open. I stared in disbelief. Middle House was on fire. I could think of only one thing. *Cole.* I flew around the side and entered. I expected to be met with a blast of flames and be burned alive. Fat chance of that. There was heat but no flames. I rushed down a hallway and screamed.

"Cole!"

Kids were flying up and down the hallways carrying buckets and pans and bowls of water. I followed the line, which led to Miss Torvous's room. It was inundated with flames. And not just ordinary fire, but small balls of fire, wicked-looking things that ran up and down the walls, screaming as they dodged the incoming volleys of water. Miss Torvous was sitting in her chair, crying with a vengeance, sobs and moans racking her body.

A gangly kid lurched by me and tossed a pan of water at the flames, killing a couple of them. They hissed as they died. Gangly shouted at me.

"Don't just stand there! Help us!"

He took off. I couldn't move, couldn't stop staring at Miss Torvous, who was overcome with grief. She was clawing at her cheeks, dragging her fingernails over them. The more she cried, the more flames appeared. I took a closer look. The tears that fell from her eyes morphed into tiny flames and then grew and grew. Un-freaking-believable. She was shedding tears of fire.

"Miss Torvous!"

It was Cole, behind me. He wrapped an arm around my shoulder, tightly. Too tightly. What was going on? I tried to squirm away but he wouldn't let me.

"She's here! See? Right here!"

Miss Torvous looked over. Her eyes were huge, at least twice the size of normal. She looked like some kind of freakazoid zombie and her chin was trembling. She stared at me. I swear she could read my mind.

"She was just outside . . . up on the roof," said Cole.

"That's why we couldn't find her," said Zipperhead.

He and Dougie, Lucy, Darby, and Cameron had all showed up—looking sickly—carrying buckets of water, but they dropped them because the fire was rapidly dying out on its own, just magically disappearing, the result of Miss Torvous's will. Things returned to normal, and oddly enough, nothing looked like it was charred. There'd been no fire—it was all a spectacular illusion created by the headmistress to torment her charges. Her eyes were locked on me.

"Come here, little one . . ."

All my inner voices were screaming, *NO WAY!* And yet when prodded by Cole, I stepped toward her, slowly.

She smiled at me in a loving way and held out her arms. I took two more baby steps.

"NOW!" she screamed.

That was it! "Okay, lady, you can go screw yourself." I turned to run but Zipperhead, Darby, Cameron, and the others grabbed me.

"Sorry, Echo," said Darby. "She's been wacko, tormenting the hell out of all of us."

"She took away all our food. All our privileges," said Zipperhead. He looked truly pained to be ganging up on me.

"She's been working us like slaves," said Lucy. I looked at her and the others. They looked absolutely terrible, depleted, exhausted, and gaunt. Like they'd been exerting themselves for hours and hours.

"What does it have to do with me?"

"Nobody knows," said Dougie, who was sweating like a pig in the desert. "But we have to do what she wants or there's going to be more hell to pay."

"Just do what you're told," said Lucy.

I wasn't going anywhere without putting up a fight. I kicked and screamed, but I was overpowered and finally delivered into the waiting grasp of Miss Torvous's talon-like grip.

"Where have you been, my lovely?"

"Out doing what I'm *supposed* to be doing. Finding out who murdered me!"

Her face jerked violently, then she calmed herself down by touching her own cheek and then mine.

"No one murdered you. You're right here. With me."

"But . . . I'm not alive."

She appeared alarmed, then threw her head back and laughed.

"Of course you're alive! Look! I can touch and feel you!"

She began touching me affectionately. I was getting more confused with each passing second. This woman was batshit crazy.

"Why are you doing this?" I said.

"I'm only trying to comfort you, my darling . . ."

She relaxed her grip and I used the opportunity to wrench free of her iron grasp and flew toward the doorway, feinting left and going right, which enabled me to bypass Darby and the others, who were slow due to their sickly state.

I flew down the hallway. Miss Torvous's screeching voice bounced off the walls.

"Get her!"

They were after me in a heartbeat. Darby and Lucy and Zipperhead and Cameron and dozens of other kids, too, hands grabbing at me. But I was getting out of there once and for all. I pushed through a wall and was met by four kids who rushed right at me.

"She's over here!" one of them screamed.

I somehow managed to kick into overdrive and flew incredibly fast, leaping up and squeezing through the ceiling. I was alone, in a hallway. At the end was an open window. I made for it like a hawk, flying fast and straight. Liberation was at hand. I was only three feet from the window when Cole stepped out of the shadows and blocked my path.

"This isn't the way, Echo."

"It sure as hell looks like it to me!"

"No. I mean running. Listen to me!"

I was in no mood to listen to anyone. I tried to duck around him but he grabbed me, pulling me close.

"Echo . . . you have to trust me."

Dammit! Even now I loved his stupid bedroom eyes. My

chest heaved and my heart pounded. But his eyes . . . they held nothing but calm and adoration. I relaxed my shoulders and in a tiny mouse voice I capitulated.

"All right, Cole, I'll do whatever you say."

In two seconds, the hallway was flooded with other kids, all forming a barrier around me as Cole escorted me back.

We stood in her doorway. Miss Torvous looked at me now like she had when I'd first arrived, like I was some unsanitary, unwanted pest. She dismissed me with a wave of her hand.

"Put her in the chamber."

The chamber?

Cole and the others nodded. Miss Torvous's door shut of its own accord. I glared at my captors.

"Guys! Will someone please tell me what's going on?"

Cole whispered in my ear.

"Trust me. We're not going to put you—"

He had to stop because Miss Torvous had flung open her door with a bang and pushed out into the hallway.

"Sometimes people have to be taught a lesson," she said.

She latched a talon onto my wrist. I was terrified and squirmed to get away. Wasn't going to happen.

I was marched downstairs through the laundry room and into some kind of subbasement, down a narrow hallway—an access thing, really—at the end of which was a large, round chamber with a door in the middle. Cole opened it. We stared inside. The walls were coated with a crusty white substance.

"What is that gunk?" I said.

"Plaster mixed with sea salt, cinnamon, and garlic," he said.

"She made us build it when you were gone," said Darby.

"We worked like slaves—it sucked. I kept wanting to puke," said Zipperhead.

I remembered that sea salt and burning sage had made us all queasy at Mike Walker's office.

"What's the point?"

"She calls it a 'time-out' chamber," said Lucy.

"Well, I'm not going in there."

I tried to push my way past Cole and the others but there were too many of them. I screamed as they forced me inside and shut the door.

"Cole! COLE!"

I searched frantically for an exit that didn't exist. But there were a dozen holes that had been drilled in the walls, holes just big enough for an eyeball to see through, and they were out there . . . peering in at me.

"Cole, help me!"

There were crusty clumps of salt on the floor. I picked some up and threw them at the eyeballs. They disappeared as the watchers backed off, but soon they reappeared, gawking.

The walls of sea salt had a horrible effect on me, making me queasy and weak. I found the centermost part of the room and sat down. A salt chamber. How very clever. I had to give her badass credit. Miss Torvous was one devious, sadistic bitch. My head was spinning. Dizzy, I lay down. Minutes passed. I felt like I was going to vomit my guts out.

The door opened and Cole entered. He came to me and knelt down.

"Why didn't you stop them?" I whimpered.

"Are you okay?"

"Do I look okay?"

"You look like shit. But still pretty."

He smiled weakly.

"Why is she suddenly fixating on me?" I asked.

"I don't know but I promise we'll find out."

"I feel like I'm going to die." The irony hit me quick, but it wasn't enough to make me laugh. This sucked.

"Cole . . . I have to get out of here. You have to help me."

"I know; I have a plan. Just . . . curl up here like you have been, and I'll be back."

He started to go and I clutched his leg.

"Cole?"

"Trust me, Echo—you have to trust me."

"With my life?"

"Yes. Now play dead."

That I could do. I closed my eyes and dreamt the dream of the dying.

INTRUDERS

In the chamber I could barely feel my heartbeat. It had slowed down considerably, my pulse steady but sluggish and fading. My consciousness was slipping away, my thoughts thinning into wispy strands of nothingness. I was dying . . . again. I tried to open my eyes but didn't have the strength. I heard noises but couldn't identify them. A shriek, I think, and its echo, like a continuous reverb. I finally opened my eyes. Then things came into focus.

Miss Torvous was in the chamber with Cole, trembling.

"I think she may be dead," said Cole.

"I never . . . I didn't think . . ." stammered Miss Torvous.

"Let me pick her up," said Cole.

Miss Torvous nodded. She was in shock. Her head tilted back and forth like her brain was gyrating.

"What have I done?"

What she'd done was kill me. My afterlife was coming to an end.

I felt arms scooping me up. I could smell Cole's scent. I felt myself being moved—he was carrying me out of the room. Then I heard the earsplitting slam of a door and a scream so loud and terrifying it made my eyes pop open. Cole held me in his arms. Darby had just slammed the door of the salt chamber shut, locking Miss Torvous inside.

"Let me out of here!"

She pounded on the door.

"LET ME OUT OF HERE NOW!"

More pounding on the door, followed by a moaning, keening, braying kind of sound.

"Oh my god, was that her?"

"Yeah. You want me to put you down?"

I looked up at Cole. I liked it in his arms and didn't particularly want to be put down just yet.

"Um . . . can you wait a second?"

"Sure."

Darby shot us a look. Then backed away from the salt chamber door.

"She's gone mental, that's for sure. Something happened to her when you arrived, Echo. We all talked about it and didn't want to say anything to you. You were scared enough already."

"No one knows what, but you sure as shit triggered something in her," said Cameron.

I wanted to stay in Cole's arms a long, long time, but my head had cleared, my stomach felt fine, and I knew it was time to get busy—on my own two feet.

"You can put me down now."

He did. I stood upright, the effects of the salt chamber having now abated.

"Man, that was horrible in there. I thought I was going to croak."

"And here I thought you already had," said Darby.

"Ha-ha. I mean it. It felt like I was dying all over again. Is that how you 'kill' a ghost?"

"No," said Cole. "We're already dead, so we can't die. From what we've learned, you can go into a prolonged sort of stasis, kind of like a coma, I guess, but you won't die. That's why we decided to pull this little stunt to get Miss Torvous in there."

"And keep her in there," said Zipperhead.

"At least until we can find out what to do about her freaking out," said Cole.

"Well, thank you," I said.

"Don't mention it. It was nothing," he answered.

His face was flushing and he was getting all *aw, shucks* on me. I looked at Darby.

"Thanks. You risked your butt for me. I appreciate it."

She wasn't used to being thanked, or to anyone being nice to her at all, for that matter. So she mumbled, "Um, no sweat . . . You're, uh . . . welcome."

I smiled at her and she was about to smile but looked away, uncomfortable showing any emotion except for ballistic anger.

We went upstairs and though we swore our core group—me, Cole, Darby, Dougie, Cameron, Zipperhead, and Lucy—to secrecy, a girl who called herself Zen (death by hanging, but she swore it wasn't suicide) had ventured down into the subbasement and gotten an earful from prisoner Torvous before she passed out. Zen spread the news and now Middle House was party central. Without Miss Torvous to keep everyone reined in, none of the usual protocols or schedules were adhered to.

Anarchy and chaos sound fun conceptually, but when put

into practice, a house without rules can quickly degenerate into pandemonium and become a loony bin that makes you want to pull your hair out. Kids ate whenever they wanted, hardly anyone made their beds or picked up after themselves, and the place quickly became a jumble. Within hours, the kitchen and dining hall were disaster areas and kids squabbled about who was to blame and who should be doing what.

Every ghost in Middle House had their own unique power, their own way to inflict bodily harm or at least terrorize, so when fights broke out, it was time to dive for cover. A petite girl named Joanne (death by being pushed in front of a subway train) had telekinetic powers and she got into it with Lawrence (beaten to death with a baseball bat). Lawrence could conjure at will any earsplitting sound he chose, and between the dishes and furniture flying across the room and smashing into the walls and Lawrence's cacophony of shrieks and roars and bomb blasts, the whole thing was becoming unbearable. Middle House was coming apart at the seams.

Cole managed to intercede, halting that fracas, but other altercations and squabbles broke out. It looked like it was only a matter of time before our happy home would implode under the weight of its own bedlam.

Cole and Darby patrolled the hallways, trying to restore order with only minimal success. Who wants to follow rules when the one cardinal rule—thou shalt not kill—was the one broken that got you here in the first place? I understood why a mob of murdered kids would want to blow off steam. Hell, I wanted to join them, maybe burn the damn place down. But then where would I be?

The chaos came to a screeching halt when a relentless pounding sound echoed through Middle House. It gradually dawned on everyone that it was someone—a real, live human being, no doubt—knocking steadily on the front door. The place fell into a quiet so deep we could hear each other breathe. Cole and I and the others rushed to the front door and peeked out. Two people were standing on the front porch, doing their best to peer in through the windows past the drawn blinds.

Cole identified them immediately. They were Mr. and Mrs. Reiner, the frumpy middle-aged neighbors. Mr. Reiner was short and stocky with a paunch and wore a sunshade hat and horn-rimmed glasses. Mrs. Reiner, though pudgy pretty in the face, had a very large butt.

"Hello?" said Mr. Reiner.

"It sure got quiet all of a sudden," said Mrs. Reiner.

Her hands fidgeted around like two small birds trying to find a place to land.

"Maybe we should call the police," she said.

"Susan, don't be an idiot. She pays me well to tend the grounds. I don't want to mess that up."

"When's the last time she paid you?"

Mrs. Reiner pounded on the door zealously. WHAM! WHAM!

"Been a couple of months, anyway," said Mrs. Reiner.

"That woman is so odd and the sounds that come from this place . . . Honestly, I don't know what she could be doing here, all alone like this. I'm not moving from this spot until she comes to the door and you get paid, AND we get a satisfactory explanation for all the noise," said Susan. WHAM!

"She's just . . . eccentric," said Mr. Reiner.

Cole and I exchanged a look. I stared down at the door. It had a slot mailbox, the kind the mailman could drop things through, or someone could deliver something out. Mr. Reiner knocked on the door. Mrs. Reiner pounded on it. WHAM! WHAM! WHAM!

"Mrs. Eddingham?"

Aha. That was Miss Torvous's "front" name? The one she used to dupe the living? Cole grabbed me by my arm and, after motioning to Darby and the gang, whisked me down the hall to Miss Torvous's room. We began searching. Did she keep cash somewhere?

We looked in her old rolltop desk and found utility bills and letters and a diary written in what appeared to be hieroglyphics. Zipperhead bounced on her bed. Darby yelled at him.

"Knock it off!"

"What's the point? We're gonna get found out and booted outta this joint and I'm never gonna find my killer. I know that for sure. I can feel it in my scars."

Zipperhead looked scared, so I went and helped him off the bed.

"Um, you're not really helping. Just . . . chill. It's going to be okay."

His jumping had dislodged a framed picture—the corner of which now stuck out from underneath the pillow on the side of the bed next to where Miss Torvous slept. I lifted up the pillow and saw a faded image of a girl with long brown hair. I was about to take a closer look when Cole's voice snapped my head around.

"I got it!"

He'd found a large, thick book, the center of which had been cut out and held cash. Lots of it.

"How much?"

"I don't know," I said. "There's thousands there."

"I mean, how much do we pay him?"

"Oh, well, he said he tends the grounds. A few hundred should do it, I think."

Cole grabbed the bills and we raced back to the front door.

"Mrs. Eddingham? It's imperative that we speak with you," said Susan Reiner, pounding yet again on the door.

I lifted up the slot and Cole slid out five one-hundred-dollar bills.

"Oh. My. Well, here we go," said Mr. Reiner, clearly delighted. "That's very kind of you. I appreciate the advance. I'll see you next month, then."

Eager to keep the dough and skedaddle, Mr. Reiner pulled his cranky wife along behind him and they departed. We watched as they walked up the long driveway, Mrs. Reiner glancing back skeptically. We'd held the fort, kept the land of the living at bay—for now. I wondered how long we could hold out without Miss Torvous.

CHAOS

That night, dinner was a glum affair. Everyone knew we were on shaky ground. Darby and Cameron assembled a passable meal of cheeseburgers, fries, and coleslaw with ketchup. Zipperhead had taken my words to heart and was doing his best to chat up a girl or two, without much luck. But he kept on going, from one to another. Eventually, I thought, he'd find someone who would see his inner cool.

After dinner, Cole and Dougie and I cleaned up the kitchen. There were only a few miscreants up for battle now, as our future seemed tenuous and uncertain. With Miss Torvous in a salt coma in the basement, we lacked structure and discipline. Kids meandered around, eating and sleeping when they felt like it. Any semblance of a schedule had been tossed out the window.

I sat in my room with Lucy for a bit but couldn't relax. I had to get up and move around. I looked for Cole. He wasn't in his room, so I went up to the roof.

It was a clear, cool night. He was by himself.

"Can I hang with you?"

"I was hoping you'd come up."

I sat next to him. Time passed as we listened to night sounds: the crickets, the wind rustling the leaves in the trees. After a while I opened up. I told him about going to see Andy and about how trying to connect with him had resulted in a near tragedy.

"I'm lost. Completely and utterly lost," I said.

"It won't last," he said.

He was trying to comfort me. It wasn't working.

"But I don't know what to do."

"We'll find your killer. *That's* what we'll do."

"But what about Andy?"

Cole looked away from me into the night sky. He found a star he liked and fixated on it. After a moment, he spoke slowly and evenly.

"I have an idea."

"What is it?"

"You might not like it."

"Try me."

"You have to get Andy to fall in love with someone else."

His assessment had been correct. I didn't like it. In fact, I frickin' hated it. Anger boiled up inside and I was concocting a string of expletives, a real scathing diatribe, but I couldn't very well explode, because when I asked my heart of hearts what I should do, I knew Cole was right. Setting Andy free was the right thing to do.

"Still speaking to me?" asked Cole.

"Yeah. It's just . . ."

"It sucks."

"Yeah. A little hard to process. But you're right."

My life, or rather my death, had become much more complicated. I had to find my killer and bring him or her to justice before I could move on. But now the clock was ticking. I had to somehow fix Andy before he did something stupid. Nothing else mattered except making sure Andy let go of me. Because if anything happened to Andy, even if I did find my killer and made him or her pay, it wouldn't matter, because all I'd want to do is find the deepest hole in hell and crawl into it forever. Time was not on my side.

I had to go back to school.

Cole, Darby, and the gang came with me. It was a Friday night, and under the lights at Mustang Stadium, our football team was clashing with crosstown rivals, the point of which seemed to be to inflict as much pain on each other as humanly possible. I began to wonder. What did it *mean* to be human? I thought I'd known when I was alive. Now that I was dead, I wasn't so sure. It had to be more than *shit happens and then you die.* What was our purpose? Was it *really* to get as much stuff and have as much fun as you could before you croaked? I had no answers but plenty of questions. Being dead was allowing me a lot of time for introspection. Ironic, pondering how one should live their life after they're dead.

The plan was to get Andy to fall for some other girl. I was sure the task would be herculean, if not downright impossible. But maybe that was just my ego talking. Why *wouldn't* he eventually move on? What was so special about me? Other than the fact he loved me with every beat of his heart and almost killed himself in order to join me in death. I flashed back to our first date together.

We were cruising the mall at Northgate after seeing a movie. I pointed out a killer indigo shirt in an upscale store and begged Andy to try it on. He did, and it looked great on him. But once he saw the price, he wouldn't buy it. I made sure he left it in the changing room, then herded him to the food court. I said I had to go to the bathroom while he got us some tacos. I went back to the store, acted like I was trying something on, then slipped the indigo shirt in my purse. I was so smart I even asked for a store bag on the way out. When I gave him the shirt, his eyes lit up but then he looked conflicted and I always wondered if he thought I'd stolen it. I justified the theft in my mind by telling myself I was doing whatever it took to keep him, to make him happy. Remembering this forced me to peel away another layer. I was pretty far from being the good girl I'd once imagined myself to be.

"Do you see him?" Cole asked.

I'd zoned out thinking about Andy, going further down memory lane than I'd intended.

"Um, not yet," I said.

I started scanning the stands, taking in all those bright young faces, kids doing their best to act too cool to be there, too cool for school, too cool to be alive. If only they knew. I wanted to rush up to the ones I knew and scream in their faces. *Wake up! This life you have is precious! Don't waste any of it!* I remembered Granddad saying that youth was wasted on the young. Now I understood what he meant. Boy, did I *ever*. I had a ton of regrets and I was only sixteen years old. I wished I could go back and live my life over again. But that wasn't going to happen. The best I could hope for, it seemed, was to do better next time around. If there even *was* another time around.

I found him in the stands. He was sitting all alone up in the back row—where we used to sit—and he looked miserable. A couple of guys approached him with beers under their jackets and offered him one, but he shrugged them off. They let him be and swaggered away.

"He's up there," I said, and started to climb the stairs. I could have flown up, but for a few moments I wanted to feel like I used to, being alive, just kickin' it at a football game.

Cole and the others were bird-dogging me, floating above,

waiting and watching to see what I did. Before I reached the top of the stairs, Andy got up and headed for the upper deck to the snack bar and bathrooms. I followed him. He went into the boys' bathroom. I stayed outside. Sure, I could have gone in after him and no one would have seen me, but I'd never wanted to slip into the boys' bathroom when I was living, and didn't want to now. That was totally a guy's fantasy, being invisible and traipsing around the bathrooms or girls' locker rooms or whatever.

Three girls emerged from the bathroom. Andrea Johnson, Tabitha Welsch, and Carly Hockney. Out of the three of them, I thought Andrea was the most likely candidate to become Andy bait. I'd once seen her and Andy kicking a soccer ball back and forth, some serious foot flirting going on. But then again, that was back in third grade, so I wasn't sure there was still much of a connection between the two of them. But who knew? Maybe she was deeply embedded in Andy's brain as a future girlfriend.

As I was pondering this, Cole floated down and landed next to me.

"Cute," he said. Referring to the girls. Truth be told, they *were* all pretty. I had no idea why it bothered me that Cole was thinking these girls were attractive. I told myself he could have all three of them for all I cared. I was really good at lying to myself.

It was hard for me to imagine Andy falling for any of these girls, but I guess we had to start somewhere. I had no idea what to do or how to begin.

"Um, okay, cute is cute, so . . . just exactly what am I supposed to do here?"

I knew I sounded like a whiner but I didn't care. I hated the whole game plan. I was going to be a rat bitch and I knew it.

"How about you don't stress out and just watch," said Cole. "I have an idea."

It was halftime and the snack bar deck was starting to fill

up, getting jammed with kids giggling and poking and wolfing down junk food while they scoped out the competition. Cole rose up and zipped above some girl, singling her out. My eyes were on him, not her, and then Andy was coming out of the bathroom. Cole pulled the girl's scarf from her neck without her noticing. He dropped it to the floor. Andy bent down and picked it up.

"Hey," he said to the girl. "You dropped this."

The girl turned around. It was Dani.

SEDUCTION

As she gazed up at my boyfriend, her eyes shined with gratitude. I wondered just exactly how you could kill a ghost, because that's what I wanted to do to Cole right now as he floated down next to me. He saw the malice in my eyes.

"Easy. Take it easy. I know it's going to be hard."

But he didn't know. He had no freakin' idea how hard it was watching Dani flutter her eyelids and move her body, sending unmistakable signals to Andy. *I'm yours if you want me.* I couldn't hear what they were saying, but it didn't matter. The nonverbal communication was what counted here, and Dani was making short work of him, consoling him now with another gentle hug. She hooked her arm through his and tried to get him to walk with her. But he shook his head. He wasn't ready yet. *Good!* I thought.

Spurned and hurt, she turned away from him and headed for the grandstands. Darby was waiting for her there and deftly spilled a drink on the metal stairs. Dani slipped and fell. And screamed.

I watched Andy rush down to help her. He didn't just lean over and console her—no, he had to go and scoop her up into his arms! She leaned her head on his chest. Her hero.

He carried her out to *our spot* and sat her down and examined her ankle. She winced in pain. I flew over and could see that she was fine but was milking the moment for all it was worth.

"Does it hurt?" said Andy.

Hell yes, it hurts, I thought.

"A little," said Dani. "It feels better when you touch it."

Andy blushed. The scene was making me nauseous. She was such a little pro. I felt myself being yanked backward. It was Darby.

"Come on—you're not doing yourself any favors getting your panties in a bunch being so close like this," she said.

Darby was strong—she had to be to pull me away, because Andy was like a giant magnet to me—and she dragged me up to join the pack on the stadium roof. We had a ringside seat for the little play unfolding before us. I would call it *The Seduction,* starring Dani and my very own beloved Andy.

"I gotta give her props. She is good," said Zipperhead.

"What the hell would you know about it?" said Cameron. "You never even reached puberty."

"You don't need puberty to fall in love," said Zipperhead.

"Guys, not the time," said Cole.

As I watched Andy caring for Dani, I endured a wave of pain. I should have been the one he was caring for. *She's not even hurt, for god's sake, and I'm freakin' dead!* I was sad and confused and wanted to fly into outer space and never come back.

"I can't bear watching this," I said, not taking my eyes off them for one second. She was stroking his cheek.

"So don't watch," said Dougie, who then blew an icy-cold breath that found Andy and Dani. They shivered and found warmth by hugging each other.

I tore my eyes away from the love scene and stared up into the black sky. I couldn't take one more second of any of this, so I flew over and landed on the roof of the school's clock tower. It wasn't long before Cole and the others joined me.

"I got dumped by my first girlfriend at summer camp," Dougie said. "Ruined the whole trip. I put maggots in her sleeping bag but it didn't make me feel any better."

"I once kissed a girl," said Zipperhead.

"No way," said Cameron.

"Her name was Christen Zettlemeyer. She had red hair and she was really pretty."

"I call bullshit. How old were you?"

Zipperhead's ears turned red. "What does it matter?"

Cameron started laughing.

"Okay, we were . . . young, for sure, and it was on the cheek, but that counts, right?" Zipperhead asked.

"Of course it counts," I said. "Any kind of love counts."

"Dying before you even get to experience love completely sucks, you know? I mean, it hurts—it really, really hurts," said Zipperhead. He had tears in his eyes.

"We all know how you feel, Zip," said Cole.

He put an arm around Zipperhead, who bucked up, wiped away his tears, and smiled. My opinion of Cole just kept rising higher the more I got to know him.

But Zipperhead's words had a real effect on me. I'd fooled around to be sure, but I was still technically a virgin—I'd planned on saving myself for Andy—and now I was going to stay one forever. Zipperhead was right. It sucked soooo bad. I looked over at the stadium and saw Andy and Dani. He had both arms around her now. They looked like a couple already.

"Every time I think things can't get any worse, they do," I said. "If he hooks up with her, I don't think I even care what happens after that—I mean, what's the point? I'm so . . . miserable."

We sat for a moment. Cole made a motion and I felt something like a breeze behind me. I knew the others were taking off at his urging. He was going to bust a move. I could have told him not to bother. I could have flown off. I could have done about a thousand things. But I just sat there and waited for it.

"Maybe this will help."

He leaned in, lifted my chin, and kissed me for the second time. I didn't protest. I needed it, needed it like I needed my next breath. Cole knew what he was doing, and we had this incredible energy flowing between us. My eyes were closed and I felt wind rushing through my hair. I opened my eyes. We weren't on the roof any longer; we were spiraling through the night sky, lifting up. I caught my breath as I broke away from the kiss.

"What are we doing?"

I looked into his eyes. They shimmered the most amazing blue, reflecting the stars.

"I don't know—call it anything you like. Maybe ghost dancing?"

Ghost dancing. I liked that. He was smiling. His touch felt amazing. He was holding my waist and my hands were gripping his shoulders as we spun around, whooshing higher and higher. For the moment, Andy was a distant memory and my heart felt still. Cole hummed, and his deep voice echoed through the sky, growing louder and yet more distant, as though it were emanating from the patches of clouds. I hummed along with him and we were in tune, in sync, equals harmonizing in the night. It was the most beautiful sound. A voice inside asked if I was falling in love. I knew the answer.

I was blushing and let go of Cole. Like a gentleman, he released his hold on me, too. I closed my eyes and let out a deep breath and sank down, descending.

We were back on the roof now, both so embarrassed we couldn't look at each other. Cole spoke in a low tone.

"Um . . . that was . . ."

"Nice. Really nice," I said.

"Kind of better than nice, don't you think?" he said.

"Yeah. It was pretty spectacular."

We still couldn't look one another in the eye. I was afraid if I looked at him I would smile so wide I'd crack my face. So I just stared at the roof.

The football game was ending. Our home team had been given a solid drubbing and people were streaming into the parking lot, fleeing the scene of the massacre.

"So, now what?" I said.

"We have two choices. We could stay like this forever, which gets my vote because I don't ever want you to leave me," he said.

I was tingling from head to toe. But my left brain, my logical voice, urged me on.

"What's the second choice?"

"We go find your killer," he said.

"Cole . . ."

I looked at him and he saw everything in my eyes. He saw that I had fallen in love with him like he'd fallen for me, but also that I couldn't just leave things like this, that I had to resolve my life, my love for Andy, my afterlife.

"You don't have to say it. Let's get going," he said.

I grabbed him and kissed him one more time. It only lasted five seconds but had the feel of eternal bliss. Then we flew off into the night.

Yep. I was totally screwed.

OUIJA

There's a water tower on Balmor Hill that we used to throw crab apples at when I was a kid. Now I was all grown up and dead and a ghost and landed on top of it with a ghost boy. Things change. We sat and talked as we looked out at the city lights.

"You got any suggestions on how I should go about finding that wonderful person who snuffed out my life?"

"Well, we do what cops would do. Make a list of suspects and then vet them one by one."

"Vet them?"

"Yeah, examine them, scrutinize, get to the truth."

"And how are we supposed to do that?"

"We do what ghosts do best. We scare the shit out of them.

People tend to start acting crazy when they're being haunted, and more often than not, the truth comes out."

"You mean they just blurt it out?"

"Sometimes, if they're haunted fast and hard enough. But there's a risk with that."

"Such as?"

"Such as, if they're innocent . . ."

I nodded my understanding. "We'd end up messing with their heads and possibly screwing up their whole lives."

"You got it."

"So we have to be selectively terrifying."

"Now you're getting it. So, who's first on the list?" said Cole.

I had someone in mind.

Denise Wiggins lived with her parents and snotty little brother in a two-story Tudor house on the tallest hill in Kirkland. They had four cars, a rose garden, and a rich-person's view of Lake Washington. When we arrived, we found thirty or so cars parked haphazardly in the circular driveway. Several of the cars had "Go Mustangs!" bumper stickers on them, so I concluded Denise was throwing one of her massively popular soirées, the kind that I was never invited to.

Japanese techno pop was thumping. We passed through the front door without bothering to open it. Charlie Boder from my French class was doing his beatboxing thing. He was really good at it and I always liked him. I was going to miss him. Then I remembered a time in class when he'd been doing that and I'd given him a basic "you suck" kind of look and he'd shut up. The poor dude was probably trying to impress me and I'd shut him down and hurt his feelings. Why had I been such a bitch? I wished I could zip back in time and take back all the crummy crap I'd done. I wished I could change it all. But I couldn't. Not in a thousand years. All I could do was look to the future, and that meant finding and outing my killer.

We looked all over the house and finally found Denise in her dad's library doing vodka shots with her posse. As soon as Cole and I entered the room, she was blinking and rubbing the back of her neck, scared. She took two quick shots and her chief acolyte, Laura Stellini, was uber concerned.

"Jesus, Denise, take it easy or you'll pass out."

"What do you think I'm trying to do?"

"Why are you so freaked?" asked Laura.

Denise did something then that gave me the willies. She jerked her head around like a deer that just heard a twig snap. Her eyes narrowed. Could she see me? No. I knew by looking in the mirror behind her that she couldn't. I had no reflection. She hugged herself.

"I can't take it anymore. Ever since that Dumpster thing at school—she's just been . . . messin' with me. I gotta do something; I know she's out there and she blames me," said Denise.

"You're just imagining things," said acolyte number two, Carley Moore.

"Whatever," said Laura. "We have to help her. I say we do a séance, try and call her out."

"I'm up for it," said Denise.

They marched past us and went upstairs. Cole and I watched.

"Wait a second—this is way too weird," I said. "Why is she thinking about me and doing this now? I mean, right at this moment?"

"Because you're here. She senses your presence. Maybe not consciously, but in her unconscious mind, the one that connects with the unseen universe, she knows you're hanging around and she wants you to move on."

"So when a ghost hangs around someone they used to know, they just pop into their mind?"

"Something like that. Just accept it, Echo—she's thinking about you because you're right here next to her."

I was thinking about Cole because I was right next to him,

too, but I didn't want to tell him that. I had so many conflicting feelings inside that I thought I was going to explode. Every time I was in Cole's orbit, I was growing closer to him.

"Maybe you should go in first, okay?" I said.

He gave me a weird look and then moved up the stairs. I watched him from behind and enjoyed being able to stare at him all I wanted without him knowing I was doing it. He had a really nice body. For a ghost, I guess. I thought about what it would be like to have him hold me again. *What am I doing?*

Cole entered the attic and I went in after him. We found Denise, Carley, and Laura sitting on the floor. They had lit candles, which cast spooky shadows. Denise pulled something out of an old chest. A Ouija board. Maybe this was going to be productive *and* fun.

"God, it's cold in here," Denise said.

"Maybe Echo's ghost is in here," said Carley. "Whenever ghosts are around, the temperature drops."

"Where'd you find that out?" asked Laura.

"I saw it on YouTube."

"Oh, then for sure it's gotta be real," said Laura, rolling her eyes.

Cole and I exchanged a look.

"We do have a tendency to make things rather chilly," he said.

I offered a little smile. I didn't want to tell him the truth, that whenever I was around him, I felt the opposite of cold—I always felt a warmth spreading through me.

Carley touched the Ouija board.

"So how does it work?" she asked.

"Don't you, like, know *anything*?" said Laura.

"I know you're bulimic and won't cop to it," said Carley.

This much was true. I'd seen Laura throwing up after lunch on more than one occasion, and though she was rail thin, she obsessed about her weight.

"Shut up!"

"Both of you shut up!" said Denise. "You put your fingers on this thingy . . ."

"It's called a planchette," said Laura. She looked smugly at Carley.

"But just lightly, so you don't really move it yourself. The . . . spirit you're talking to moves it."

"This is so creepy," said Carley.

"My whole life is creepy right now, so if you don't mind, please shut your piehole and help me out here, or just get the hell out of the room, okay?"

Carley nodded.

Denise's fingers trembled as she laid them on the planchette. Nothing happened.

"What do we do now?" asked Carley.

"You can either ask it a yes-or-no question, or just wait to see if it . . . oh my god!"

Now the planchette was moving.

Because my fingers were on it, too, and slowly I spelled out a word. Starting with *m*. Then I moved the planchette over to the *u*.

By the time I moved it to *r*, Denise was beginning to put up resistance on the planchette, terrified of what was coming at her. Carley and Laura were trembling. I kept it up. I thought I smelled urine but couldn't be sure. Was Denise wetting her pants?

"Oh my god, oh my god, oh my god!" said Carley. "It's spelling . . ."

MURDERER

All three girls shrieked and Denise's fingers flew away from the planchette like it was scalding hot. She started whimpering.

"No . . . no . . . no . . ."

"What the *hell*, Denise?" said Carley, her face now ashen. "Did you freaking kill Echo?"

"No!"

"Jesus, Carley, you are so damn dumb. We were *with* Denise the night Echo was killed. Over at Jason's, remember? You drank, like, seven beers and a Moscow Mule and he grabbed your boobs. Duh!"

"Oh yeah. What an asshole."

Laura turned to Denise and stroked her hair, consoling her. "Sweetie, don't pay attention to this thing," she said. "It's just a stupid kid's game is all."

"Why did it do that?"

"*It* didn't do anything; it's just your subconscious mind, your fear acting out. Don't think about it anymore," said Laura.

I backed off and watched them from a distance.

"What do you think?" asked Cole.

"Denise has an alibi. I think she couldn't have done it."

"I feel like I have worms crawling on me," said Denise. "I have to know something."

She put her fingers back on the planchette and spoke.

"Echo . . . Echo, are you here? Here in this room, right now?"

I couldn't help myself. I floated over and moved the planchette to spell out

YES

Denise's face looked like it was going to slide off her skull.

"Oh my god . . . oh my god . . . OH MY GOD!"

She sniffed and snuffled and burped and, for all I knew, farted. The tension was overtaking her.

"I'm so sorry I tried to destroy your artwork, Echo. And I'm sorry for being mean to you. I really am!"

She was coming completely unglued. Laura's eyes blazed.

"What do you want, Echo? What should she do? What do you want Denise to do?"

I whispered to Cole.

"If I told her to jump off the roof, do you think she'd do it?"

"She just might. But she's innocent. Asking her to do that would be . . ."

"Mean and spiteful, I know. But it's the first thing that came into my mind. I always thought I was a good girl. Now I'm beginning to wonder."

"She's waiting. Tell her something."

I moved the planchette one last time and spelled out

NO MORE BITCH

"Oh God, I'll change, I will, I promise!"

Denise collapsed into a blubbering heap, her acolytes cooing and stroking her hair. I had the feeling that Denise *would* change, that she'd become more aware of other people's feelings. She'd tormented me, but I doubted she would torment anyone else. Hell, she might even join a convent. I led Cole from the room. Our work here was done. But I racked my brain. *Who killed me?* I'd eliminated suspect number one, Walker, and now number two, Denise. I thought of the anger that lived in Andy's father, Hank. He was shaping up to be suspect number three.

MOTHER

When we got back to Middle House, Darby and Zipperhead were waiting with solemn looks on their faces. Kids were fighting and using their powers to spook each other's brains out. I ducked as a fireball whooshed by and slammed into a wall that burst into flames. Darby screamed down the hallway.

"Knock it off or I'm gonna kick your ass to the curb!"

Cameron ran up and used his power to douse the fire with a stream of water from the bathroom.

"Getting damn sucky around here," he said, coughing through the smoke.

Darby was shaking her head and made a motion with her hand as she looked at Cole and me.

"What's up?" said Cole.

"You better come with us," she said.

We did as she asked, following her down the stairwells into the subbasement to the salt chamber.

"It's bad. It's so bad. It's really bad," said Zipperhead, nervously rubbing his scars, causing tiny sparks to shoot out.

When we got to the salt chamber, we peered in through the peepholes. Miss Torvous was splayed on the floor, her feet and hands bent at weird angles. No fingers or toes wiggled. Her chest wasn't rising and falling.

"It's all going to go to crap," said Zipperhead. "They're going to come for something and she's not going to be there and they're going to close this place down, maybe sell it or something, and what are we supposed to do then?"

"How about for starters you stop jabbering like an idiot and help us figure something out?" said Darby.

"Nothing to figure out. We're screwed," said Zipperhead. Tears spilled down his cheeks and he took off upstairs.

We continued to peer in at Miss Torvous. She looked dead. A pretty neat trick for someone who already was.

"Do you think she's . . . ?"

"Somehow gone?" said Cole. "I don't know. But I think we better find out."

"I'm not going in there," I said.

Always the brave one. The concept of awakening a sleeping monster who had serious issues with me was not, in my mind, the best course of action. I figured we could probably get along just fine without her lording over us, if only we banded together and kept our wits about us.

Dougie came down—shirtless, as was his constant habit now—and was chewing on his fingernails like a raccoon going mental.

"They're on my case!"

"Who?" said Cole.

"Everyone! They said it's cold enough in this drafty old place without me making it colder. And I wasn't even doing anything. Oh, and there were some guys out front taking pictures."

Cole tensed up.

"What was that about, you think?" I asked.

"I don't know. They could be cops, or realtors, or journalists— who knows? The only thing I know is that it's not good having humans poking around."

He stared in at Miss Torvous.

"Sooner or later we're going to need her," he said.

"I know what you're thinking, but don't do it," I said.

"I'm going in."

He pulled Dougie and Darby and me over to a rusty, old metal storage bin and opened it. There were a dozen or so pairs of thick leather gloves piled up, along with several bags of sea salt. He handed us each a pair of gloves.

"Here, put these on."

We did as he asked. Then he handed Dougie the bag of sea salt. I felt queasy. Dougie burped.

"Man, this stuff is rank, dude."

Cole continued to be all business.

"She might be in some kind of coma, but if she isn't and starts kicking up a fuss when I bring her out, go ahead and toss some of this on her."

We waited with the gloves on and the bags of salt at the ready. Cole seemed to be in the chamber for a long time and it was making me nervous. I moved over to a peephole and looked in. He was kneeling down and ever so gently scooping her up into his arms. She was limp, like a bird that had crash-landed. His tenderness struck a chord in me, and again my mushy brain was thinking about how he was such an awesome guy. He did have one glaring flaw. The whole "dead" thing. Other than that I was having a tough time finding fault in him.

He carried Miss Torvous toward the door. I backed up. Dougie and Darby braced, ready to defend themselves.

"She better not try anything!" said Darby.

Their concern wasn't necessary. It was clear that Miss Torvous was totally out of it.

We followed Cole as he carried her up the long flight of stairs. In the hallway, kids hushed and stared. She never once stirred. Cole took her to her room and we proceeded with him. He laid her on the bed where she sank into the thick down comforter. Cole stepped back and joined our ranks. Miss Torvous was absolutely still. We stood in silence, staring at her for a long time. You could hear the old clock with no hands in the hallway ticking away.

It was eerie, as if she were some kind of ancient tomb or something we were paying our last respects to. I'd never before noticed how utterly beautiful she was. Cole was the first to break ranks. He moved closer to her, then closer still, his face now inches from hers. He was listening . . . feeling . . . perceiving. Cole motioned to me as he leaned even closer to her.

"I can't tell if she's breathing. Help me."

I was petrified, but I did what he wanted and stepped forward, moving my face close to hers. She didn't look completely dead, just very ill. I was contemplating if and how a ghost could die when I felt a tiny stream of breath coming from her nostrils.

"She's . . . breathing, I think," I said.

"I think so, too," he said.

"The effect of the salt is wearing off," said Darby. Her voice was shakier than I'd ever heard it before. Cole spoke again to try to calm everyone down.

"We're going to be okay. When she wakes up, all we have to do is talk some sense into—"

Her eyes popped open.

"Miss Torvous, please don't be angry. We just wanted—"

Cole couldn't finish his sentence. Quick as lightning she grabbed him around the neck, her grip swift and sudden. Her nostrils flared. Her face flushed crimson.

"You'll pay for this!"

We threw gobs of salt on her. As it rained down, she screeched like a velociraptor. Cole wrenched himself free but she leapt up and was on him like a crazed lioness.

Dougie and Darby were pelting her with the sea salt, but all it was doing at this point was pissing her off. Cole looked sick as a dog. I remembered the small framed picture that Zipperhead had dislodged while jumping on her bed. Was it Miss Torvous as a girl? Was it her sister? Mother? Daughter?

I remembered how she looked at me when I'd gone into her room before she melted down. She'd called me "darling." Her gaze had been soft as though she adored me. She felt some connection to me—I just didn't know what it was, but I had to take a shot.

"Mommy!"

She released Cole. Her head swiveled on her body as though she were a giant doll. Her eyes found mine. Was she looking at me? Or looking into the past?

"Corrine?"

I felt a tingling on the back of my neck. Darby's and Dougie's eyes were bulging. They couldn't move. I spoke gently to her.

"Please don't hurt him. It's me you want."

She softened and rose to her feet.

"You came back to me," she said.

She floated over—it was weird because we'd *never* seen her ghost float before—and she touched my cheek with her cold hand, cold on cold.

"Came back?" I whispered, terrified.

"Yes, Corrine . . . I've missed you so much."

I had to play along. I placed my arms around her.

"I've missed you, too."

I looked at Darby and Dougie and did my best to speak with my eyes. *Get him out of here!* They understood and helped Cole from the room, gently closing the door behind them.

"Can we sit down?" I asked.

"Of course, darling," she said.

We moved to the overstuffed settee and sat. She cupped my face in her hands.

"I loved it when you called me Mother."

I smiled. But I was getting nervous. I bit my lip and couldn't keep my foot from tapping.

"Miss Torvous . . ."

She hardened slightly and cocked her head to one side.

"Darling, you don't have to—"

"Who am I? I mean, who do I remind you of?"

This was it. I was going to find out the truth. She was going to destroy me.

"Corrine, sweetheart . . ."

"My name is Echo. Echo Stone."

She wouldn't look at me. Instead, her gaze bounced around the room. She rubbed the back of her neck and clenched her teeth.

"I'm not Corrine, Miss Torvous."

She looked like she might explode again. Who knew what she was capable of? But I'd gone this far and couldn't back down.

"You can work us to the bone, but that's never going to bring her back. Please . . . tell me?"

I took another chance and ever so gently placed my hand on top of hers. She looked down at it. It was do-or-die time. Was she going to destroy me or open up and share her dark secret? It was so quiet I thought I could hear my own heart beating.

She raised her gaze slowly up to mine. Her eyes welled with tears. She pointed a long, slender finger at the bureau.

"Top drawer. Under the clothing."

I couldn't imagine what was in the drawer, but I knew whatever it was, it would change everything.

TRAGIC

I rose and opened the drawer. Under a stack of a young girl's clothing was a newspaper. A page-two article with the headline "A Tragic Fatality."

I looked over at Miss Torvous. She was as still as a stone. Her lips barely moved as she said, "Go ahead and read it."

She clenched her eyes shut tight, as though expecting to be struck. She spoke again.

"Out loud."

I did as she asked.

"Shortly after midnight on July 19th, paramedics responded to a call from 4581 Moorland Street, where they encountered the body of a young girl, apparently the daughter of Mrs. Emily Torvous, 34, who was incoherent at the scene.

The girl was rushed to Saint John's Hospital where doctors were unable to revive her. The cause of death was reported to be severe head and neck trauma. A medical spokesperson stated that the injuries sustained were consistent with being struck by a car. Mrs. Torvous has been admitted to the Bonner Hills Mental Facility for evaluation."

I looked over at her. She was shaking her head and let out a long, low moan. Her voice trembled.

"I couldn't live with myself after that. Phenobarbital. Ten grams. It did the trick."

So that was it. She'd run over her daughter, then taken her own life.

"It was an accident," I said. I didn't know if that was true, but I felt like it had to be and I wanted to ease her pain.

"I was drunk."

There wasn't much to say to that. She'd made the worst mistake I could possibly imagine: getting smashed and running over your own kid. No wonder she went off the deep end. I didn't blame her and it was way too late to judge her. I went and put my arms around her.

"I'm sorry."

She let me hold her for a moment.

"Will you let me call you Corrine? And hold you?"

"Yes. Of course."

"Sweet Corrine," she said. And put her arms around me and sobbed. She needed this. And I missed my own mother so much that maybe I did, too. I began to sob along with her, and after a few moments, we'd cried all the tears that were due.

She wanted to hold me and, truth be told, I didn't mind being held. So we stayed that way, mother and surrogate daughter, for a long, long time, and eventually fell asleep.

Then we heard a pounding on the front door. It was morning. Cole and Darby entered quickly.

"Miss Torvous?"

She was starting to zone out again, going back into the delusional trance that was keeping her terrible guilt at bay.

"Leave me alone. I'm with my daughter!"

The banging on the door continued. I moved to the window. Snoopy Mrs. Reiner was on the front porch with two policemen, one short, one tall.

"I'm telling you, there's something going on in this place! I heard things all night long!"

"We can't search the premises without a warrant, ma'am," said Shorty.

"But what if she's dead? What if some teenagers or gang members broke in and killed her?"

The cops exchanged a tired look.

"I'm not going to let up on this," said Mrs. Reiner. "I have a sixth sense about these things. I know for a fact that there's something *abnormal* in this house!"

She had that right. Boy, did she ever. The cops stepped away from her and were conferring. It didn't look good. Especially when the tall one went to the squad car, popped open the trunk, and lifted out a battering ram. Shorty put a hand up.

"Probable cause?"

"The lady says she heard sounds of violence. That's enough cause for me," said the tall cop.

They were about a minute away from smashing open the front door. And if they found Miss Torvous like this . . .

I had to act quickly. I went to her and took her face in my hands. I couldn't be Echo if I wanted to get through to her brain from her heart.

"Mother?"

Her eyes were glazed over.

"Mommy, listen to me!"

I grabbed her by the shoulders and shook her.

"I forgive you. It wasn't your fault."

"Corrine?" she said.

I had broken through. "I'm not Corrine, not your daughter. But believe me when I tell you that I am speaking for her. She's speaking through me. And she forgives you."

Miss Torvous closed her eyes and took a long, deep breath. She sobbed again, her chest heaving, then pulled herself together, dabbing at her eyes. She finally heard the loud banging on the front door.

"What's going on? Cole?" she said.

She stood up, her back ramrod straight.

"It's the police. I think they're trying to break the door down. They think you're dead or something."

"Well, they're not entirely wrong," she said.

A tight smile formed on her lips, then was gone in a second. She was back to her old self.

She marched to the front door and opened it. Mrs. Reiner shuffled back a step and blinked, her mouth opening.

"Hello, Mrs. Reiner," said Miss Torvous, cool as can be. "Is there something wrong on the grounds?"

"Um . . . no. Are you all right?"

"Of course. Never better. How can I help you, gentlemen?"

She smiled at the cops. It was a wonderful power she had, being able to put on a façade so that living people could see nothing but a normal human being when a ghost lurked inside. The cops exchanged a glance, then gave a dirty look to Mrs. Reiner.

"This was just a routine check. Nothing to worry about."

Mrs. Reiner wasn't satisfied.

"But . . . she . . . the noise . . ." she said.

"As I said, just a routine check," the tall cop stated.

"You have a nice day," said the shorter of the two cops.

"I intend to," said Miss Torvous. "Tell your husband the back hedge needs trimming, will you, Mrs. Reiner?"

Mrs. Reiner was nodding numbly as Miss Torvous closed the front door.

The headmistress turned to us.

"Let's get this place cleaned up," she said.

Everyone moved very quickly. Torvous was back. We worked for hours getting things back to normal, sweeping and mopping and cleaning, and dinner that night was a pleasantly quiet affair, with only a few kids fooling around. Cole walked me to my room where we lingered in the doorway. Lucy, in her cat incarnation, was asleep on her bed, her tail twitching.

"You did fantastic today," said Cole.

"I only did what I had to."

"Don't get mad, but . . . seeing you like that, acting so smart and cool under pressure, it made me . . ." His voice trailed off as he blushed.

"It made you what?"

"It made me want you even more. And I didn't think that could ever be possible."

I wanted him, too, wanted to tell him so, but I had to hold back. I had business to take care of and I was terrified that if I let my feelings for Cole ripen and mature, I would fall into an abyss, plunging into a crushing love that would consume me forever. So instead of telling him what I felt in my heart, I stared at some imaginary point behind him and told a lie.

"I don't know if that's such a good thing."

My words shredded him. He tried to cover it up and did a crappy job. I could tell I'd hurt him.

"I . . . I don't understand, but I respect you, Echo. I'll do whatever you want me to do, even if that means leaving you alone."

It felt like a fist was squeezing my heart.

"I think that's the best thing," I lied again. *What is wrong with you, Echo?* said one voice. *You're trying to do the right thing!* said another.

Cole nodded ever so slowly, then turned and floated down the hallway, his shoulders slumped. I wanted to cry out to him,

Come back here—I'm falling in love with you! But I just watched him go. I wasn't sure if I was the bravest girl in the world or a big, fat coward. In seconds, he'd turned the corner and was gone.

That night, I willed myself to sleep thinking of Andy. But after I'd fallen asleep, I dreamt of Cole.

In the morning, I looked for him but he wasn't there.

VETTING

I told myself I was going to Andy's house to investigate his father, Hank, but a nagging voice was calling bullshit on me.

All you really want to do is check on Andy, be physically close to him—you're still holding out hope, you idiot.

It was true that I wanted to be close to Andy. I loved his smell, his laugh, and the way he touched me, like he really cared for me. Of course that was all in the past now, so I wasn't really sure what I was doing. Maybe I'd stung Cole so badly I was afraid I would lose him forever, too. I told myself that I couldn't *love* Cole; I didn't know him well enough yet. My nagging voice called bullshit again. *You dumb-ass! You already love Cole so much you can feel it with every breath you take.*

It was true. I was caught in the middle. Not alive and not

all the way dead and gone. In love with a living human boy and a ghost boy at the same time. They were both pulling at me. If I didn't fix things soon, I felt like my heart would be ripped in half.

It was early on a Sunday morning. Andy was in bed sleeping. I hovered above him for a long time, my face just inches away from his. I loved feeling his warm breath on me. I wanted to kiss him in the worst way, but I just floated there above him. I didn't want to wake him up or freak him out in case he could sense me. He stirred in bed and pulled the sheet away from his body. He wasn't wearing a shirt and I felt an ache as I stared down at his sculpted stomach. I wanted to crawl in bed with him, wanted to press my body against his. But I didn't *have* a body, so he wouldn't feel a thing, except maybe something like a cool breeze. I was starting to feel pervy for spying on him like this.

"I miss you, baby. I'll always miss you," I said. Then I added what I thought I needed to, to convince myself that what I was doing was the right thing, and not completely insane.

"I want you to be happy, even if it's with . . . Dani."

I almost choked when I said her name, but I had to say it because at some point I really would have to start believing it. I didn't now, not for a second, but I had to keep working on that. I loved Andy with my whole being, and loving someone is supposed to mean that you care more about them than you do about yourself. At least that's what my grandma Tilly used to say. I clearly had a lot of self-work to do. For starters, I had to stop worshiping my former (god, how I hated that word) boyfriend and find the ass face who murdered me. Was it Hank? I would do everything I could to find out.

I heard some pots banging around downstairs, so I headed down. Hank was in the kitchen, cleaning up his breakfast dishes. Even when he was alone he looked mean, and I didn't like getting too close to him. He was dressed in slacks and a nerdy short-sleeved white shirt and went into the hallway where he grabbed a clip-on tie and put it on. Then he went into the family room and opened the drawer of an old desk and pulled out a King James Bible.

He checked himself in the mirror, slicked his hair back, and went out the front door carrying the Bible. I followed him.

Saint Augustine Church was the oldest church in Kirkland, boasting a tall, carved gray-stone bell tower topped with a white cross. I went in and slipped into a back pew. It was an early service with not too many parishioners in attendance. The priest was fit and young looking with a shaved head and a hipster goatee. He was a smiler, a joyful-looking man who spoke in a robust voice, and after giving Communion, wrapped things up. After a brief hymn, people began filing out. Hank watched them, then caught the priest's eye and made a beeline for the confessional.

I looked up at the statue of Jesus and wondered if he would forgive me for eavesdropping on a confession. I figured that with all that had happened to me, the Big Guy would cut me some slack.

The confessional was dark and cool. A latticed grate separated the priest from Hank.

"Forgive me, Father, for I have sinned."

"Only the Lord can forgive you. I can help lighten your burden. Tell me. What's going on?"

"I have been mistreating my son. He's . . . distraught . . . filled with grief over this girl. He was in love with her. *So* in love."

Hank sniffed back a tear. I thought I might fall over. In my mind, this brute never cried.

"I see," said the priest.

"I don't think you do. She's dead. Murdered. You probably heard about her. Echo. Echo Stone?"

"Yes. Your son's grief is normal, a necessary process."

"I know, and I've been riding him about it, real hard. You see, she was an amazing girl, one of a kind."

I was taken aback. Hank thought I was *one of a kind*? Then why on earth did he—

"I watched her grow up. She was a clumsy little girl."

I was not!

"And she blossomed like a flower, the most beautiful flower I've ever seen. I loved her long before Andy ever even gave her a second look."

The *eeeewwwww* factor was rising exponentially with every word Hank uttered. So the old guy had been perving on me! Yuck!

I flashed back to a memory involving Hank. I must have been about thirteen. He was working on his roof and I was in my room, dancing, doing my best impression of Katy Perry, with a tied-up blouse and foofy skirt and stockings, singing "I Kissed a Girl" over and over.

I didn't see him watching me at first, but when I did—just caught him out of the corner of my eye—I didn't stop. I should have closed my curtains and shut the whole silly schoolgirl act down, but I didn't. I flipped my hair and danced like a fool. Every time I looked at Hank, he looked away quickly, pretending he hadn't seen me. But I knew he had. And yet . . . I kept on dancing. The good girl trying to act bad. So stupid. That didn't mean he wasn't creeping on me; it just meant that I could have stopped and didn't. Because some warped part of me thought if I could get Hank to like me, by any means, then Andy would, too. The memory put yet another smudge on the sterling image I'd had of myself. Hank continued with his confession.

"I haven't been honest with Andy. I don't know how to tell him how I thought about her so much. When Andy's mother died, it left a hole in my heart. In some stupid way, I thought that girl could fill that hole."

"So you had desires?"

"I . . . just wanted to hold her. I guess those are what you'd call desires. I know they were wrong, and I fought them. I never acted on them. Not once. But they haunted me, and I feel like if I just told my son . . ."

"Some things are best confessed only to the Lord. Not all things must be said to everyone, especially if they would do harm," said the priest.

"And you think it would harm Andy if I told him?"

"I can't make that judgment. Only the Lord can do that. Ask the Lord for guidance. It will come to you."

"Thank you, Father. I feel so bad inside. So filled with guilt. See, the night she was killed, she should have been with Andy, but I was half in the bag and ornery so I made Andy go to the library and do homework. Maybe if I'd let him go out with her, she'd still be alive. I hate myself for it."

So Hank wasn't my killer. When I'd entered him, I'd misinterpreted his rage. He didn't hate me, he hated himself. The priest spoke to him with great compassion.

"The first thing you must do is forgive yourself, as God forgives you."

"I don't think I can do that, Father. The only way I can make this right is to find the son of a bitch who killed her and make him sorry he ever walked a single day on this earth."

"Vengeance is not the path to salvation."

"We're going to have to agree to disagree on that one, Padre. Thanks for your time. I'll say some Hail Marys."

I waited outside the confessional. Hank emerged, looking sideways, both directions, like a criminal. I had a lot of thoughts about him. I was disgusted but also felt sorry for him. He'd loved and lost his wife. He loved Andy. Mostly I was relieved.

He wasn't my killer. It was time to move on to suspect number four. There was just one problem. I didn't *have* a suspect number four. I had to think back. Who was at my funeral that was so evil they would kill me? How could anyone do that to me? I had no clue. Then I thought, maybe I had to go at it a different way. Maybe I had to start asking, *What did I do?*

THEFT

I followed Hank back to his and Andy's place. I told myself again that I was just doing surveillance but the truth mocked me. I wanted to be around Andy. I waited in the woods behind his house, sitting on a tall branch, listening to the birds and feeling the sun on my body. The sun's rays were different than when I was alive, but I could still feel them. Maybe it wasn't real, like the phantom pain someone feels in a missing limb. But I didn't care. It felt good to imagine.

I sensed movement above me to my left and thought for a second it was a bird. But it was too large for a bird. And there'd been no shadow. Ghosts don't have shadows. I spun around and there was Cole, perched in a tree about twenty feet away.

"What's up?" he said. Casual. Cool. Acting as though last

night had never happened. Did I really dump him? Or was it a dream? I was hoping it hadn't happened but I knew what was real.

I tried not to smile. I was so glad to see him but I didn't want to let on. I was still in the let-him-go mode.

"What are you doing here?" I asked.

"We can't always do these things alone. I want to help."

I nodded. *Okay. He's here to help—that's it. Nothing more. It's not like he's over there singing out his love for me to the treetops. This is all business. Sure.*

"It wasn't his dad. I heard him confessing in church."

"Ooooh. Listening in on a confession. Pretty slick move," he said.

"I know it was sleazy, but I just—"

Cole flew over suddenly and landed right next to me.

"It wasn't sleazy. There are no rules. We do what we have to do."

"And then?"

"And then we join the Afters."

I nodded again. I knew all this.

"I can hardly wait."

Andy's front door opened and he came out. He was looking good, like he'd washed some of the grief off himself. I had mixed feelings about that. Forgotten so soon? My heart sank a little. He got in his Jeep and took off. I glanced at Cole. I knew he saw the pain in my eyes.

"Echo?"

"Yeah?"

"Do you want me to come with you?"

"What else are you going to do? Hang around in the trees, maybe build a nest?" He smiled like he'd just won the lottery. I put a serious face on and did my best impression of someone important.

"Let's go."

We took off after the Jeep.

Andy ripped across town with the stereo blasting heavy metal. Which was weird, because he usually only listened to heavy metal when he was lifting weights or psyching himself up for a martial arts bout, a sport he was awesome at. I once asked him about it and he said the music made him just the right amount of crazy. He pulled into Dani's driveway and she was out the door in two seconds and jumped into the Jeep next to him. I tried to be cool, but she made it hard by giving him a kiss on the cheek *and* a hug and then rested her hand on his knee as they took off. They were heading down Chalmers Road, which took them straight toward the school. I wondered what was up. Why go to school on a Sunday? My thought process was scrambled as her hand kept inching upward until it was on his thigh. I imagined hitting her over the head with various objects. I heard growling. It was me. Cole pursed his lips.

"Keep it under control, Echo. Keep cool."

I swore under my breath. Yeah, you betcha. Where was he taking her? When they pulled into the school parking lot, I thought to myself, this makes no sense. Andy stopped the Jeep by the side of the main building and checked the grounds. Not a soul in sight. Except us ghosts.

He put it in park, kept the engine running, and got out. He pulled Dani over into the driver's seat.

"Get ready to hit it when I tell you," he said.

"What are we doing?" she said.

"You promised to help me. If you don't want to, I can take you home."

"No, I'm good; I'm in," she said. She didn't want to piss him off in the least.

He pulled a crowbar and heavy-duty bolt cutters out of the back of the Jeep and went to a side door. He cut through the padlock in two seconds and was inside. I zoomed in after him with Cole right behind me.

"What's he doing?" said Cole.

"How should I know?"

"Well, for one thing, he was your boyfriend."

There was that word again. *Was.* I wasn't on board with *was.* I still wanted *is.* Dammit!

The hallways were dark. Andy ran right to Mr. Hemming's photography classroom. Then it hit me. The sticky note on Andy's corkboard wasn't about *his* fourth-period class, it was about mine. I had photography fourth period. With Mr. Hemming. The classroom door was locked but the top half of the door was glass. Andy used the crowbar to smash his way in.

"What are you doing, Andy?" I said.

Why was he vandalizing Mr. Hemming's classroom? I watched as he moved through the classroom to the teacher's desk. He picked up the small glass piggy bank Mr. Hemming kept there and put it in his pocket. That's what he'd broken in for? A piggy bank? Again, none of this was making a stitch of sense. But then again, neither did my murder. I heard footsteps and zoomed down the hallway. Mr. Mack, the old security guard, was limping his way toward us.

I whooshed back to Andy, who was still searching the desk. There was nothing of value on top. He yanked on the desk drawers. Locked. He pulled the crowbar from the back of his jeans. In one sudden, violent motion, he popped open the desk drawer. More footsteps. Mr. Mack was closing in.

"You have to get out of here!" I shouted.

I didn't want him to get caught. He'd be suspended, or worse—thrown in jail. He pulled a laptop out of the drawer and ran from the room, rushing past us right before Mr. Mack let out a croaky, pathetic, "Stop!"

Andy ran back outside, legs pumping, his jacket flapping. The little glass piggy bank popped out of his pocket and fell to the pavement, shattering. Andy stopped and scooped up the coins that had been inside. I wondered if he was losing his mind.

He jammed the coins into his pocket and jumped into the Jeep. Dani slammed her foot on the gas and they were gone, leaving Mr. Mack cursing in the doorway. He fumbled in his pocket and called a number on his cell phone, but I was pretty sure there was no way he could have seen the Jeep's license plate. Andy had gotten away with it. This time.

AXE

We followed the Jeep to Vista View Park where Andy opened the computer and scanned through the files. I had no idea what he was looking for, but by the expression on his face, he clearly wasn't finding it. He kept looking and looking until finally he slammed the computer shut.

"Son of a bitch!"

"What's wrong, sweetie?" said Dani.

Oh, so now it was *sweetie*? I gritted my teeth. Andy started up the Jeep.

"Now where are we going?" asked Dani.

"Into the belly of the beast," he said.

Dani was as confused as I was as Andy punched the Jeep forward.

"Any clue what's going on here?" asked Cole.

"Not at all," I said. "But we're going to follow them."

We soared above the Jeep as it sped through town then screamed south on Lake Washington Boulevard. Andy turned left up a side street and parked with a screech in a cul-de-sac, two doors down from an upscale brick Tudor. It was Mr. Hemming's house. Again thoughts of my photography teacher brought up an inward smile. Things were coming back to me slowly. I remembered coming to this house, remembered being nervous. I must have been dropping off an assignment or something, because I was rarely nervous around my teachers. I was a fairly good student, not a cheater or anything. I never had anything to hide.

Andy had Dani wait in the Jeep while he moved into the backyard of the house adjacent to Mr. Hemming's place. A dog barked, but it was behind a fence down the street and posed no threat to Andy, whatever he was planning on doing, which at this point I supposed was more searching, or possibly even a confrontation with Mr. Hemming. I wondered what Andy thought Hemming might know about my murder? It wasn't possible that he was a suspect. He was a guy who smiled *all* the time. If you Googled *friendly,* his picture would probably come up.

Images appeared in my brain, each one causing a wave of pain. Suddenly I wasn't smiling, I was afraid. I tried to dig deeper but they went away just as Andy entered Mr. Hemming's house through the back door.

I rushed into the house and looked around frantically. Moving down the hallway, I passed a set of framed family pictures. Hemming with his arm around a girl, probably his daughter. In one picture, the daughter was smiling by a cake that said "Happy birthday, Marie" on it.

I found Hemming in his office at the computer. He'd heard something and stood up and looked around. For a few seconds, he was looking right at me. I spoke his name.

"Mr. Hemming?"

I wasn't sure why I kept on talking to living people when I knew damn well they couldn't hear me. Hemming looked away and appeared suddenly nervous. He hadn't heard me or seen me, but *maybe* he'd sensed me. I was learning from the gang that this was common. As a living human being, you couldn't see or hear ghosts, but you could sometimes sense their presence. I thought about just scaring Hemming and entering him, but I remembered Andy was coming.

I flew through the house until I saw Andy. He was moving quietly, taking careful steps. He and Hemming were on a collision course. I flew back to Hemming. He'd been alerted. He glanced down a hallway and saw Andy. Instead of confronting him, he backed up into another room, probably to call the cops. Andy was going to get busted after all. But Hemming wasn't picking up the phone. He was picking up an axe from next to the fireplace. If I didn't do something, he was going to split my boyfriend's head like a melon.

My mind raced, a jumble of confusion. I forced myself to focus. I rushed outside.

"What are you doing?" asked Cole.

"No time," I said.

I reached the Jeep in seconds and swirled around Dani, causing her hair to rise up. For good measure, I opened and closed the glove box, slamming it hard twice.

"What the hell?" she yelled.

Good. She was plenty scared. I entered her. Her psyche was jumbled because of the fear, but she wasn't full of terrible images or anything, just worrisome thoughts. I took a deep breath and screamed like a warrior woman, then flung myself from Dani's body and rushed back inside.

Andy was just about to go into Hemming's office when he heard the screaming, which was enough to scare the pants off anyone because it was relentless and sounded like it was coming from someone who just fell into a pit of fire. Hemming was poised behind a door with the axe, ready to chop.

Andy ran from the house. Hemming lowered the axe. My distraction had worked. Hemming moved to the living room window and peered out.

Andy got into the Jeep and shook Dani to stop her from screaming.

"Jesus, Dani, what's wrong? What are you *doing*?"

Dani stopped screaming abruptly and slowly shook her head back and forth. She was clearly dazed.

"I . . . I thought something bad was happening to you. I had these, these thoughts. I don't know where they came from—they just sort of jumped in my brain. I was so scared!"

Her whole body trembled. She wrapped her arms around him.

"Can we get out of here? Please?"

Andy shot a look at the house and saw Hemming standing in the living room picture window.

"Just you wait, you piece of shit," he muttered.

Andy jammed his foot on the gas. The Jeep's tires smoked on the pavement.

I'd saved Andy twice now. I wondered what I'd have to save him from next. Cole and I pursued them. They drove back to Vista View Park where Andy parked, got out, and went to the bluff, staring bleakly out at Lake Washington.

It wasn't long before Dani joined him and slipped her hand around his waist.

"Are you going to tell me what's going on now?"

He wrestled with the difficult words, and they finally came out.

"Hemming and Echo had something going on."

Dani's eyes got big.

"You mean . . . ?"

"I don't know what I mean yet, I just know there was something. The way they looked at each other and stuff."

Dani opened her mouth to speak but thought better of it. She was thinking. And so was I. *Was* something going on between Hemming and me? Was I having an affair with him? Was I *that* bad? Maybe I was, and maybe Andy had caught me. What if, in a jealous rage, it was Andy who had killed me? My head was spinning and the more I tried to find clarity in my brain, the worse it hurt.

Dani touched the back of Andy's neck, stroking him to calm him down. They sat in the grass. I had to watch as once again she busted a move on him, kissing his cheek.

No way had Andy killed me, I thought. You don't kill the person you love. But in my logical mind, I knew better. One phrase kept leaping up. *Crimes of passion.*

Dani was still working on Andy. He didn't look like he wanted affection but eventually gave in and kissed her. I felt like a crazed butterfly was trapped in my heart. But thankfully the kiss didn't last very long. Andy pulled away. He didn't look like he'd enjoyed it at all. A victory for me, but thinking that thought made me feel small and bitter.

"Is something wrong?" she said. Her voice was soft and plaintive. Andy didn't answer her. She sighed.

"I get it. It's too soon. Well, I'm in no hurry; I can wait. You're worth it."

She put her head on his shoulder. It was obvious that he had zero chemistry with her. Their kiss hadn't been like any of the kisses we'd experienced—the kind that curl your toes and tingle your spine. I missed those kisses. By the look of things, so did he. It made me feel warm. *Concentrate, Echo!*

I became plagued wondering about Mr. Hemming, my head pounding. Andy took the coins from his pocket and held them in his palm. One of them wasn't a coin at all. It was my missing Saint Christopher medallion.

GIRLS

"Are you sure the medallion is yours?"

I gave Cole a withering look.

"Okay, I believe you—it's yours. But it doesn't prove that he killed you."

"Well, it appears he has violent tendencies. He was about to chop my boyfriend's head off."

It was a small thing, but when I said "boyfriend," I saw a flicker of hurt in Cole's eyes. He set his jaw and moved me back from Andy and Dani. She was still snuggling next to him and I was glad to back off, too, so I followed Cole. We floated up and sat on the roof of a nearby house.

"Hemming was in his own house—he could have thought it was an intruder or something."

"Why are you defending him?"

"I'm not; I'm just playing devil's advocate to be safe. I want to find your killer as bad as you do. I just don't want to rush to judgment. You have to try and remember what happened."

We sat together, just thinking. Then Cole had an idea.

"Does being around Hemming bring back any memories?"

"Yeah, but only positive things."

"Are you sure?"

"I think so. Maybe . . . some other things, but they're vague. I really have a hard time thinking he's the one who did me in. It makes no sense."

"Maybe you should just enter him."

He was right. I should try. Andy had suspicions, and that meant I should, too.

We left Andy and Dani and zoomed back to Hemming's house, passing through the side wall.

Hemming was in his office working at his computer. He was deleting files from his hard drive. Hundreds. Maybe thousands. He was in list view, so I couldn't see what he was deleting. It could have been anything. But I had an uneasy feeling. Hemming had a thin line of nervous sweat rimming his upper lip.

I had to get him to stop so I could take a look.

"Just enter him if you can, right now," Cole said.

"No," I said, "the answer is right here. Cole, I need you to get him out of the room."

"Any suggestions?"

"No, just please do it, and now, okay?" My voice was sharper than I'd meant it, but time was slipping away. Cole zoomed out of the room. In seconds came the sound of a fire alarm. Mr. Hemming jumped up from his desk and ran out of his office.

I got right on the computer. My fingers manipulated the keys, trying every combination I could think of, but I was getting nowhere. The files were disappearing in a blur. Then I had a flash of memory. In private Hemming had called me his "little goddess." I tried it. It worked, because the screen froze. On a naked girl. So he's into porn. Big deal—what man isn't? I was thinking this whole Hemming thing was a false lead. Then JPEGs began opening up in a flurry. My hands flew protectively to my chest. I was stunned.

There were more photos of girls, around my age, some even younger, in compromising poses. More and more and more photos popped onto the screen. I felt an onslaught of shock as I recognized some of the girls—my classmates. Hemming was a twisted pervo! Several of the most prim-and-proper girls in school had shed their clothing and let Mr. Hemming capture their nakedness. Images of myself flashed in my mind. I saw expressions on my face that I knew were sultry, not my usual style. I tried to remember being alone with Hemming, maybe even posing for him. But I couldn't get my brain to cooperate.

The kitchen alarm stopped. I highlighted as many of the photos as I could and created a folder on his desktop and dragged them into it. There were dozens and dozens.

"COLE!" I screamed.

He was in the doorway in an instant.

"I need another diversion!"

He was gone as quickly as he'd appeared and I heard Hemming coming. He was heading back to his office when he stopped in the doorway, angry.

"Goddammit!"

I could hear water running somewhere in the house. It sounded like a shower. Cole must have turned it on. It would buy me precious time. Hemming went to turn the water off.

The files finally finished copying. Then I logged into my e-mail account and sent the folder to myself. It was a large file and was taking forever to upload and send.

I heard Hemming coming back from turning off the shower. My first instinct was to run, but why should I? How could I be afraid of him now? I was already dead. I flew to the door and slammed it right in his face, literally, hitting him hard.

I rushed and unplugged his computer. Something made me stop and stare at the side of it, where you'd attach an external hard drive. A flash of lightning went off in my head as I had a quick memory of a hand yanking out a hard drive cord.

Hemming rushed into the room. He was sweaty and nervous. His eyes darted around from the closet to the windows and back to the doorway. He was trying to figure out what was going on. He had no answers, but he wasn't panicking. He calmly plugged his computer back in and froze when he saw that his computer was somehow logged into my e-mail. He shivered, clearly creeped out, then pulled himself together and deleted the e-mail and attachment. And emptied his trash folder. So much for my tech-savvy detective work and plan to expose him via e-mail.

He slowly scanned the room, then stared down at the keyboard. I knew what he was wondering. How had this happened? He closed his eyes and took a long, deep breath. He had a look of fear on his face, then acceptance, then determination.

He logged on to a meditation site. Ocean waves. Then he sat on the floor and assumed a lotus position and began to hum along with the meditation. Creepy.

Cole came in and stood by me as we watched Hemming. He looked like the nicest, most passive man you could ever meet. Cole was confused.

"I don't get it. I mean, you really think he's the one who—"

"He's a sicko who manipulated a lot of girls into posing nude for him. His computer had thousands of pictures on it!"

Cole's eyes went wide, then narrowed as he nodded, not saying anything just yet, but I could tell he was formulating a question that he didn't yet have the guts to ask me. So I just flat-out told him. Or started to, anyway.

"Um, Cole, I think I might have . . ."

I couldn't finish the sentence, because I was too damn embarrassed and I wasn't 100 percent sure I'd actually done what
I was afraid I'd done. My words had given birth to an idea and
by now Cole knew exactly what I was talking about. He spoke
very softly.

"You posed for him?"

"I don't know!" My words were like bullets. I didn't mean
to fire at him like that but it just came out. "Sorry."

"It's okay—you're only human."

"Was."

I felt ugly and shameful.

"Echo, no matter what you did, you're still human in my
book."

I could see the truth in his eyes. It didn't matter what I'd
done when I was alive. Cole cared for me now. I walked back
and forth in front of Hemming. I had to know the truth.

"I'd enter him and try and see what happened, but look how
calm he is right now. He's like some freakin' Zen master or
something."

Cole and I looked around. Hemming had bookshelves full
of books on not only psychology and sociology, but meditation
and spirituality in a dozen different cultures. He was into mind
control big-time.

Cole used his power to fling a dozen books from the shelves.
Amazingly, Hemming barely flinched. I lunged at him but
couldn't enter him. He was too calm.

"Okay, just stay here with him for a minute. See if you can
remember anything."

I did what Cole asked. I looked at Hemming. Like before,
every time I tried to recall anything, my head began to pound
unmercifully. I tried again and again but it wasn't going to
happen.

"I can't do it."

Cole took my hand in his.

"There's another way to retrieve memories," he said.

He just kept staring at me, like he was trying to memorize every square inch of my face. I blushed.

"Are you going to enlighten me or do I have to guess?"

"Follow me," he said.

He led me to Hemming's bedroom and beelined to the closet.

"Pick out something you've seen him wear."

My eyes found it immediately. A burgundy cotton pullover sweater. I took it from the hanger.

"Let's go," said Cole.

"Where?"

"Somewhere quiet."

Sweater in hand, I followed Cole. We went back out through the front door and then ran until we flew. Anyone watching would have seen a burgundy sweater being swept through the sky by the wind.

We found a forest glen. Cole saw a comfy spot of grass and sat down, and beckoned me to do the same, holding out a hand. I took it, and he pulled me down onto the grass. Slender shafts of sunlight filtered through the overhead sylvan canopy. I felt like I was on some kind of dream date. But there was business at hand.

"Okay, now hold the sweater with both hands. Touch it as much as you like, even with your cheek."

After seeing the pictures of all those girls, I didn't want to touch the sweater, let alone with my cheek!

"Go on," said Cole. "You have to be open to the truth."

I touched the sweater, rubbed it, ran my fingers along the seams. I felt incredibly stupid.

"This isn't working."

"Stop rushing, stop pushing," he said.

"Yes, sir."

"What are you thinking about?"

I was thinking about how the sweater would look great on him, especially if he wasn't wearing a T-shirt.

"I'm thinking of a bajillion things at once."

"Try to clear your mind."

"How?"

"Focus on your breathing."

I did that, and the many thoughts and images that were clamoring for attention in my brain gradually began to subside. I could feel the sweater more intensely now, and I imagined the essence of Mr. Hemming flowing through it and into my arms, into my veins, and up into my brain.

Nothing happened for a long time. But then, like a blurry, old home video, images began to take shape.

"It's . . . I'm . . ."

"Shhhh . . . ." said Cole.

I breathed in slowly through my nose and exhaled through my mouth.

"Maybe close your eyes," said Cole. "And let yourself just . . . be."

I was so freaking nervous the last thing I wanted to do was close my eyes, but I did. I breathed deeply. After a long moment of letting myself calm down, I began to smell the scent of the pine needles and wild grass. I felt the air on my pale ghost skin. I wasn't trying to force anything, I was just holding the sweater. And then it happened. The images began to come to me in waves. My scalp tingled. I was remembering.

I felt my body slacken, as though I were folding into myself. My chin began to tremble. I spoke in a whisper, describing everything to Cole as the memories came to me. I saw Mr. Hemming's face after school one day. He was smiling, trying to be a regular guy, a "buddy," but he couldn't completely hide his sleazy, leering grin. The worst thing was, I felt so insecure that

I almost liked it, liked the fact that a man could find me, little old me, attractive. The images kept coming, everything gradually sharpening into focus.

I was in the den at his house on a settee. He had his camera. I was wearing this very same sweater. That had to be why I chose it—it was my unconscious speaking to me. Hemming's voice was velvety smooth as he coaxed me into pulling the sweater this way and that and into finally removing it entirely. He was talking about the movie *Titanic* and how brave Kate Winslet was when she posed nude and now how "brave" I was and so very, very, *unsettlingly*—that was the word he used—beautiful. In those moments I had lost myself and I did feel beautiful as his words washed over me, caressing my ego.

"Don't be ashamed, be proud. Shame and regret are simply constructs of the ruling class. To keep us in line. You're not doing anything wrong here, Echo. God, you're really something."

He kept firing away with his camera and his mouth.

"You can have total control of your mind and what you think of. You just have to shift your focus when you think of something that makes you feel bad."

"I . . . I don't know how to do that . . ." I said.

"It takes mental effort—that's all."

He told me that I could have total control of my mind by simply guiding my thoughts where I wanted them to be. He told me to think of myself as what I was, a great beauty posing for a great artist. A Mona Lisa. His words resonated and I did his bidding, his soft voice a siren song, his words manipulating me into moving in ways I'd only dreamt of in private.

"You have no idea the power you possess with your beautiful body, do you?"

"No," I said.

Hemming had me trapped in his web—I was powerless—until I heard other words from other voices, my parents, my aunts and uncles, and the room began spinning. Mr. Hemming kept shooting, the shutter firing off like a machine gun, short bursts of clicks. When it stopped, an ugly silence settled on the room. Feelings bubbled up inside me. I knew I had done the wrong thing and was filled with shame.

Mr. Hemming kept praising me—"Good girl, good girl . . ."—like I was some dumb dog.

Anger and shame built up inside me. I got up quickly and put my clothes on.

"What are you doing?" he said.

"I . . . I have to go," I said.

"Come here. Please? I just want to touch you—that's all."

I backed up, afraid.

"Life is what you make of it," he said. "If you think it's bad, it can be bad. If, on the other hand, you think that every moment, every experience, is a blessed gift, then that can be your truth. Our truth."

He approached me and touched my shoulder and looked like he was going to kiss me or something. I felt like throwing up. I backed away from his touch.

"I . . . I want you to delete all of those," I said.

"That's not going to happen," he said. His voice was clipped and angry. But then he got all warm and fuzzy again.

"What you're experiencing is a common feeling, and it will pass. You're beautiful; we've just made art together. Okay?"

I knew it was useless to argue with him. So I just nodded.

"This is between us, our secret, right?"

I nodded again—what the hell else was I going to do?

I let myself out the front door and began walking fast. And then I ran. My lungs were aching as I made it home and crawled into my bed. I tried to fight the tears, but I cried like a baby for an hour. Then I heard a knock on my door. I prayed it wasn't who I thought it was.

MURDER

Andy stepped into the room. He asked why my eyes were all red. Had I been crying? I mumbled some lame excuse about allergies. But he knew better, knew something had happened. His eyes hardened but he didn't press me on it and we never talked about it again.

I opened my eyes and looked at Cole. He'd heard my whole narration, everything, all the sordid details, and yet I saw no judgment in his eyes.

Leaves made shuffling sounds as a cool breeze swept through the glen. Cole spoke, his voice warm and forgiving.

"Can you keep going?"

Closing my eyes again, I continued to clutch the sweater. I

could. I spoke softly, telling Cole everything I saw. Again I saw Hemming. Only now he wasn't smiling. His face was twisted in anger and he was yelling. Things shifted. I was at school, in his office, at his computer, typing furiously. I heard a noise but didn't look up until it was too late. Mr. Hemming ran into the room and lunged for me. But I was quick. I unplugged his external hard drive and ran for the door. He grabbed at my shoulder and I bit him, hard. He yelled in pain. Then I was out the door.

I was breathing heavily now but the memory of my fateful day and night was coming back to me in bursts so fast that I could hardly keep up. I ran to the parking lot. Then I was speeding in my mom's car. My eyes were bloodshot from crying. I tried calling someone on my phone but my battery was dead. I kept looking in the rearview mirror so often I almost ran over an old lady struggling with her aluminum walker on the curb. I cursed. A car was behind me. I couldn't tell if it was Hemming or not. I slammed my foot on the gas.

The memory was making my head feel light, as though it might detach from my body and float into the air. My breathing was hard and fast. I hoped I wouldn't pass out. Cole touched my hand. It anchored me and I held on to the memory and rode it through.

I skidded to a halt in front of my house. I looked over. Andy wasn't home. Dammit! Neither was Mom or Dad. The safe haven I'd counted on hadn't materialized. Squeezing the hard drive in my fist, I ran into the house, slammed the door, and locked it. My chest was heaving, my heart pounding like a jackhammer. I risked a glance outside. No one was coming after me. Yet. I ran into the kitchen and plugged my phone into a charger, then to the front window and prayed. Maybe he'd given up. Maybe he knew that I would turn him in and he was already packing up to get the hell out of town. I almost relaxed, thinking of him running away from me. But then my heart jumped. Hemming's car slid silently like a shark into the driveway. He'd cut the engine.

I ran upstairs into my room. There was no lock on the door. My parents had always respected my privacy. In my mind, I moved a bunch of heavy furniture in front of the door, but what I actually did was just pick up my Magic 8 Ball, the plastic one that answered questions. Like a complete moron, I shook it and asked if I was going to die. I stared as the little letters came into focus. *Outlook not so good.*

Adrenaline was pumping through my body, skewing everything sideways. I felt like I was in some sick haunted house. Everything was deathly quiet. Then I heard Hemming come in through the glass sliding deck door, the one we never locked. I heard his syrupy, sickening voice.

"Echo? Come on, sweetie, this is just plain silly. You don't have anything to be ashamed about. Those kinds of things are all in your mind. I can help you with that. I can help you make those thoughts go away."

He was a teacher, all right, but he was so wrong. The feelings would not go away. I felt cheap and dirty and it was his fault. If Andy had taken the pictures it would be one thing. But Hemming was an old man.

"It's just art, sweetie. There's nothing to be ashamed of. Trust me."

Nice argument, but it wasn't going to cut it. He was going down. If I survived.

I heard him coming up the stairs. In one hand I had his filthy hard drive. In the other I clutched the Magic 8 Ball that I planned on bashing his skull in with if he came after me. He opened the door to my room. I'd climbed up onto my bed and was ready to pounce.

"You have no right to steal my private property," he said,

his voice raspy now, not so calm. He had Mike Walker's eleven-inch hunting knife in his hand.

I concluded that it was time to negotiate.

"Mr. Hemming, if . . . if you leave right now, I won't call the cops and turn you in, if you promise to get help."

I let that offer hang in the air. He considered it. Then sneered.

"You stupid little bitch . . ."

A low growl rumbled in my throat.

"Get away from me, you sick asshole!"

He changed his mind, folding back his anger. He shook his head and put on his sad face. He held his hands out like a priest ready to hear my confession. *My confession!*

"I'm going to count to three and you'd better get out!"

"Or what?" he said, mocking me. "You'll do what?"

"I'll kill you!"

He laughed. *He actually laughed.* That's what triggered my leap. I saw the shock in his eyes as I flew through the air, the stupid 8 Ball raised with deadly malice. I pictured it knocking him out cold, blood flowing from his scalp. That didn't happen. He was quick and strong and caught me, twisting the toy away from me as we fell to the floor.

"Give me the hard drive!"

I leapt to my feet, shaking.

"No!"

Softly, he said, "Don't make me cut you."

So calm. So measured. I wanted to kill him.

"Go ahead and try!"

I have no idea why I said this. His lips went tight on his teeth. Was he going left or right? He lunged. I guessed correctly. He slashed at my right shoulder and I ducked and tumbled left and got past him. I was free! *Run, Echo—run like hell!* He grabbed me from behind at the top of the stairs. We grappled, I could feel my hands being cut, then we tumbled down the stairs together, bashing against the walls, knocking off pictures, landing in a horrific crash at the bottom as we collided with a table. I felt a sharp pain in my ribs—like the kind you get from running too hard for too long.

I grabbed my side. I was clutching the knife. And I was bleeding. Mr. Hemming had his hand on the knife, too. He looked surprised as he slowly withdrew it.

"Jesus, Echo, what did you *do*? What did you *do*? I wasn't going to hurt you; I just had to try and scare some sense into you!"

Holding the knife, he paced back and forth like a panther in a cage, biting his lips and rubbing his free hand up and down his pant leg.

"God, I loved you, and now look what you've done!"

The pain in my side was like a scalding-hot poker. I gasped. The life was draining out of me. I didn't want to die. My voice was garbled and wet with blood.

"Please . . . Help me . . . Call an ambulance . . ."

My eyes were filled with all the pleading and peace and love and humanity I could possibly muster. Surely he would act fast now and help save me. He'd stopped pacing. *Get the phone! Take out your cell phone and dial!* But he didn't. He didn't reach for his phone. He'd weighed the options and made a decision.

"I'm sorry, Echo." His voice was sad. "We both know I can't do that."

Haunting words like blows to my chest.

"Please . . ."

"You were my favorite. But you must know, sweetie, that I can't let you live. This has gone too far. You'll ruin my life—"

"No!" I blurted. "I swear . . ."

"It's too late."

He was so hideous in this moment, everything ugly and violent and corrupt—the seconds ticking by in slow motion on the wall clock—as he put the tip of the knife to my heart.

"Good-bye, Echo. You were always my number one girl."

With one forceful thrust, he shoved the knife in. The pain was unbearable, exploding out from my chest to every cell in my body. Now my life was truly leaking away. I curled into a fetal ball. Everything went blurry, then dark.

I felt myself drifting up and away and in moments I was watching the whole scene from above. Hemming moved so slowly, so confidently, as he walked halfway up the carpeted stairs to retrieve his hard drive, which had slipped from my hand. He picked it up and slid it into the pocket of his jacket. I floated above him, watching as he methodically searched our house until he found a container of disposable antibacterial cloths, which he used to wipe down my hands and my neck and face, anywhere he might have touched me. He wiped down the sliding glass door handle, then quietly let himself out. I floated out through the door and watched him get in his car and drive away. He rolled his window down and played a song on the radio. "DJ Got Us Fallin' in Love" by Usher. Freakin' weird.

Without knowing why, I followed him, or what was left of me did. He drove slowly at first, then sped up, taking the ramp onto the freeway and then opening it up, rolling the other windows down, the wind whipping the interior of the car, as though he were trying to blow the sin off himself. It didn't work. I was sitting in the back seat, calm as can be.

He drove out to Fall City and wound up along a logging road, parked, then got out and popped his trunk, took out a shovel, and walked fifty yards off the road into a dense thicket where he dug a deep hole and buried the knife. He filled in the hole, tamped it down, then walked back to his car, tossed the shovel in the trunk, and took off.

I opened my eyes and was with Cole again. I no longer wanted to hold the sweater. I wanted to burn it. I balled it up and threw it. Cole went and picked it up.

"I'm proud of you, Echo."

"Proud of me?"

A slut who took her clothes off for one of her teachers?

"You fought him—you fought him as hard as you could."

"Not hard enough. I didn't win."

"No, but you will. I *promise* you will."

He came back over holding the sweater.

"Do you think you could remember where he buried the knife?"

"I don't have to touch that stupid sweater again to remember. I know exactly where it is. My dad used to take me up there when he'd go fishing. I've been on that road. I can find it."

"Perfect. You did great, Echo."

I fought tears but lost. Cole touched me hesitantly, and I collapsed into his embrace, hugging him tightly. He whispered to me.

"He's going to pay for what he did."

"I know," I said, but I wondered if I was right. There would be so much work to do. Fortunately, I was highly motivated and had at my disposal an amazing team of ghosts who were very good at one thing in particular. Haunting the living shit out people.

POWER

Over dinner at Middle House, Darby, Lucy, Cameron, Dougie, and Zipperhead listened raptly as Cole told them what had gone down with Hemming, pausing only when Darby would spit out an apt expletive about the twisted teacher.

"I am so going to mess him up," she said.

"Not before I get my sparks on him," said Zipperhead.

"I'll freeze his nuts off," said Dougie.

"We'll all get to contribute," said Cole.

We agreed to get a good night's sleep and take on the task of haunting Mr. Hemming the following day. I tossed and turned while Lucy purred. I couldn't sleep and went up to the roof. After a while, Cole came up, too. The night was overcast and chilly. Cole had brought a blanket and we covered up. Even ghosts get cold. And lonely.

"Can I ask you something?" I said.

"You ought to know by now you can ask me anything."

"Meryn. The girl you loved . . . the one you pretty much died for? Do you still think about her?"

"Sometimes."

I waited for him to continue. But he kept quiet. I had to know.

"Do you still . . . love her?"

"Yeah, a part of me does," he answered after a moment.

"That must be hard," I said.

"It is, except for one thing."

"What?"

"Except for the fact that everything I've ever done in my life, including getting murdered, led me here. To you."

He'd done it to me again. I could feel the blood rising in my cheeks.

"Not that it means anything," he said. "I know you have what you have in your heart and nothing I can do can make you change that. I'm not even sure I'd want you to. I want what's best for you. Whatever makes you at peace."

There he was, being all chivalrous again. A part of me was hoping that he'd stop saying and doing the right thing all the time and for once just throw it down and make a righteous play for me. But he was right. He knew what was in my heart. Andy.

"Um, remember you told me how you died? I was wondering—what happened to the guy who hit you with the pipe? What did you do to him?"

"Nothing yet. He's too stupid to kill. I'm still working the whole thing out."

"No need for you to be Mister Nice Guy when it comes to some knuckle dragger who murdered you."

"He stood over my body and I thought he felt bad. But then

he laughed. It kind of freaked me out. I was so shocked and angry that for some reason I blanked out on his face. I can't remember what he looks like."

"I'd say he's got some horrible payback coming his way. I think you should let me help you find him."

"Maybe someday. First we've got to deal with your killer."

"Why do I come first?"

"Because I say you do."

When a guy puts your world, your feelings and troubles and problems, before his, it does something to you, something that feels really good inside.

But something else was telling me that outing Hemming wasn't going to be as easy as everyone thought. I hoped I was wrong.

"By the way," I said, "do you have a power?"

"Um . . . yeah . . ."

He seemed embarrassed. I smiled at him.

"Okay . . . ?"

Like, was he going to tell me? He didn't say a word. But he smiled slightly, then looked down at the garden, staring intently, his eyes slowly narrowing. I watched, my heart beginning to flutter as a single stemmed rose snapped free from a bush and leisurely floated up until it was right in front of my eyes. It bloomed, just for me. Wham. I felt it in my heart.

"Telekinesis. I can make things move," said Cole.

"You sure can." My voice was barely a whisper.

That night in bed, I kept thinking about Cole. I was hoping he was in his bed thinking about me. But my heart beat on and on and spoke to me. Andy. Andy. Andy.

Morning took a long time to come. Time passes slowly when you have something you're looking forward to, and I was looking forward to tormenting Hemming until he begged for mercy.

For months, maybe even years, he'd been taking advantage of young girls and getting away with it. It was time for retribution.

After breakfast, we went for a flight. I led the way, with Cole, Darby, Dougie, Cameron, Lucy, and Zipperhead following. We swept over the treetops, gliding effortlessly. I knew my way around King County and would have no trouble finding the Fall City logging road Hemming had taken to the place where he'd buried the knife. We needed it. We had plans for it. We soared over Lake Sammamish and were cresting over Fall City in another minute. I swept down to the main road and looked for the turnoff.

I was confused. It wasn't where I thought it was. I backtracked and came in from another angle but with even less success. I was getting disoriented. So many new roads, new buildings, houses, and developments since I had been there when I was a kid. Cole read the confusion on my face.

"What's wrong?"

"It's . . . not there . . ."

"It hasn't moved; things have changed—that's all," he said.

He was right. I just needed to keep looking. I remembered riding with Hemming, sitting in the back seat of his car, the departed passenger, watching trees rush by on either side of the car. I remembered a field with tall grass growing around the skeleton of a rusty, old green John Deere tractor.

We flew down to ground level, the same level I'd been at when Hemming was driving. I zoomed down road after road, my eyes like lasers, scanning, searching . . . hoping . . . praying. And then there it was. The tractor.

I recognized a grouping of tall pines by the turnoff.

"Here!" I said. "Right here."

I found the general area, maybe because I was actually remembering, or maybe because some kind of fate was drawing me there. I dropped down, let myself become earthbound, and felt the ground beneath my feet. I walked on the damp grass, my new friends by my side.

"How do you know where it is?" asked Zipperhead.

"I don't," I said. "But it's here. I can feel it. Right here." I pointed to my chest.

It was true. I could feel a very light stabbing pain in my heart and as I moved deeper into the pines, the pain grew stronger. If I veered one way or another, it would either increase or diminish. I had what amounted to a cosmic divining rod in my spectral body and it was going to lead us to the weapon that had killed me. In another minute, the pain in my chest was so intense that I collapsed. Cole caught me in his arms before I hit the ground.

"I think it's here," I said.

Cole carried me backward while the others sank down into the cold earth. No need for a ghost to dig. We can pass easily into the ground. It welcomes us.

It was Lucy who found the knife. Hemming had wrapped it in a rag and it hadn't been buried that long. Cole suspended the knife in midair and studied it carefully.

"It looks like he's wiped it down. I don't see any marks. And there's no blood, nothing to connect it to you, Echo."

The blade was sharp and deadly. It gave me the willies.

"He stuck you with this thing?" said Darby, grabbing the knife out of midair and hefting it.

"That must have hurt like a mother," said Zipperhead.

"Duh," said Lucy, looking a little peeved. "About as much as having your skull impaled on spikes, right?"

Zipperhead frowned and looked like he was thinking. "I dunno; both suck. The way we all got it sucked."

Everyone nodded his or her silent agreement. Reliving the various ways in which we'd been undone was not a joyful pastime.

"Well, we can't just drop off the knife and call the cops and hope they find some DNA, right?" Cole said.

"Yeah, I don't see that working," said Cameron.

"So then. Let's go do some haunting," said Cole.

We took off into the sky, the blade of Walker's eleven-inch hunting knife glinting in the sunlight.

As we approached the school, I wondered if Hemming would even be there. We didn't have a concrete plan, so we left the knife stuck high in a tree and went in and wandered the halls, watching as life went along just fine without us. I noticed that this time around, Zipperhead, Darby, Dougie, and Cameron were having a hard time hanging around a school full of living, breathing teenagers. The fact that they'd been cheated out of the most formative years of their lives was apparent on their faces and it made me sad. But they were there for me, ready to right the wrong that had been committed. I knew that wouldn't repair the damage that had been done to them, but busting Hemming would help. Eventually, we found him.

We bird-dogged Hemming throughout the day, watching as he wore his sticky-sweet smile, chatting up girl after girl. I wondered why I'd never noticed how he paid so much more attention to girls than guys. Now I knew. He was a predator.

We were in no hurry, and collectively decided that a haunting on the school grounds would have too much collateral damage to be feasible. There were plenty of kids at school that I would have loved to give a good scare to, but there were kids that I liked, too, friends and people who I knew were mostly okay, even if they acted like jerks so they wouldn't be picked on.

The main thing was I wanted to keep my eye on Hemming in case he made a run for it. I didn't want to lose him. After observing him for an hour or so, I concluded that there wasn't much chance of him bolting. Even after all that had happened, he was cool and calm, the picture of patience and understanding as he taught his Psych 101 and Photography as Art classes, smiling at the girls as always.

When the 3:00 p.m. bell rang and the school emptied out, Hemming lingered only briefly at his desk, copying some files onto another hard drive. I sat with my ghost posse in the empty desks, watching him. Out of habit, I sat in my old seat, the one I used when I was alive. At one point, Hemming shivered as if he was cold and scanned the classroom, his eyes finally settling close to me. He was looking at my desk.

"Echo . . ."

His voice was sympathetic and soft.

"You were my favorite. My princess."

I wanted to throw something at him. The others shifted in their seats. Darby stood up, the veins in her temples throbbing.

"I gotta tell you, I do not like this SOB. Why don't we just scare the shit out of him right here, right now?"

It was tempting. He was alone in his classroom. But I knew the best thing to do was to keep watching and waiting. He shook his head slowly, his eyes looking far away.

"You shouldn't have blamed yourself. The only bad choice you made was to try and crush my world."

I rose slowly from my desk. He wasn't talking to *me*, was he? I got very close to him. He sucked in a breath. But he didn't reach out to touch me. He was talking to his memory of me— that was all. But still, it was creeping me out.

He glanced around the room, then ejected the hard drive, put it in his briefcase, and went out to his car. He was clever and skillful. Even now I had the uneasy feeling he was manipulating me. I was terrified he would somehow get away.

"Get the knife," I said.

ZEN

Zipperhead flew up and pulled the knife from the tree and we followed Hemming to his house. As he parked alongside it, Darby used both hands to sink the deadly knife into his front door.

"He's going to shit himself," said Dougie.

But he was wrong. When Hemming approached the door, he didn't even flinch. He stared at the knife, then turned and looked up at the sky where we were. It felt like he saw me, maybe all of us. He didn't seem afraid, just curious, as though we were a flock of migrating birds or something.

"He's pretty calm for someone who just saw his murder weapon stuck in his front door," said Cameron.

"Maybe he senses us. Maybe he's just trying to act cool," said Dougie.

"Or maybe he's some kind of freak who doesn't get scared," said Zipperhead.

"Everyone gets scared," said Cole. "We just have to find his weak spot."

Hemming removed the knife from the door and went in his house. We followed him.

As we entered through various doors and walls, seeping our way in, the strains of an opera filled the house. It was Mozart's dark and violent piece, *Don Giovanni*. I knew it well because my father had, for reasons unbeknownst to me as a child, taken a liking to the piece as he sipped his gin late at night. Me, I hated opera. I'd rather listen to fingers on a chalkboard. Again I passed the good teacher's few "family" photos on the wall, young Marie smiling on a bicycle, a remembrance of his past life, and I figured that his wife probably dumped him because of his lying, cheating ways.

Hemming was at his desk, the knife at his side. With one hand he was casually fondling it. His other hand was on his mouse and he was scrolling through pictures on his computer, his eyes intent.

It was unsettling. Not only was he unfazed by the appearance of the knife—like *that* happened every day—he had retrieved all his "work" and was looking at pictures of girls he'd photographed, shifting them around, moving his trophy collection to satisfy some kind of internal need for order. Watching him do this, my desire for revenge built like an angry boil. I was ready for the smackdown.

"Let's get this started," I said.

"All over it," said Cole.

Cole used his power to cause the knife to quickly zip up into the air. Then it slammed down and sank into the desk, right next to Hemming's mouse pad. He leapt up, his breath quickening, and looked around the room. Then he nodded, as though he somehow understood what had happened.

"It's all right," he said. "It's okay."

He pulled the knife from the desk.

I moved close to him, got right in his face and stared into his eyes. He blinked. Even though he couldn't see me, we were glaring at each other. Did he know I was there?

"Leave me alone, Echo."

He *did*!

"We both know I can't do that," I said, echoing his killing words back to him.

He didn't react. He hadn't heard me. These were just mind games. I was determined to win. I decided I would enter him. I took a few steps back, screamed to holy hell, and rushed him, ready to get in his head and try and do some damage.

But nothing happened. How could I have been so stupid? He wasn't frightened. He sat back down and kept right on gawking at his trophy pictures.

"God, he's such a perv," said Darby.

"Scare him! I need someone to scare him good," I said.

"I'll start by freezing his eyes closed!" said Dougie.

"Then he couldn't see shit, dipwad," said Zipperhead. "I'll zap the shit out of him!"

"I think we should take it slowly, ease into it," said Cameron.

"Good idea," said Cole. "Lucy, you want to do the honors?"

"Purrrfect," she said.

Lucy shrank down as she morphed into her cat self but stayed invisible. Cole used his power to turn the music off. Hemming cocked his head and listened. What he heard was purring. Then he looked down at his leg. Lucy was circling his left leg, still invisible, her tail entwined as she purred. Hemming flinched but then closed his eyes and relaxed.

"Nice kitty," he said.

Whoa. I had no idea what to make of this. The "kitty" he was talking to was invisible. Lucy changed tactics and began to yowl and leapt up onto his desk. She made herself visible and hissed in his face and took a swipe at him. He jerked his head back but, again, was strangely unfazed by the sudden appearance of a cat materializing out of thin air.

"Let me get you some milk . . ."

Hemming rose from his desk. We tagged along as he walked into the kitchen and opened his refrigerator. When he did, Dougie created an arctic blast that blew Hemming back on his ass. He had frost on his face and hair. He stared at the contents of his refrigerator. Everything was frozen solid. The contents in glass and plastic containers expanded. Some of the glass bottles exploded.

I tried rushing him again but struck out.

"I can't get in!" I said.

I backed off. Hemming wasn't freaking at all. Instead he closed his eyes and concentrated, going to some inner place.

"What the hell is going on with this guy?" Zipperhead yelled.

We'd expected Hemming to behave like any rational human. But he clearly wasn't rational.

"I'm not sure," said Cole.

Zipperhead sent a stream of sparks at Hemming, who jolted as though he'd touched a live wire, and his hair stood out from his head like he'd been touching a Tesla ball. But somehow he managed to remain calm and kept his eyes closed.

"What the HELL?" shouted Darby.

Dougie was creating a deep freeze and Cameron was turning on water all over the house. Zipperhead was sparking the place up while Lucy yowled.

"Everybody calm down," said Cole.

Hemming straightened his hair, flattening it against his head with his hands. Then his eyes opened and he looked right at us. Again I wondered: Could he see us? No. But he knew we were there.

"I can feel you, Echo. And others, too. There's something you should know," he said.

We waited. I was holding my breath.

"I believe in ghosts," he said. Calmly. Simply. Matter-of-factly.

He got up and walked past us into his study to a bookcase. My eyes went to the titles. He had dozens of books about the afterlife. Titles with the words *poltergeists, apparitions, phantasms, specters, accounts of hauntings.*

"Let's see how he likes this," said Darby, waving her arms, creating a hallucination for him. A thousand cockroaches poured out of every crack and crevice in the room, a horrific sight that would have terrified any normal person. But Hemming was clearly not normal, on several counts. He merely observed the hallucination, seemingly recognizing it for what it was.

"Screw this!" Cameron shouted. He created a horrific sideways torrent of rain that made Hemming drop to the floor and cover his head, but the objective, to get him to freak out, wasn't achieved. In a few seconds, Cameron gave up.

"Never seen anything like this dude," he said, raising his arms in anger.

Hemming collected his dignity as he stood, calmly got a towel from the kitchen, and dried himself off.

Darby was getting pissed off and she conjured the image of a corpse, which was unmistakably Hemming's own. The corpse rushed at Hemming and screamed. Hemming was startled and scared this time, falling backward onto his couch.

"Now we're getting somewhere!" Zipperhead cackled.

He created a flash of sparks that danced around the periphery of the corpse apparition for good measure.

Hemming was breathing heavily and felt his chest, as though

taking his pulse. Then he closed his eyes again and retreated into his meditative safe place.

"That which you resist, persists," he repeated, four times in a row.

"What the heck's that supposed to mean?" said Darby. "Why's he talking in stupid riddles?"

"He's controlling his thoughts, which control his emotions," Cole said. "He's a smart guy. Sick, but smart."

Hemming kept meditating. We watched him, impotent. Seconds ticked by, then a minute or two. Hemming slowly opened his eyes and searched the room. He was looking for me. Of course I didn't appear. If I could have, I would have. But I was powerless against his will. All my fear and disgust swept through me like an icy wind.

"I hate you!" I screamed.

Hemming flashed a sad smile and went and sat at his desk.

"You have to move on," he said. And kept repeating the phrase until it began to rattle around in my brain like a spiked marble. I turned to Cole. He looked very, very sad.

"I got nothing."

Hemming spoke to the room, his eyes wandering around, searching, wanting to make sure that he connected with me, with us. He used his teacher voice.

"Then the Lord said to Moses, 'Make a fiery serpent, and set it on a standard; and it shall come about, that everyone who is bitten, when he looks at it, he will live. And Moses made a bronze serpent and set it on the standard; and it came about, that if a serpent bit any man, when he looked to the bronze serpent, he lived.' "

"What is he talking about?" Lucy asked.

"Shhh . . . he's not done," said Cole.

"The people were plagued by poisonous snakes, and Moses used an image of those snakes, the very thing that had struck fear into their hearts, to give them courage. The Christians did the same thing. For one hundred and fifty years after Christ was crucified, the cross was used as a means of terror, to cause fear. But you know what? The Christians took the cross and made it their own. They embraced their fear! And that's what I'm doing. You cannot frighten me, Echo, for I embrace you! I welcome you into my arms!"

I rushed at him. And bounced right off. He was laughing. I tried again and again. But I couldn't enter him.

"What are we going to do?" I shrieked.

"I . . . I don't know," said Cole. His calm bravado shaken, he sounded nervous and uncertain. I looked to the others. They could only shrug. They'd given it their best shot and zip. Nada.

Moments crept by painfully, each second like poison in my veins.

"I guess not everybody has a vulnerable spot," said Dougie.

We all glared at him.

"I'm just sayin' . . ."

"We can't just give up! We have to do something!" I pleaded.

Nobody had an answer. Zipperhead shot a few sparks. Darby conjured a corpse. Hemming was unfazed.

We were beaten. My shoulders sagged. Darby made an angry low noise in her throat. Dougie shuffled his feet, agitated. Cole winced. We left defeated, our tails between our sorry legs. A fine lot of ghosts we'd turned out to be. I'd never taken failure well in my life, and in my afterlife it wasn't any easier.

Knowing who my killer was and not being able to do anything about it, not being able to bring the monster to justice, was a feeling worse than any I'd ever had. I felt powerless, like my entire life *and* death had been meaningless. We flew slowly past a park where humans did what humans do: walk and talk and play and live. I missed doing stuff like that. Especially with my parents. I wished I hadn't been such a typical moody, stick-in-the-mud teenage girl. But I was who I was, even though the more I learned about myself when I was alive, the less sparkling my self-image appeared to be. I saw a father pushing his daughter on a swing. Her giddy laughter lifted like musical notes into the air.

And then I had an idea. It was dark. Loathsome. But maybe you fought evil with evil. Maybe Hemming had a weak spot, after all. Could his Achilles' heel be what I thought it might? There was only one way to tell. It made me sick to think about it, but I could almost hear the universe calling to me, *Do it— there's no other way.*

"Darby, how specific can you be when you conjure things? I mean, images?"

"What do you mean? As specific as you would want me to be, I guess. All I have to do is picture something in my mind and I can make it appear."

"So if I showed you a picture, you could conjure that?"

"Hell yeah, easy-peasy."

"And . . . if I showed you a face, could you put that face on another body?"

"No sweat. That's me, a regular walking, talking Photoshop."

"Super. We're not done with this yet," I said.

I felt a glimmer of hope. I dropped straight to the ground. The others followed and formed a circle around me.

"What's up, Echo?" Cole asked.

"I have an idea . . ."

Their eyes widened expectantly. I smiled at my new friends. Maybe Hemming wasn't so invincible after all.

CRACK

When we got back to Hemming's house, he was meditating on the couch in his study. He looked so serene, a finger pressed to his smiling lips. *Smiling!* If my plan worked, we were going to wipe that smile off his smug face. He would be anything *but* serene. I took Darby into the hallway and planted her in front of a picture of a girl, a girl not that much younger than me, maybe by a couple of years. Marie. Hemming's daughter. I had no idea about his divorce or if he even had custody of her on weekends or anything. But my plan counted on one thing. I was hoping that somewhere within his twisted psyche, he had a sliver of human decency. That he loved his daughter. Darby continued staring at the picture.

"You got it?" I asked.

"Locked, loaded, and ready," she said.

Darby and I went back into the study and joined the others. They were staring at Hemming and looked skeptical. I hoped against all hope that my plan would work.

"What do you want us to do?" asked Zipperhead.

"I think Darby and I have it covered. You can just kick back and watch," I said.

I went to Hemming's computer. It was easy to load up the last thing Hemming had been looking at, his gallery of victims. They began to appear. Hemming opened his eyes and looked over at the screen. He was only mildly interested. Until something happened that made the hairs on his neck rise.

"My god . . ." he said.

He jumped off the couch and ran to his computer and gaped. Darby was doing just what I'd asked her to. Superimposing the face of Hemming's daughter, Marie, upon the girls he'd manipulated and abused. More and more images popped up on the screen, each a variation of the same thing, as though Hemming had turned his own daughter into something he could never imagine. He began to unravel.

"No!"

He tried to shut off his computer but Zipperhead sparked him every time he reached for it. When Hemming tried to run from the room, Cole used his telekinesis and forced him back in front of the screen, even going all *Clockwork Orange* on him and forcing his eyelids open. Hemming had no choice but to bear witness, each image like a knife in *his* gut. Now it was *his* turn to be stabbed.

"Oh god . . . oh god . . ."

He writhed and screamed like he was being burned at the stake.

"Nooooo! Echo, stop it! For god's sake, stop it! Please! I'm begging you! Make it go away!"

Hemming's whole body was shaking now and he began to

weep. I rushed at him and entered easily. The twisted but very effective images Darby had conjured were smashing around through his brain. He was feeling shame and regret on a major scale, a tsunami of pain. And then other images appeared. It was me, being killed by him—the images all too familiar to us both—but this time instead of my face in agony as the knife plunged in, he saw his daughter Marie's.

"Marie! No! Nooo!"

He screamed until his throat was raw. And then everything bled into a deep, dark-red nothingness.

I found myself lying on the floor next to Hemming's body. He was alive but in shock. Cole helped me to my feet.

"Are you okay?"

"Yeah, I think so. But *he's* not."

"Echo, you're brilliant!" said Cameron.

"You smoked his ass, babe!" said Zipperhead.

"That was wicked. I mean, I thought I was badass, but you are amazing," said Darby.

I wanted to say thanks, but what I'd done was sadistic and terrible and I felt awful. I knew he deserved it, but I still felt regret.

We watched as Hemming had some kind of rag-doll seizure, his body jerking violently for a full minute. Finally, he stopped.

"Is he dead?" said Zipperhead.

"No, look—he's still breathing," Cameron answered.

Dougie blew a breath and an icy-cold wind blasted Hemming. He opened his eyes and immediately started fisting them, rubbing them harder and harder, as though he could somehow erase the images that we'd planted in his brain. When he opened his eyes, they were so bloodshot they looked like two skinned beets.

He clawed at his neck like an animal, then regained his bearings and sat up.

"I didn't mean . . . I wasn't . . . Oh god . . ." he said.

I felt thoroughly creepy for what had happened, but it *had* to be done. It made his whole sordid life real to him. By forcing him to think of all those girls as someone's daughter, like his own daughter, he was compelled to face the truth, the reality, and it had twisted up his psyche and snapped it like a twig. He stood on wobbly legs, a man rising from his grave. He zombie-walked over and picked up the knife and hard drive. He began to wail in pain.

We followed as he walked out of the house. He was wailing and crying openly and didn't bother getting in his car. Instead, he took his shoes off and walked, his pink feet stepping on rocks and glass, suburban penance. He walked and walked. And cried like a little boy, sobbing in hot, harsh jags. People stared at him, this crying man with the knife in one hand and a hard drive in the other. He marched past the playground where the father was still swinging his daughter. When the father saw Hemming, he pulled his daughter off the swing and held her in his arms so she wouldn't have to bear witness.

Hemming marched the mile into town and onto Main Street where he tore at his shirt, ripping it open. Using the knife, he made small cuts on his neck and shoulders, drawing blood.

"Yuck, that's disgusting," said Lucy.

Hemming kept bawling, his eyes a fountain of tears.

"I think he's . . . broken," said Cameron.

"He's toast," said Zipperhead. "Great job, Echo—you completely obliterated him."

Mark Hemming would never be the same man he was, not even close. He would never go near another girl. I had broken him down and destroyed the evil part of him. I hoped it would never surface again.

By the time he got to the police station, he was weak from the loss of blood and babbling incoherently. He collapsed on the front steps. Kirkland's finest spotted him and took him into custody in less than a minute.

Watching as all this came down, I felt nothing. You always imagine when the bad guy gets it—especially the bad guy who killed you—that you'd do a victory dance or whoop with joy. But for me that didn't happen. All I felt was emptiness inside. I was relieved, but my heart was vacant.

DAISIES

Darby, Zipperhead, Lucy, Dougie, Cameron, and Cole and I set sail for Middle House, taking a purposefully meandering, winding route, skimming over the treetops. Dark clouds clotted the sky but soon dissipated, allowing sunshine to warm the landscape. When we got back, we found Middle House back on an even keel now that Miss Torvous had, with a little help from yours truly, exorcised her demons. A more relaxed, almost playful vibe permeated the place now, though the underlying need everyone had for vengeance was still present. I wondered if, now that my killer had been brought to justice, I would move on and join the Afters. How and where would I do it? As usual, Cole had a frustratingly simple, pragmatic answer.

"You'll know when you know."

Yeah, I guessed I would. I searched inside, doing a moral inventory, and found that I couldn't entertain the notion of leaving this existence without attending to a couple of important matters.

A few days passed. One of the younger boys, with the help of his friends, haunted the sicko who'd abducted and then killed him. The man was so remorseful that he not only turned himself in, but hung himself to death in his jail cell with a wire coat hanger. The authorities couldn't figure out where the man had gotten the hanger. But *we* all knew. Justice had been served.

I kept waiting for something to happen to me. I wasn't beamed magically up into the sky so soon after our haunting like Mick had been. I was going to have to be more patient. I let my mind wander, not trying to force anything. But the same thoughts kept visiting me and I shared them with Cole.

"I have to say good-bye to my parents," I said.

"I know," said Cole.

"And to Andy."

He measured me carefully.

"Not easy tasks. Let me know if you need any help."

"Thanks, but I think I'll go it alone."

I went to my old house and found workmen fixing the gutters, replacing a broken window, and applying fresh coats of paint, inside and out. Everything had been moved out of the house. A For Sale sign had been planted in the front yard. My parents wouldn't be back to this house ever again—I knew that. I said good-bye to my old place, risking a glance over at Andy's house. I knew I'd have to come back and figure out some kind of closure with him, too. But right now I wanted to see my mom and dad.

It wasn't hard finding them. I simply waited for my mom to finish work at the dental clinic where she had her practice and followed her home. They'd rented a cute one-bedroom condo in Kirkland with a view of the lake. Mom brought groceries in from her car and prepped a simple dinner of pasta and seafood. She opened a bottle of wine. She sipped it and looked around the place. They'd already unpacked all the boxes except for one on the foyer table, and she went to it.

I watched as she lifted the lid off the box. There were three framed pictures of me inside. Mom stared at them a long time, fighting back tears. I wanted her to take them out and hold them, hug them, kiss them. When she put the lid back on the box, I began to cry. I couldn't bear to be put in storage and forgotten.

When she went back into the kitchen, I gave the box a push. It toppled, the pictures spilling out. Mom was startled, her eyes darting around the empty house. She went to the box and kneeled.

"Oh, Echo . . . baby . . . I'm so sorry . . ."

She picked up all three pictures and cradled them in her arms.

"I'm the one who should be sorry," I said.

I wrapped my arms around her—I could tell she sensed me—and we cried together for many minutes. It was hard letting go.

When she'd cried herself out, I released her. She seemed to have gathered strength from our encounter. She looked at the pictures. I thought she would put them back in the box. But she didn't. She retrieved a hammer and some small nails from Dad's toolbox and carefully hung them on the wall. I was gone, but I would never be forgotten.

Dad came in and looked beat, like he'd been working his ass off, diving in deep, trying to escape the trauma that had battered him and Mom so profoundly. As he approached Mom, he saw the pictures and hesitated.

"I thought you couldn't . . ."

"I changed my mind. She was here. She spoke to me."

"Oh, honey . . ."

He gave Mom a long hug. They both had such grief in their eyes.

"In that case, I got a little something . . ."

Dad went out and came back in with something he'd left in the car. A small bouquet of daisies, my favorite flower. He handed them to my mom and they held each other.

I could hardly bear it. How could I possibly leave this world knowing they were in such pain? But then Mom reached up and turned Dad's mouth to hers and kissed him gently on the lips. I thought it must have been the first time they'd kissed since I'd been murdered, but maybe I was just assuming that. The good thing is that the kiss evolved into a deeper, longer, lingering kiss. Their skin flushed and then my father swept my mother up into his arms and carried her up the stairs. I lingered as they went into their new bedroom. As soon as I heard my mother's breath hasten, I whispered words I knew that they couldn't hear but hoped they would feel.

"Good-bye, Mommy and Daddy. I love you both so much."

I flew down the stairs and out the door and high up into the sky, buoyed by the feeling that they would be okay. They were young enough. Maybe they'd even have another kid someday. If they did, I hoped it was a girl.

I flew for hours, letting the wind carry me along whenever I got physically taxed, which honestly ghosts don't often do. The whole lack-of-a-corporeal-entity thing paves the way for limitless amounts of mobility and energy. Only our psyches become overwhelmed to the point where we must sleep. I wanted to sleep now, in the clouds, if only to avoid what was coming next. My last date with Andy.

ANDY

Andy and I used to play on the neighbor's swing set when we were kids. It had rusted and was in disrepair but still stood. I sat on the remaining workable swing and swayed gently back and forth, looking at Andy's house, remembering times gone by. Barbecues and water balloon fights; sneaking out at night to meet and kiss; whispering long, heartfelt proclamations of love. We meant every word.

The chain squeaked softly. Leaves tumbled across the grass. Anyone seeing the swing would conclude it was the wind blowing it back and forth.

Andy. My Andy. The first time we'd met, we'd had a brawl. A couple of four-year-olds pushing and shoving in a heated contest over a toy elephant. Andy was a chubby little beast and as soon as I picked up "his" blue elephant, he bull-rushed me and shoved me over onto my butt. I remembered my ears getting hot as I jumped up and pushed him right back. His little eyes went wide with shock and he fell backward and dropped the elephant. I grabbed it and ran home as he wailed until his mother—who hadn't died yet—came and soothed his bruised ego. Our initial encounter was brutal. Clearly love at first sight.

Now I had some heavy lifting to do. I had to say good-bye to my soul mate. I wanted to let him know he could have the blue elephant, forever. I stepped off the swing and floated over and into his house. He was at the kitchen table. His father was old-fashioned and still had the actual newspaper delivered. Andy had cut out various articles about Hemming and had them spread on the tabletop.

His eyes were red and he looked like crap. Apparently Hemming's confession and subsequent incarceration hadn't brought to Andy the same sense of closure it had to me. In fact, Andy looked more miserable than ever. His father, Hank, entered the kitchen, went to put a hand on his son's shoulder but thought better of it, taking a swig of OJ from the fridge.

"Have a good day, son," he said.

Hank waited for a response, got none, didn't press. He went out and got in his car and departed, leaving Andy alone with his misery.

"I'm sorry, Andy," I said. "I really messed things up."

He was shaking his head, his hands balled into fists. I didn't want to leave him like this. In fact, there was only one persistent thought that found its origin in my heart and reached up into my brain. I didn't want to go. I didn't want to leave him. Ever.

But I knew I had to. I was stuck. Maybe this would be my purgatory, forever next to him, unable to consummate any kind of earthly love.

When Andy's phone rang and Dani's avatar appeared, he

looked conflicted. He reached for his phone, then withdrew his fingers like it was too hot to touch. The ringing stopped and the message icon appeared. Andy didn't listen to it. He picked up his phone and opened the photo app and looked at old pictures of me instead. The tears that fell from his eyes might as well have been falling from mine. His phone rang. It was Dani again. I knew what I had to do.

I moved over and as he was pondering whether or not to answer the phone, I opened the window, and warmth from outside tumbled in on a breeze. Andy picked up his phone and answered.

"Hey, Dani." Smooth. All charm.

He listened. She wanted them to meet for dinner. He didn't seem thrilled with the idea but at the same time must have known that he couldn't wallow in pity forever, so he said okay. Eight o'clock at Jonathan's Home Port. She had a Groupon. I knew I had a mission. I had to become Cupid.

I flew into the nearby woods and sat on a branch, contemplating my afterlife and doing my best to gather enough courage to do what needed to be done. Later, I flew over to Dani's place. She lived in a sandstone house with a tile roof on a cul-de-sac in a project near Totem Lake. Her parents had money. Her car, a late-model Bimmer, sat in the driveway, pink dice hanging from the rearview mirror. I went inside and found her primping in her room.

I shook my head back and forth like a judgmental schoolmarm. She was doing everything wrong!

"Jesus, Dani, will you please get your shit together here?" I said.

She sniffed like I'd just farted. I measured her carefully. I'd have to do an almost complete makeover. She had her hair piled up in a princess bun, which Andy hated. Like almost all boys, he loved my hair flowing down around my face and onto my shoulders. She was wearing a hideous burgundy top and yoga pants. This would not do. Andy hated burgundy and liked to see me in skirts, liked to see my legs. He loved it when I wore black knee-high stockings, too. And she'd gone way overboard with the makeup and mascara! It was like she thought she was auditioning for a Disney movie starring a raccoon.

I pulled the clip from her hair. She jerked her hand and tried to catch it but watched in the mirror as her hair fell down.

"Hmmm," she said.

She shook her fingers through it, making it fuller, and thankfully decided it would look better down. She ran a quick brush through it and put on lipstick. I had to get creative here and so I guided her hand so she smeared her cheek. I blew powder at her and she sneezed, which allowed me to toss even more of it onto her mug. She looked like a clown and decided to start over. She went into the bathroom and washed and dried her face.

When she came back to her makeup station, I'd removed and hidden most of the offending makeup choices.

"What the hell? This is sooo stupid! Mom!"

She looked around, yanking open and slamming drawers, then checked the time on her phone. She couldn't dick around. She had to kick into gear. So she applied only a modicum of makeup. Just the way Andy liked it. Less is always so much more. Her unfortunate wardrobe choices were easy to rectify—a spilled liquid here, a pulled thread there—and after a few minutes of manipulation, I was able to guide her into a brown blouse and skirt with black stockings and ankle boots. She took a look at herself in the mirror.

"This is so weird!" she muttered to herself, and I thought, *Kiddo, you ain't seen nothin' yet.*

DANI

Jonathan's Home Port was an upscale restaurant on the shore of Lake Washington in downtown Kirkland. Dani drove nervously and fast, running two stop signs, and got there early. That was never a smart move, according to *Cosmo*. A girl should always let the guy wait for her so he can see her enter. I had to cause a slight makeup malfunction—a minor smear—to buy some time. Dani spent ten minutes in the little girls' room (I managed to jam the lock on her stall), which gave Andy enough time to arrive and be seated first. I sat down next to him and watched him carefully. His clothes didn't seem to fit right. His jacket was too tight and he kept digging at the heel of his shoe. The plain truth was he didn't want to be here with her. He wanted to be here with me.

"I miss you so much."

"I miss you so much."

My body shivered. We'd both said the same thing at the same time. It was like an echo. How ironic. All I wanted was to crawl onto his lap and have him hold me. Emotions were welling up inside me, my wants and desires overpowering. I wasn't thinking clearly. I was on a date with my boyfriend, my childhood playmate, the man I planned on having children with and spending the rest of my life with. It was inspiring, uplifting, and, owing to the fact that I was dead, ultimately soul crushing.

Dani emerged from the bathroom. You know those shots of people walking right at the camera in slow motion looking all cool, like they're being watched by everyone on the planet? That's how Dani looked now. I had to give it to her. She had a great figure and all the parts were moving together in perfect sync. She was killing it. Andy's eyes took her in and he stirred in his seat. He may have still been thinking about me but he liked the way she looked.

My heart was in rough shape, but behind that feeling, in the part of my being where reason and logic dwelled, I was hopeful. It was best for Andy to move on. To forget all about me and evolve, to put the past behind him and forge a new life with a new girl. The concept hurt. But I knew what was best. When she approached the table, he stood and pulled out her chair for her.

"Why, thank you—how gallant," she said.

"You look . . . nice," he said, still stunned.

"Thanks. So do you. I like your shirt."

Andy looked down at his shirt as though seeing it for the first time. It was a terrific shirt, blue to match his eyes, with thin white stripes.

As they engaged in small talk, I studied them. Andy was clearly trying to stay interested in what she was saying, which was plenty, her nervous chatter coming out like flocks of tiny birds from her mouth. I wanted this to be over with. My goal was to get them to kiss, to get him to put his hands on her, and then, that seed planted, I could hopefully retreat into the night, alone forever.

But little Miss Chatterbox was talking too much. All the how-to blogs said you should get the guy to open up about himself and act as interested as possible. I read all that stuff but never had to worry about it because Andy had always been over the moon about me. Now it was up to Dani. But after her initial smoking-hot entrance, she was fading.

Dani did all the stupid stuff: tried to play footsie with him under the table, held his hand too long, glomming onto it and not letting go, giggling too loud at the things he said, and batting her eyelashes like freakin' Bambi.

She talked on and on. Deep down, she was a good person, and actually mustered a few intelligent and relevant things to discuss, but she was sloppy due to nerves. When she moved over and sat next to him after the main course, I knew she was busting a move to get him to kiss her. She touched his lips with her fingernails and licked her own lips. Though it pained me, this was it. This was the make-it-or-break-it moment. I practically willed their heads together and then their lips met.

My heart ached, but the pain was a good one because I had hope—hope that I was doing the right thing for the boy I loved. For a brief moment, I flashed on the times that Cole had kissed me, but the images blew away like specks of dust. All I could see was Andy kissing Dani. It was over for me and I didn't like it; in fact, I hated it.

They broke apart. Dani was smiling. Andy wasn't. She tried to kiss him again. He wouldn't let her. She tried a third.

"I loved that," she whispered. "Did you?"

Andy's eyes said it all. He *hadn't* loved it. My heart leapt up—until I realized how stupid it was for me to be happy about the current turn of events. I decided I wanted him to fall for her, and I wanted him to do it now. They had to lock lips, passionately. There might not be another chance. I had to think of something, and quick. The only way to get Andy to feel like he did when he kissed me while he was kissing Dani was for me to *be* Dani, or at least inside her. I hoped I could pull it off.

I took flight and swirled around Dani, causing her skin to pebble with goose bumps. I moved faster and faster until she drew in a gasping, frightened breath. It was all I needed, the slightest opening of fear, and—pouncing like a cat—I leapt into her.

She was a jumble of giddy joy mixed with terrifying negative thoughts, images of Andy pushing her away. She had a joyful inner aura about her and I saw childhood memories, happy times with parents and siblings who loved her. She also had a wonderful, earnest, honest yearning for Andy. So did I. I heard myself say, "Let's go outside and look at the stars."

As I rose, I looked in the mirror. I was in Dani's body but I was looking at me, at myself—the eyes were unmistakable. The feeling was incredible. I was corporeal again!

Being outside at night was something Andy and I used to love to do—just lay on our backs in the grass and gaze into the starry sky, holding hands in between kisses, not having to say a whole lot. Who needed to yammer when you could listen to the whispers of the universe?

When we stepped out the back door and onto the deck, Andy looked up at the sky.

"I bet we have the best view in the whole universe," I said.

He looked sharply at me. This is something he always said when we went star gazing. He nodded and smiled at me. At Dani.

I was in no hurry. Andy was tapping his fingers on the wooden railing. He was deep in thought. I knew he was thinking about me.

"Dani, uh . . . listen . . . my life . . . it's just . . ."

I had to make my move. I couldn't let him start blurting out how much he loved me and missed me. It would ruin everything for Dani. So I wrapped my wrists around his neck, like I always had, and moved my lips closer and closer. I could feel the breath leaving him as he relished the anticipation.

"I . . . I . . ." he muttered.

"Shhhh . . ."

Our lips met. So softly. So perfectly. Then our tongues explored and a hunger rose in both of us as I pressed my body against his. If I could have bottled that moment and kept it, just stayed like that for eternity, I would have. It felt so good to be alive again! This was it. This was the second chance I'd been dreaming of every hour of every day for the last week.

And then everything changed abruptly.

"What are you doing here?" I said. I was frowning. At Cole.

He was at the far end of the deck, watching. Andy was taken aback.

"What? I'm . . . kissing you, obviously." He was confused.

"I know, and I'm kissing you. Do you . . . like it?"

In answer, he kissed me again and the sky exploded. I was sure I'd gone through the process and ascended into my afterlife. That's how glorious the feeling was that pulsed through every cell in my—or rather, Dani's—body.

Cole then did something weird. He used his telekinesis to freeze the scene. Andy was as rigid as a sculpture. I could move, and I walked Dani's body over to confront Cole.

"What are you doing here?" I asked again.

"You've gone inside her," he said.

"Yes."

"And something's different."

"I know."

He was right. I was. And there was no turmoil. I wasn't battling anyone. Unlike everyone else I'd entered, Dani was placid, accepting, even welcoming, or so my mind was telling me.

"You did it to kiss him one last time, didn't you?"

"I had to. She was totally dying; she was going to ruin everything."

Cole made a face. He wasn't buying it

"And it so happens that I couldn't help it," I said.

Cole's eyes bored into me, seeking the truth.

"Is that what was happening, or what you were *hoping* was happening?"

"I . . . I don't know for sure. But Cole, I love this."

"Of course you do."

I did. The feeling of being human again, of being alive, being able to touch and smell and kiss—it was heaven on earth. Things we take for granted meant everything to me right now. Every single breath I took in Dani's body was like a precious gift.

"Cole, let us be. Let me play this out, please?"

Cole nodded, the pain in his eyes as obvious as if he'd had a sign on his head that said *But I love you, too!*

"How long have you been in?"

"I don't know. Feels like a long time."

"And she's not rejecting you, not trying to cast you out?"

"No. Not yet."

"Do the right thing, Echo. It's your choice."

KARMA

The word *choice* hit me hard. It was rapidly occurring to me that I *could choose*. I could choose to stay. I could stay alive in Dani's body. I could make Andy love me—I was halfway there already—and I could start over. This truly was the universe giving me a second chance! Cole released his freeze hold on Andy, who turned to me and reached out.

"This is so weird," he said. "It's like I had some nerve thing, I guess. I couldn't move. And I thought I heard you talking."

"It's okay," I said. "Everything's okay."

He shook his head and looked at me with those beautiful eyes and said, "Yeah, I know. Everything's perfect."

And then he pulled me to him again. My toes curled inside my shoes. This was it; this was my new life.

"I . . . can't believe this is happening," said Andy.

"I know. Me, too."

I felt a thousand pinpricks all over my body. Then an image of Dani as a little girl flashed through our brain—it was ours now; we were sharing it—and I drew back. Her dad had just won her a huge pink teddy bear at a carnival and she was on cloud nine. More images appeared—and then quickly faded, images from Dani's young life. It was as if they were being erased. Me being in her was causing this. Every action has its consequences. Dani's consciousness, her being, was fading because I was taking over. My thinking changed. The reality of what I was contemplating hit me hard.

I thought about how Dougie was tormented, how he'd smacked his kid brother and made him cry. It was a stupid thing to do, and he'd been trying to take it back ever since. But you can't take the wrongs back. They follow you to your grave . . . and beyond. I couldn't take someone else's life, even if it meant I could be reborn myself. I realized that in the short term I would be riding on a cloud of bliss, loving and being loved by Andy, my dream of all dreams. But in the long term, Dani's demise would come to haunt me, my own bad behavior stalking me like a shadow, always there, always reminding me of the selfish choice I'd made.

I'd wanted Andy back so bad and this was my chance. But I couldn't do it. Even though it was a dream come true, even though it was the one thing in the world I wanted more than anything, I couldn't stay human. Because I would be stealing a life, a life yet to be lived. Dani had committed no crime other than poor fashion choices. She didn't deserve to have her existence snuffed out. I had to do what Cole said. I had to do the right thing. And the right thing was to stick with my original plan, get her and Andy on the track to love, and then withdraw and accept whatever fate awaited me.

In my journey as a ghost, I'd learned a lot about myself.

I hadn't been as good and giving and pure as I'd imagined myself. I'd made tons of mistakes and hurt people in the process.

I'd sometimes been manipulative and selfish, convinced that
the ends justified the means. Now I knew that the means were
everything. It wasn't what you got in your life that mattered; it
was how you lived it.

Maybe next time—if there *was* a next time—I could do better. I wanted better karma when I was reborn. I hoped this
would help my cause.

I grabbed Andy and kissed him one last time. He moaned.
I pulled away. And then I called him his pet name, the name
that only I knew.

"Wolfie . . ."

He was rapt.

"What the . . . Echo?"

"Echo's . . . gone."

"Is she?"

I couldn't help it. I kissed him again and moved my tongue
in a dance so familiar that he had to know it was me. We'd done
it a thousand times.

"Jesus Christ," he said, pulling away.

I hugged him, putting my face on his shoulder so he couldn't
see my tears.

"Oh, baby. Promise me something."

"What?" he croaked.

"Promise that you'll love me forever and ever—will you do
that?"

"I promise. I swear. I'll never stop loving you. Never."

I wiped the tears from my eyes and looked at him. I was
looking at him with Dani's eyes now.

"You are some kind of kisser," Dani said as I started to pull
away.

Andy was shaken and looked like he might fall over. I held
on to him until the last possible second.

He leaned on the railing for support. And then, in a sudden, swift movement, I wrenched myself free from Dani's body. She was on her own now. Andy was blinking as he stared at her.

"I'm . . . so confused."

"Um . . . me, too."

She was trembling.

"But it's going to be okay, isn't it?" she said.

He looked deeply into her eyes. What he saw I can't say, but with every passing second, his eyes began to sparkle a little more with joy and hope.

"Yeah. It's going to be okay."

I watched them go back inside. I looked up at the stars and felt Cole beside me.

"Congratulations. You just screwed up a once-in-an-afterlifetime opportunity. You could have stayed. And lived."

"Taking someone else's life isn't living. It's called murder." Cole smiled.

"Yeah. I guess we know all about that."

I started to walk away across the deck. At first I didn't look back at Andy. I wanted to imagine that he and Dani were back inside, holding hands, gazing into each other's eyes. But I couldn't help it and sneaked a look. They were. I would remember what I'd done forever. I felt light, knowing I wouldn't be forever weighed down by the heavy shroud of regret. I would take this to my afterlife and I would be proud.

Cole walked with me. "Want to fly?"

"It feels good to walk. You go ahead."

"Nah, I'll walk with you. That is, if you don't mind the company."

I took him by the hand. We walked for what seemed like miles, doing nothing but breathing in the damp night air and listening to the sounds of life going on around us. We reached a small wooded area of towering pines and entered. I climbed the tallest one and stood on top, reaching down and pulling Cole up next to me.

He knew me well enough to know he didn't have to say any-thing and he seemed happy enough just to be holding my hand. The moon's glow made everything look like it had been brushed over with a silver glaze.

"Cole?"

"I'm right here."

"Do you think you could do me a favor before I . . . you know, go?"

He smiled warmly.

"You know I'm going to say yes. What do you want me to do?"

"I want you to kiss me, just like you did the first time."

He gulped. I mean, actually gulped, like a nervous little boy. I didn't let up. I wanted what I wanted.

"Do you think you can do that?"

"Um . . . sure. You know . . . okay . . ."

He was working up the nerve to do it when I held his face and looked him in the eye.

"Not right now."

"Oh. Um . . . then when?"

"When the time is right. You'll know."

I put my head on his shoulder and we watched the moon.

STAY

Six days and six nights passed. The moon stayed true in the sky as I wondered what fate awaited me. The truth was, I didn't want to go anywhere; I was attached to Cole and growing more so every day. We talked about each other's "alive" lives and I learned he wasn't very good at sports, and that this caused aggravation for his father while his mother was secretly pleased that he preferred drawing and writing songs to clashing with his peers on the gridiron or hardwood floors in the gym. I hadn't known he liked to draw and I found out in a way that made my stomach tingle. On night seven of watching the moon on the Middle House roof, he had something with him, and after some coaxing on my part, he showed me that all along he'd been making sketches of me.

The drawings were really good. I was apparently some sort of goddess in his eyes, because the girl in the sketches was more than pretty—she was beautiful, with eyes alight and a face with smooth but strong features. The fact that he was obviously embellishing meant that in his eyes I was gorgeous, and that made me want him all the more.

I could've stayed up here forever with him just staring at the moon. But the moon clouded over and the skies became angry, releasing claps of thunder and spitting cracks of lightning. And then the rain came down. It was light at first but swiftly evolved into a downpour driven by raging winds. Cole wanted to go inside but something was pulling me into the night and I grabbed his hand. We flew hard and fast into the dark sky, the pounding rain whooshing through our phantom bodies. It didn't take long before I sensed that the others were behind us.

"What's up?" asked Darby.

"Just going for a little rain dance?" said Lucy.

She shook her body, clearly hating the rain, but she was there with us, compelled, just like Cameron and Dougie and Zipperhead, to accompany us, their sixth senses telling them that this was no ordinary night.

"Easy to wipe out when it's wet," said Zipperhead.

"Yeah, you could get killed," said Dougie.

We were laughing when the rain eased up and then stopped, and we landed in one of Seattle's many wooded refuges, Seward Park. Lucy shook from head to toe. We all looked up at the sky. There was a break in the clouds and a diffuse moonbeam was breaking through and finding us, exactly where we stood.

Well, what did I need? God on a megaphone, yelling, "Hey, this is it—this is your time, kiddo"?

No, I understood that the universe was talking, had lured me here—lured us all here—for a reason. We knew we'd been summoned here to send me off but no one wanted to say it. I'd grown close to all of them, this band of freaks and misfits, and it wasn't going to be easy leaving them behind.

"Um . . ." said Zipperhead.

He was on the verge of blurting something out.

"Yeah, you know, Echo . . ." Cameron muttered.

Darby's hands were on her hips and she was trying to defy destiny and looking formidable.

"Maybe this isn't it," she said.

Her voice dropped off into the night as the moonbeam grew brighter and now was quite irritatingly appearing to single me out.

"Okay, I don't need a chorus of angels. I get the point," I said to the sky.

A light breeze was stirring, coming from the north, and another, stronger one was churning in from the mountains in the east. The effect was that my hair was dancing around my head in a swirl as the moonbeam glowed brighter.

"Looks like this is it," said Zipperhead.

"Thank you, Mister Obvious," said Dougie. "Anybody else hot?"

They all rolled their eyes at him. No one was hot. It was a cool, wet, windy night. But that was Dougie.

"Listen . . . Echo . . ."

I moved to Dougie and gave him a hug. He was, as usual, cold as a block of ice. But I kept the hug going for a few more seconds, and he actually warmed up, feeling almost . . . human. I pulled away and we smiled at each other.

"Thanks, Dougie. You know I couldn't have done it without you."

He started pacing and patting his arms. Now he was cold, his breath coming out in little bursts of fog.

"That's not true," he said. "You're the one who kept putting it all together."

"Yeah, you're a natural-born detective," said Zipperhead.

"And a leader," Cole added.

"I'm . . . I'm no leader," I said.

But their eyes told me differently. Their eyes told me that all along they'd been following my lead, backing me up as I'd plunged headlong through my journey.

"We all know what we know," said Darby. "I bet if you'd stuck around, you would have helped me find the subhuman dipshit who shot me in the face."

"Darby, I want to help you—you know that."

Now it was my voice that was trailing off into the night. Darby wiped her cheek. Damned if she hadn't shed some tears. This was harder than I'd thought it would be. Once upon a time, I was psyched to rise up into the great beyond to join the Afters, to take my place in line in the cosmic evolution. But now . . . I was plagued with doubts and fears. What if being an After meant being nobody, nothing? What if instead of meeting up with all those who'd gone before me, I landed on some deserted planet devoid of anything? I had no way of knowing what was going to happen, and I was apprehensive. I looked at Cole. He was staring at the ground. He licked his lips.

I felt someone tugging at me. It was Zipperhead.

"Gonna miss you, newbie," he said.

I gave him a hug.

"Gonna miss you, too. And don't you worry—you're going to find the sucker who shoved you and make them pay."

He smiled weakly, trying to be nice. He didn't believe a word I had to say.

"Thanks for helping me believe about . . . you know . . ." he said quietly.

"Dog, you are never going to get laid," said Dougie. He laughed—until I shot him a harsh look, and then he tried to cover it with a cough. I looked straight into Zipperhead's eyes.

"I wasn't lying," I said. "I meant every word. It will happen for you. It's just going to take time."

"That . . . I got . . ." he said.

I turned to Darby. She immediately went into defense mode.

"Don't get all mushy on me. I hate mushy."

"Okay. You suck."

"So do you," she said, a small smile creeping onto her face. Without warning, she bolted forward and grabbed me in a bear hug.

"You . . . you're about the only person who's ever been nice to me. Thank you for that," she whispered in my ear.

Then she practically flung me away from her as she turned her back on me and blew her nose.

Cameron held up a hand and we high-fived.

"I'll catch you next time around."

"Yeah."

Lucy had morphed into her black-cat self and purred as she circled my leg, her tail snaking around my calf.

"See ya . . ."

I'd said good-bye to everyone except for Cole. He was staring past me into the distance.

"Cole . . ."

"I'm wondering . . ."

He looked at the others. They backed off and gave us the space we needed.

"I'm wondering if, even if I get to live a thousand lifetimes, I'll ever feel the same about someone as I do about you . . ."

His eyes held so much love that there was only one thing for me to do.

"That thing we talked about? Now would be good," I said.

It was his cue to kiss me, and he did. I can't say for sure how long it lasted, but as our lips met and our tongues touched, it was as though we'd melded into one person, our bodies and souls merging. Every cell in my body was tingling with an unimaginable thrill. I wanted the kiss to last an eternity. I can't remember who stopped first, but as soon as we parted, I felt a crushing emptiness.

More clouds dissipated in the insistent glow of the moon-beam. My voice croaked as I said, "Take care. I mean it. All of you."

I raised my arms up, half expecting the hands of the universe to reach down and yank me up. For a long time, nothing happened. And then I began to rise. They were all staring at me with their sad eyes and I looked at them one by one, saying a silent, heartfelt good-bye. And then I looked at Cole. He mouthed the words *I love you*. My heart weighed a thousand pounds. Our eyes were locked on each other like laser beams. I continued rising up into the sky as now a galaxy of tiny lights began to whirl around me, escorting me upward to begin the next chapter of my existence.

You know that feeling you get when you're doing something and you're convinced to your core that it's the completely right thing, that somehow you've stumbled into your destiny, riding a wave of what you've known all along would and should be happening? This *wasn't* one of those feelings. This was com-pletely the opposite. This felt like I'd just taken a wrong turn down a one-way alley into a black hole. Everything was back-ward and convoluted.

I tried to think about my future and what it would be like to be reincarnated as someone else. I tried to lift my spirits as my ghost body was ascending with such grandeur. But my thoughts kept coming back to Cole and my ghost life at Middle House.

I wanted to help Zipperhead find out who had pushed him to his death. I wanted to help him experience love. I wanted to lead the way as the gang discovered who shot Darby and then haunted the SOB until he paid the price. I wanted to help Cameron and Dougie and Lucy solve their murders and move on, too. But most of all, and I know this was totally selfish, I wanted to be with Cole. I wanted to be by his side when he found his killer and brought him to justice. And if we should happen to work in another astonishingly beautiful kiss or two along the way, then that would be just another one of the perks of being a ghost.

The realization came down on me like a landslide. I wanted to go back. So I lowered my arms. I continued to rise and I swear I could hear harps—or maybe it was just night birds chirping or my brain shorting out—and then the whole night went silent as a tomb. This was it, my moment of truth.

I began to float back down. I tried not to be too happy about it, in case I reversed the flow, so I closed my eyes. I asked the universe to do with me what it wanted. *Take me or leave me—it's up to you.* I repeated these words over and over, silently in my head. And then I felt my feet on the ground. I opened my eyes. The whole gang was smiling at me and looked like they might burst into a cheer.

I'd come back. Why? I might not know for a very long time. But it was clear that I wasn't done on earth. Cole stepped forward.

"Welcome back. It looks like you have some unfinished business."

"Yeah. Looks that way."

He smiled. And then pulled me into his arms.

ACKNOWLEDGMENTS

I would like to acknowledge my fabulous, talented editor, Brendan Deneen, at Thomas Dunne Books/St. Martin's Press for his cogent guidance; my tireless manager, Patrick Hughes, whose faith in my work continues to inspire me; my sister Marsha Holand for her unwavering encouragement and support; and my dear friend Mike Karson for generously lending me his sky castle to dance with my muses.